Love In Between

SANDI LYNN

Photo & Cover Design by Sara Eirew @Sara Eirew Photography

Models: Jonathan Dumas & Madison Bennett

Editing by Lucy D'Andrea

And B.Z. Hercules

Music Acknowledgement

Clouds

Music and Lyrics by Letters and Lights

I want to take this opportunity to thank, Eric Knudsen, of the band, **Letters and Lights** for graciously allowing me to use the lyrics to his song "Clouds" in Love In Between.

You can connect with Letters and Lights on Facebook:
https://www.facebook.com/lettersandlights

https://twitter.com/letters_lights

TABLE OF CONTENTS

Prologue

"You're the most beautiful bride I've ever seen."

"You have to say that; you're my mom." I smiled.

I stared at my white A-line strapless dress, embellished with rhinestone flowers that cascaded asymmetrically over the bodice as I ran my hands down my sides. I turned my head to make sure my cathedral bridal veil was placed perfectly amongst my elegant curly updo.

"I can't believe you're finally getting married!" Giselle smiled.

"You're picture-perfect, Lily Gilmore," Gretchen spoke as she snapped a picture with her phone.

I was so nervous and my hands were beginning to sweat. I couldn't believe this day had finally arrived. The past year of planning the perfect wedding was torturous, but exciting. Hunter stood by my side and had agreed with everything that I liked. I think he just wanted to keep the peace, or he just didn't care. He didn't want a big wedding. He wanted to run off to Vegas and get married at one of those drive-by chapels. I've always dreamed of a big wedding, and he understood, so he nixed the idea of Vegas. Plus, my mother would have killed us both if we eloped.

People were gathered in the church, waiting for the ceremony to begin.

"Lily, where's your sister?"

"I'm not sure, mom. She said she had to go get something and that she'd be right back."

"She's your maid of honor, and she needs to be here. The ceremony's about to start."

I sighed and headed out of the dressing room. I walked down the long hallway that connected to a small kitchen. I figured she probably went out behind the church to have a cigarette, so I proceeded through the kitchen and stopped when I heard a noise coming from one of the rooms off to the side. I placed my hand on the knob and slowly turned it as I pushed opened the door. Nothing had prepared me for what I saw.

I pulled the door shut and ran out of the church. My heart was racing, and my stomach felt sick. I heard my mother's voice following me from behind. I stopped when she called my name in a panic. I put my hand on my head and paced in circles, not believing what I just saw. My breathing was rapid as I looked up and saw Hunter standing there, looking at me, and my sister standing behind him. Tears began to stream down my face as he slowly started walking towards me. I put my hand up before he took three steps.

"Don't you dare come near me, you bastard!" I screamed.

"Lily, Hunter, what the hell is going on?" my mother asked.

I stood there, pointing my finger. "Why don't you ask that cheating bastard over there and his dirty whore standing behind him?!" I spat.

My mother turned her head and looked at my sister, Brynn. She stood there, shaking her head as she stared at both of them. By this time, a crowd of people had emerged from the church and were gathered around to see what all the commotion was. The way my mother was looking at Brynn and Hunter gave me the feeling that she knew what was going on between them.

"Lily, please let me—"Hunter started to say.

"Don't you ever say a fucking word to me again!" I screamed, cutting him off.

I stood there, feeling about as small as an ant, and raised my arms up in the air. "Well, it looks like there isn't going to be a wedding today, folks! Unless, my whore of a sister over there wants to marry this cheating bastard!" I yelled as I pointed to Hunter.

"Lily! That's enough!" my mother commanded.

I looked at her with disgrace and slowly walked towards her. "You knew, didn't you? You knew they were screwing behind my back!"

She stared at me with a look of guilt. She didn't have to say a word; her reaction said it all. I shook my head as I looked at my sister who was standing on the steps, crying.

"Why are you crying? Isn't this what you wanted? You can have him, baby sister, because the two of you were made for each other!"

I ripped off my veil and threw it on the ground as I turned on my heels and stomped away. Giselle and Gretchen followed behind, and we took the limo back to their hotel room.

Stepping into the hotel room, I immediately sat on the edge of the bed. The only tears that fell were the ones outside the church. I was still in shock until Giselle sat down next to me and told me that it was okay to cry. I broke down as she held me. Gretchen walked over and sat on the other side as all three of us hugged each other.

"It's going to be okay, Lily," Gretchen whispered.

"How could he do this to me?" I sobbed.

"He's an asshole, and it's better that you found out now," Giselle said.

"She's right, honey. It's better now than five years from now," Gretchen spoke.

I sniffled and Giselle handed me some tissues. "What are you going to do now?" Gretchen asked.

"Gretchen!" Giselle scolded.

"It's okay. I don't know what I'm going to do. I can't go back home, and I can't face my family. I can't believe my mother knew about Hunter and Brynn. How could she keep that from me after what my father did to her?"

"I don't know, sweetie. It's pretty fucked up that she knew, and your sister, my God, why would she do that to you?"

"I feel like I'm going to be sick," I said as I sprang from the bed and into the bathroom, shutting the door behind me.

***

I stayed in the hotel room for an entire week. I didn't get out of bed except to use the bathroom. I kept my phone off and gave strict instructions to Giselle and Gretchen not to let anyone know where I was staying. They went out and bought me a new cell phone so that we could keep in touch, because they needed to get back to California for their jobs. I ordered room service when I felt like it, but I mostly stared at the ceiling, thinking about how much my life sucked. I cried until it felt like my eyes were going to fall out, and I didn't understand why Hunter would do that to me. Oh wait, yes I do. It's because he's a man, and that's what men do. They're cheating, lying bastards who can't commit to one woman. Are all men like that? I started to believe they were. Then, there was my sister.

***

It was Wednesday, so I knew my mother would be at her charity meeting and that my sister would be having lunch with her friends. It was something they did every Wednesday. As the cab pulled up to the house, I stared at it for a minute through the window.

"Miss, are you getting out?" the driver asked.

I looked at him and it took my brain a minute to register what he'd asked.

"Yeah, I'm sorry."

I paid him the cab fare, got out of the cab, and stood in front of the long winding driveway that led to the only house that I'd known my entire life. I slowly entered, making sure no one was home. I couldn't face my family; not after what they'd done to me. I quickly went upstairs to my room, grabbed my suitcases from the closet, and began throwing only the necessities inside. I needed to do this quick before someone came home. I grabbed a handful of clothes from my closet. My makeup, bras, underwear, and shoes. I had two suitcases packed and ready to go. I opened the top drawer of my desk, pulled out my bank book, and I stood in the doorway, taking one last look at the room that had been mine my entire life. I headed down the stairs with my suitcases. As I was approaching the front door, it opened, and my mother walked in. She froze when she saw me, and tears started to fill her eyes.

"Lily, my baby, I was so worried about you. Where have you been?"

I looked at her with a stern look, and instantly I felt sick to my stomach.

"It doesn't matter where I've been. The only thing that matters is I'm gone and out of this family forever. What you did to me, by not telling me about Brynn and Hunter, is unforgivable. You helped me plan my wedding, knowing he was fucking my little sister. You were going to let me marry a cheater and a liar. What kind of mother are you?!" I started to cry.

"Lily, please. You have to understand that I was trying to protect you, and he promised me that it was over," she said as she walked towards me with her arms out.

"Don't you dare take another step!" I snapped. "I'm nothing like you, and I won't live my life like you either."

I walked out the front door, stopped, and turned around, staring at my mother as she stood there, crying.

"This family is *dead* to me. Tell my little sister that I hope both her and Hunter live happily ever after. Have a nice life, Mother." I threw my suitcases in the back of my Explorer, got in, and started the truck. My mother came running out of the house after me as I began to back out of the driveway.

"Please, Lily, I'm sorry. Don't do this to us. You're going to regret it."

"The only thing I regret is ever being a part of this lying, cheating family!" I spat as I peeled out of the driveway and headed as far away from this place as I could. The only thing I knew was that I couldn't stay in Seattle anymore. It was time for me to disappear and start a new life.

I drove for about three hours until my gas light came on. I had reached Portland, Oregon. I pulled into a gas station and opened my purse to get my credit card. I froze when I saw the two tickets to Aruba, which was supposed to be my honeymoon. We were supposed to leave tomorrow because Hunter couldn't get two weeks off the day after the wedding. I filled up the Explorer with gas and drove down the road to a mini outdoor mall. I took out my camera and decided I was going to take pictures of every place I stopped because I wanted to make a scrapbook of the journey to my new life. I took pictures of the shops, the signs, and the people all around.

It was a beautiful, warm sunny day, and I noticed a café with tables that sat outside. I wasn't really hungry, but it had been several hours since I had last ate. I took a seat at an open table and placed my order with the waitress. As I was looking around, taking in the fresh air, I noticed a couple sitting a few tables over from me. They were holding hands, and laughing. The guy was hot; there was no doubt about that, and his girlfriend was very pretty. There was something about his smile that struck me in more places than one. They looked happy, and from what I could see, they were very much in love. I grabbed my camera and snapped a picture of them.

I ate lunch, had a couple glasses of iced tea, and reached for my purse to pay the bill. As I reached in and grabbed my wallet, the airline tickets fell out and onto the cement floor. I reached down, picked them up, and held them in my hand, staring at them in disgust. After I left some money on the table, I had an idea. Walking over to the happy couple that I'd been watching since I sat down, I approached them.

"Hi. I know this is weird, but I have two airline tickets to Aruba. The flight leaves tomorrow, and I want you to have them."

They both looked at me like I was crazy.

"You aren't going?" the woman asked in confusion.

"No, actually, something came up, so my fiancé and I weren't able to go. I don't want them to go to waste and I can't get a refund. The two of you look like you would enjoy Aruba together."

She looked at him, and they both looked at me. "Let me pay you for the tickets," the guy said as he reached into his pocket to pull out his wallet.

"No. Please just take them. I don't want your money. Just promise me that you'll have a good time," I said as I put the tickets on the table and started to walk away.

"Wait!" the girl yelled. "Thank you." She smiled.

"Consider it a gift, and just pay it forward someday." I smiled as I walked back to my Explorer.

1

One Year Later...

Inserting the key into the lock, I unlocked the door. I slowly turned the handle and lightly pushed the door open as I stepped inside my new apartment. Setting down my suitcases, I took a deep breath. I flipped the light switch on the wall next to the door and looked around. The furniture that I ordered online had arrived, and it was scattered all over the room. I rented this apartment based off the pictures showcased on the internet. Walking around, I inspected my new home. The light gray walls and white moldings gave the place a classic look. The eggplant color couch and loveseat I bought matched perfectly, as did the glass coffee table and end tables. I walked down the hall and into my bedroom. Flipping the light switch, I stared at the empty space as the bedroom set was being delivered tomorrow. It was late, and I was exhausted since I drove fourteen hours straight from Portland to Santa Monica. My Explorer was filled with boxes, but they would have to wait until the morning. At that moment, I just wanted to feel the comfort of my new couch.

I spent the last year in Portland when my car broke down, and it took two weeks to get repaired. I guess you could say the place grew on me, and I really didn't have any other place to go. I rented an apartment, took a job as a freelance photographer for the local newspaper, and I was a substitute teacher for a few months at one of the local elementary schools. How did I end up in Santa Monica? The local newspaper shut down, and my gig as a substitute teacher had ended when the regular teacher came back from maternity leave. Giselle called me one day and said that her Aunt Chris, the principal of an elementary school in Santa Monica, was looking for a long-term substitute teacher and that I should call her. So I did, and that's how I ended up here.

Giselle and Gretchen lived in Santa Monica, and I was excited to be living near them again. They're twins, and we'd been best friends for as long as I could remember. I met them when I was six years old, when they moved into the house next door. Their father was an investment banker, and their mother was a model in her younger days. Giselle and Gretchen followed in their mother's footsteps. With their five foot ten inch height and size six bodies, they were made to be models. I was envious of their deep brown eyes and their long, straight brown hair. Our mothers used to call us the three musketeers because we were inseparable. We did everything together, and we were always there when the other one needed us. The twins were my rock, and no matter what exotic place their job took them to, we talked almost every day.

***

I opened my eyes and was startled by the music I heard coming through the wall. I grabbed my phone and looked at the time; it was three o'clock in the morning. I had been sleeping for about two hours, which had become the norm for me since I caught Hunter and Brynn together in the church. My mind was on permanent rewind, and every time I closed my eyes, that scene played over and over again. I got up from the couch, grabbed my purse, and walked to the bathroom. I wanted to wash my face, but I forgot that all my towels and washcloths were packed away in one of the boxes that sat in the Explorer.

I took the brush out of my purse and ran it through my long, blonde hair. I searched for a rubber band and pulled my hair into a high ponytail. As I looked at myself in the mirror, I couldn't help but notice the bags underneath my blue-gray eyes. I really needed a shower, so I put on my shoes, grabbed my keys, and headed out to the Explorer. As I stepped out into the hallway of my apartment, I stood there and stared at the door from which the blaring music was coming from. Shaking my head, I rolled my eyes and headed to my SUV for the box that was labeled: *BATHROOM.*

I lifted the box out of the Explorer, and then carried it to the door of the apartment building. As I was inserting the key, the door opened, and I stumbled back, nearly being knocked down.

"Hey there. I'm sorry. I didn't see you," a good looking man apologized.

He looked at me and then at the box on the ground. "Are you moving in?" he asked as he looked at his watch.

"Yes. I just got here a few hours ago, and I haven't had a chance to get the boxes from my truck."

"It's nice to meet you. I'm Sam," he said as he held out his hand.

"Hi, I'm Lily. It's nice to meet you too."

"Let me grab that box for you." He offered as he bent down to pick it up.

"No, that's alright. I've got it," I said as I put my hand in front of him.

"Don't be ridiculous. Let me carry the box for you since I almost knocked you on your ass with the door." He smiled.

It was the middle of the night, and I was arguing with a hot guy over a box. "Fine. My apartment's right there," I spoke as I pointed to my door.

Sam looked at me and smiled. "Well, look at that; looks like we're neighbors."

I opened the door for him as he stepped inside my apartment and set the box down on the floor. "So, you're the one playing the loud music at three a.m.?" I asked.

"Sorry about that," he spoke as shrugged his shoulders. "I'll tell Lucky to keep it down."

"I'd appreciate it. Thanks for the help with the box."

I spent the next hour unpacking the box and putting away the towels. I organized all my bathroom items and then took a hot, relaxing bubble bath. My hands began to wander as it had been a while since my battery operated boyfriend and I had a date. As soon as I was finished, I got out of the tub, wrapped a towel around me, and walked into the living room where my suitcases were. Opening my larger suitcase, I pulled out a pair of jean shorts and a navy blue tank top. I grabbed my phone from the couch and looked at the time; it was six a.m. Giselle and Gretchen were coming over to help me unpack around eight, and the bedroom set was being delivered between nine and eleven. I blow-dried my hair then put it back up in a high ponytail. I put on some light makeup and then decided to go for some coffee before starting my day.

I stepped out of my apartment at the same time Sam did his. We both looked at each other. "Don't you ever sleep?" He smiled.

"I should be asking you the same thing." I smiled back.

Sam was hot; there was no question about it. He stood around six feet tall with a great muscular body, sandy brown hair, and brown eyes. He definitely fit the Santa Monica image.

"Where are you off to so early in the morning?" he asked.

It really wasn't any of his business, but he was being nice, so I felt the neighborly thing to do was to be nice in return.

"I'm off to find some much needed caffeine," I replied as I stepped out of the building door, and he followed behind me.

"Me too. I went to make some coffee, but the bag was empty. I hate it when Luke doesn't tell me we're out of coffee."

"Luke?" I asked.

"Yeah, he's my BF and roommate. Hey, would you like to go get some coffee together?" he asked with a smile.

I studied him for a few moments. Sam seemed like a really nice guy, and he was gay, so I didn't have to worry about him hitting on me.

"Sure, I'll go with you, but we have to make it quick. My girlfriends are coming over to help me unpack."

I hopped into his truck, and we drove down the road to a coffee house called Brewster's. As we walked inside, Sam was instantly greeted by the girl behind the counter.

"Morning, Sam. Who's your friend?" she asked as she was wiping down the counter.

"Morning, Jamie. This is Lily. She just moved in next door. Lily, this is my cousin, Jamie. She owns this lovely coffee house."

Jamie wiped her hand dry and held it out to me as I gently shook it.

"It's nice to meet you, Lily. Are you new in town?"

"Yes. I just moved here from Portland last night."

"Great. Welcome to Santa Monica and to Brewsters! What can I get you?" she asked.

"I'll just have a large black coffee." I smiled.

I looked over at Sam and found him staring at me.

"What?"

"That's how Luke drinks his coffee. I don't understand how you can drink it with no sugar or cream. We argue about it all the time."

"Everyone has different coffee taste," Jamie said.

"Let me pay for your coffee," I said to Sam.

"It's on the house." Jamie smiled as she handed us our coffees. "Cheap-ass, Sam over here never pays. Consider it a welcome to Santa Monica gift."

"Thanks, Jamie!" Sam smiled as he grabbed a bag of coffee from the shelf. "I'm taking a bag home. I owe you!"

Jamie rolled her eyes. "He owes me every week." She laughed.

"Thank you, Jamie. It was nice to meet you." I smiled as I held up my coffee cup.

"It was nice to meet you too! Make sure to stop by occasionally and say hi."

I walked out of Brewster's and climbed into the truck. "Your cousin is really nice."

"Yeah, she's more like my sister. She came to live with me and my family when she was eight years old. Her mom and dad were drug dealers and they were sent to prison."

"Are they still in prison?" I asked.

"Yeah. Twenty years later and they're still there. She hasn't seen them in all these years either."

We arrived back at the apartment building and I climbed out of the truck. I walked over to my Explorer and set my coffee cup on the hood. Sam followed me.

"Let me give you a hand with those boxes."

"That's alright, Sam. Go enjoy your coffee. I can handle this."

He walked over to the back of the Explorer. "Nah, come on, Lily. Let me help. It's the neighborly thing to do anyway."

I sighed and unwillingly opened the hatch. Sam smiled, grabbed a box, and headed towards the apartment building. I stepped ahead of him so that I could hold open the door. Before I got up to the door, it swung open, and a guy stood there, staring at me.

"Luke, you're just in time. Hold this box," Sam said as he handed it to him.

"What are you doing?" Luke asked. "I woke up, and you were gone. By the way, there's no coffee left."

"Yeah, I know. I just picked some up at Brewster's. I have the bag in my truck. By the way, this is Lily. She's our new next-door neighbor."

"Hey," he spoke as he quickly looked away.

"Hey," I replied back.

I couldn't help but stare at him. He stood in the doorway— all six feet of him—in ripped jeans and a gray muscle shirt. He was barefoot, and his short, brown hair was messy. He was definitely one of the hottest men that I'd ever seen. You could tell he worked out by the muscle and definition in his arms and shoulders. He had a Celtic cross tattooed on his left bicep, with wings behind it. Thank God he was gay. I felt rather uncomfortable because Luke didn't seem as friendly as Sam did.

"Lily, go unlock your apartment door so we can get these boxes in there," Sam said.

As I walked past Luke, I caught him staring at me. The minute I looked at him, he turned away. As I unlocked the door and opened it, I stepped outside and held the building door open so that Luke could set the box down in my apartment. He did just that and then went inside his apartment and shut the door behind him without saying a word.

"What's his problem?" I asked Sam.

"Just ignore him. He's not much of a morning person."

I couldn't shake the feeling that he seemed familiar to me, but I knew it wasn't possible. He just had one of those faces. As Sam and I were bringing in the last of the boxes, Giselle and Gretchen pulled up. I hadn't seen them in over three months. I set the box down and ran over to them as they got out of the car. I hugged Gretchen first and then Giselle.

"I'm so happy you moved to Santa Monica," Giselle shrieked as she hugged me tight.

"Me too." My eyes began to swell with tears.

"Who's the hot guy walking towards us?" Gretchen smiled as she pushed her hair back behind her ear.

"Hello, ladies." Sam smiled.

"Sam, this is Giselle, and this is Gretchen. They're my two best friends."

"It's a pleasure to meet the both of you," he spoke as he held out his hand to each of them.

"Sam lives next door and he's been helping me bring the boxes in."

"We also went out for coffee this morning," he blurted out.

Giselle looked at me and smiled. "Did you hear that, Gretchen? Lily went out for coffee with a guy."

"I sure did, sis!" Gretchen smiled at me.

I turned and looked at Sam. "Don't listen to them. Thank you for your help. I appreciate it."

"No problem. If you need anything, just knock on my door or wall." He smiled.

I grabbed Gretchen and Giselle's hands and led them into my new apartment.

2

"So, Lily, tell us about Sam from next door and what's going on between the two of you." Gretchen smirked as she ran her hand along my new couch.

"Nothing's going on between us!" I exclaimed. "He helped me bring in my boxes; that's all."

"But you went out for coffee with him," Giselle said.

"Correction, we went and grabbed a coffee to go. Besides, he's gay anyway."

"Shut up! He can't be," Gretchen moaned.

"Yes, he is. He has a boyfriend named Luke," I spoke as I started unpacking the box for the kitchen.

"What a shame," Giselle said. "He seems like a nice guy, and he'd be perfect for you."

"First of all, I'm not on the market. I'm done with men, remember? And second of all, you've known him all of ten seconds. How do you know that he'd be perfect for me?"

"We can tell," Giselle and Gretchen spoke at the same time.

I rolled my eyes. "Come on, help me arrange this furniture." I smiled.

We moved the living room furniture around until it was perfectly placed. My bedroom furniture had been delivered, and most of my boxes were unpacked.

"What's this?" Giselle asked as she held the box labeled: *SCRAPBOOK.*

"Those are just some photos I took when I left Seattle. I was going to make a scrapbook dedicated to the start of my new life. But since I ended up staying in Portland, there isn't much in there. Just put it in my closet. I'll go through it someday."

"Oh, okay," she said as she headed to the bedroom. She came back out a few minutes later, holding my guitar. "Aren't you going to keep this out?"

I looked at her and then at the guitar.

"Yeah, I almost forgot about that. I put it in the closet so that it didn't get damaged while I was unpacking and moving things around. Just find a corner in the bedroom and set it there."

"I'm starving!" Gretchen blurted out.

"Me too." Giselle sighed.

I looked at the clock, and it was already six p.m. I realized I hadn't eaten a thing all day. "Let's order a pizza and a salad," I said.

"Sounds good. Where are your menus?" Gretchen asked.

"Considering I moved in last night, I don't have any menus." I laughed.

"I have an idea. Why don't you go next door and see if Sam has any pizza menus?" Giselle winked.

"I have an idea. Why don't you just do a search on your phone?"

Giselle rolled her eyes just as there was a knock on the door. I walked over and looked through the peephole to find Sam standing on the other side. Opening the door, I was surprised to see him standing there, holding two pizzas and a large brown bag.

"Sam, what's all this?" I asked as I pointed to the pizzas.

"I thought you ladies would like something to eat since you've been working hard all day." He smiled.

"Come in. Thank you!" I smiled. "You didn't have to do that."

"You're a lifesaver!" Gretchen proclaimed as she walked over and kissed him on the cheek. "We're starving."

"That was very nice of you to think of us, Sam. Let me get my wallet. How much do I owe you?"

"Nothing. It's on me. Consider it a housewarming gift," he said.

"Thank you, and please join us," I insisted.

"Don't mind if I do." He smiled.

I took some plates from the cabinet, grabbed some forks from the drawer, and sat down next to Sam at the table. Gretchen had already torn into the breadsticks while Giselle opened the salad. Sam grabbed a slice of pizza from the box, put it on my plate, and then smiled at me.

"Thank you," I whispered.

"You're welcome," he whispered back.

"You could have invited Luke to come over."

"I already asked him, but he refused. I told him that we'd be in the company of three beautiful women and great food, so it was his loss."

"And what did he say to that?" I laughed.

"He said he's good and just for me to come alone."

I got up from my seat and grabbed the bottle of wine Giselle and Gretchen had brought over. I took the wine glasses from the cupboard and set them on the table. Sam stood up, opened the bottle, and poured each of us a glass. He held up his glass for a toast.

"To my new neighbor, Lily. May we become great friends and share many good times."

We all smiled and clanked our glasses. "Thank you, Sam."

We talked for a few hours about our careers. Sam was an architect and worked for a well-known company called Glassman and Fillmore. I shared my love of photography and the fact that I had a teaching degree, which was the reason that brought me to Santa Monica. Gretchen and Giselle talked about their modeling careers and the exotic places they had been. It was late, so Gretchen and Giselle called it a night. I hugged them goodbye, and Sam walked them to their car.

As I was cleaning up the kitchen, a text message came through from Gretchen.

"I'm in love with Sam. Why does he have to be gay?"

I smiled and shook my head as I replied, *"All the good ones usually are."*

I finished cleaning up and looked at the clock; it was now two forty-five a.m. I turned the lights off and walked into the bathroom. Turning on the shower, I undressed, and stepped inside. It was a long day, and all I wanted to do was stay under the stream of hot water forever. After I managed to drag myself out of the shower, I put on my pajamas and looked at the guitar sitting in the corner of my bedroom. Walking over to it, I picked it up. I sat down on the edge of the bed and started strumming a few chords. Memories of my father came to my mind, and I started to play the song that he used to sing to me when I was a child. When I was done playing, I looked at the clock again, and it was now four a.m. I put the guitar back on its stand and climbed into my new bed. I prayed to God to please let me sleep peacefully.

***

My eyes flew open from the nightmare I was having. As I glanced at the clock, it was six and I had only slept two hours. I lay in bed, but did nothing but tossed and turned. There was no way I was going back to sleep. My mind was racing with the fact that I began my teaching job tomorrow. I loved kids, and I loved being a teacher, but I also loved photography and would love to make that my career. Being twenty-six years old, I was still undecided on what I wanted to do with my life. I thought I had it figured out with Hunter. My life was all planned out. We were going to get married, have a couple of kids, and live in a house with a white picket fence. I was going to pursue a career in photography while tutoring kids on the side. He was going to come home from work, and we were going to eat the meal together that I spent all day preparing. *Was I just desperate to find some normalcy in my life?*

I got out of bed and put on a cute little floral print sundress that I bought back in Portland. I dragged my ass to the kitchen for some coffee. Shit, I forgot to buy coffee. I sighed. I wondered if Sam was awake. I walked over to the wall and pressed my ear up against it. Since I didn't know the layout of his apartment, I took a chance and lightly knocked. I smiled when there was a knock back. Walking next door, I knocked on the door. I gasped when it opened, and saw Luke standing there in a pair of navy blue pajama bottoms that sat just below his hips. Instantly, I became nervous and started fidgeting.

"Can I help you with something?" he asked as he stared at me.

"Um, hi. I was wondering if Sam was around," I replied nervously.

"No, Sam isn't here."

There was tone in his voice that suggested I was bothering him.

"Oh, I'll catch him later then." I turned my back and started to walk to my apartment.

"Wait. Was there something you needed?" he asked.

I turned around and looked at him. Even though he was rude, he was sure as hell the sexiest man that I'd ever seen.

"I was just going to ask if I could borrow some coffee. I forgot to buy some yesterday, and being the caffeine addict that I am, I kind of need some, quick."

The corners of his mouth curved into a small smile. "Come on in," he said as he stepped aside.

As I stepped inside his apartment, I was shocked at how big it was. I guess being the end apartment had its advantages.

"What do you take in your coffee?" Luke asked as he opened the refrigerator.

"I drink it black. But that's ok, I'll just borrow some and make it at my place."

"You said you needed coffee quick, and I have some made, so take this cup and drink it," he growled.

"Okay." I nervously took the cup from him.

I looked around his apartment as I took a sip of coffee. It was spotless, and everything was in its place. The dark brown, leather furniture complimented the beige walls where a 65 inch TV was displayed. I was very uncomfortable, but I couldn't leave until I finished my coffee.

"You're one of the very few people that I know who take their coffee black," Luke said out of nowhere as he poured himself a cup and sipped it.

I sat down on the stool in front of the kitchen bar. Luke was leaning up against the counter with his coffee across from me. My eyes couldn't help but wander to his perfectly defined six-pack and sculpted V-line. He worked out; there was no doubt about it. I think it was time for my battery operated boyfriend and I to get reacquainted. I couldn't help but notice the scar that went from his right hip and around to his back.

"Is there something wrong with me?" he asked.

Instantly, my eyes darted up to his. "No, why would you ask that?"

"I don't know. It's just the way you were staring at me."

I wanted to die. I got lost in his body, and he caught me. I was so humiliated at that moment. I had to think of something quick.

"I'm sorry. I wasn't staring at you. I was just thinking about something."

"Thinking about what?" he asked as he walked closer and leaned over the counter in front of me.

Out of the corner of my eye, I saw an acoustic guitar sitting by the TV. "Who plays the guitar?" I asked to quickly change the subject.

"I do," Luke said.

"Cool," I replied.

He walked over to his guitar and took it from the stand. As he brought it over and handed it to me, I looked at him in confusion.

"Here. Play that song you were playing last night," he said.

"You heard that?"

"Yeah, see my couch right there? That's where your bedroom is."

"Oh, I'm sorry if I disturbed you."

"You didn't. I was up anyway. Now, why don't you play that song?"

I took the guitar from his hand and set it on my lap. I positioned my fingers on the strings and began to play. He took my empty coffee cup and filled it back up. He set the cup down in front of me as I strummed the song he wanted to hear.

"Who taught you how to play?" he asked as he leaned up against the wall next to the stool.

"My father," I answered as I strummed the last chord.

"What song is that?"

"A song my father used to sing to me. It's called 'Little Girl of Mine'."

He looked at me with a blank expression and I handed his guitar back to him.

"Your turn." I smiled.

"No. I'm not playing right now," he growled and walked back into the kitchen.

I didn't know what to say or think. One minute he was being nice, and the next, he acted as if I was bothering him. He was like a woman with severe PMS. I got up from the stool.

"Thanks for the coffee, and tell Sam I stopped by," I said with an attitude.

He didn't say a word to me. He just stared out the kitchen window with his hands pressed against the counter. When I opened the door to walk out, Sam was standing there.

"Hey, Lily. Good morning," he said with a confused look on his face.

"Tell your friend in there he needs to learn some manners when it comes to women," I snarled.

I walked back to my apartment, and Sam followed behind me.

"What the hell happened?"

"He's just rude, Sam."

Sam walked over to me and put his hands on my shoulders. "Listen. Luke's really a great guy once you get to know him. He's had a really rough year and I'm trying to help him."

"Yeah, well, so have I, but I'm not rude to people."

"Trust me when I say to cut him some slack. He's probably just nervous around you because you're so beautiful." He smiled.

I looked at him with a perplexed expression.

"I want to ask you something. Can you give me Gretchen's phone number?"

I looked at him again and shook my head as I put my hands up in front of him.

"Wait–wait–wait. Why do you want Gretchen's phone number?"

Sam twisted his face. "I want to ask her out on a date," he replied.

"A date?" I asked totally confused.

"Do you have a problem if I go out on a date with your best friend?" he asked while giving me a weird look.

"You're gay. Why would you want to date Gretchen? What about Luke? I don't think he'd appreciate his boyfriend going on a date with a woman."

Sam took a step back and put his hands up. "Whoa, wait a minute. You think I'm gay?!" He laughed.

A horrified look swept across my face. "Aren't you?" I asked carefully.

"You thought Luke and I were a couple?!" he said still laughing.

"Oh my God." I turned away in humiliation.

Sam grabbed me and hugged me. "You're so cute, Lily. I haven't had a good laugh in a long time."

I stood there with my nose pressed against his chest as I patted him on the back. "I'm glad I could amuse you."

"Now, about that phone number." He smiled.

"Hand me your phone," I said as I held out my hand. I keyed in the numbers of my phone, Gretchen's phone, and Giselle's phone. "Just in case you ever need to get a hold of me when I'm not home."

Sam smiled as he took his phone from me. A few moments later, my phone went off. I walked over to the counter, picked it up, and saw that I had a text message.

"Now you have my number if you ever just want to talk."

I looked at him and smiled. "Get out of here and go call Gretchen. She thinks you're hot, but don't tell her I said that."

Sam winked at me and laughed as he left my apartment.

3

Luke

I was sitting on the couch when Sam came through the door and started in on me. "What the hell's your problem, Luke?"

I looked at him as I took a sip of my coffee. "What the hell are you talking about, Sam?"

"You know what I'm talking about. Why do you have to be such an asshole to Lily?"

"I have no idea what you're talking about," I said as I got up and walked to my bedroom.

Sam followed behind me. "Bullshit! You know exactly what I'm talking about."

"Leave me alone, Sam," I warned.

He walked out of my room and went into the bathroom, mumbling under his breath. I opened my drawer and noticed it was almost empty. Looking over to the corner of my bedroom, I noticed my laundry basket was heaping with dirty clothes. I couldn't remember the last time I did laundry. I picked up some clothes that were lying on the floor and shoved them into the basket. Picking up the basket, I set it by the front door while I went to the refrigerator and grabbed a bottle of water. Sam came out of the bathroom just as I was walking out the door.

"By the way, Lily thought you were gay!" he shouted.

I stopped and put the laundry basket down. Turning around, I looked at Sam. "What do you mean she thought I was gay?"

"What part of 'she thought you were gay' do you not understand?" He smirked.

I rolled my eyes, shut the door, picked up the laundry basket, and headed down the hall to the laundry room. As I approached the doorway, I saw Lily putting clothes into the washer. She saw me and stopped.

"Hi, do you need to use this?" she asked while pointing to the washer.

"Yeah, but it's fine. I can do laundry another time," I replied.

I couldn't stop thinking about how I was an asshole to her this morning and how she must have mentioned it to Sam, otherwise he wouldn't have went off on me like he did.

"You can throw some of your clothes in with mine. We can split the cost." she offered.

"Didn't you just move in yesterday?" I asked.

"A couple of days of ago."

"If you just moved here, why are you already doing laundry?"

She looked at me with anger in her eyes. "I didn't do—hell, just forget it. It's all yours," she said as she took her things out of the washer and stormed out of the laundry room.

I didn't say anything wrong, so I didn't know why she got so upset. But it didn't matter anyway. I didn't care. I threw my clothes into the washer, started it, and headed back to my apartment. As I opened the door, Charley came running to me and I picked her up.

"Uncle Luke, look what my mom bought me!" she said as she showed me her silver butterfly bracelet.

"Wow, that's beautiful." I smiled and gave her a kiss on her head.

"She bought it for me as a present for my first day of school tomorrow."

"That's really pretty, peanut," I said as I put her down. "Where's your mom, Charley?" I asked as I didn't see her around the apartment.

"She went to the store. She asked Uncle Sammy if he could keep an eye on me until you came back from doing laundry."

My sister, Maddie, was a single mom, and Charlene, or Charley as we call her, was her nine-year-old daughter. They lived in one of the apartments upstairs. Her so-called dad, who denied he was the father from the start, until a paternity test proved Charley was his, comes around every couple of years. He doesn't pay child support and he doesn't call her on her birthday, Christmas, or Easter. He's nothing but a dead beat dad, and I wished my sister would get him to sign over his parental rights. He's not a good influence for Charley, and I wouldn't stand by and let him ruin her life.

"Hey, Charley, why don't you go take your crayons and paper over to the dining table and color me a pretty picture? I need to talk to your Uncle Luke for a minute," Sam said.

I walked to the refrigerator and grabbed a beer. I took off the cap and flung it at him. He caught it in his hand like he always did. I swear that boy should have been a baseball player. I think he missed his calling in life. I walked over to the couch, sat down, and put my feet up on the coffee table.

"I realized something today and I want you to know about it," Sam said.

"Yeah. What did you realize, Sam?" I asked, staring at the TV.

"I remember while growing up, my sister would come home crying because some of the boys were being mean to her."

I looked over at him as I took a drink of my beer. "Yeah, and what's your point?"

"I remember my mom telling her the only reason they were mean to her was because they liked her and they didn't know how to express it because they were scared."

"Is there a point to you telling me this story, Sam?" I asked.

"Yes, Luke, there is. My point is that I think you have an attraction to Lily and that's why you're acting like you are towards her."

"Jesus Christ, Sam, do you listen to yourself? You have no idea what you're talking about!" I spat as I got up from the couch.

"Luke, it's been a year since Callie—"

"Stop! Don't you ever say her name again!" I yelled.

Suddenly, I felt someone tugging on my jeans. "Uncle Luke, why are you yelling?"

I looked at Sam and shook my head. I bent down and put my hands on Charley's shoulders.

"I'm not yelling, peanut. I just raised my voice by accident. I'm sorry."

"Mommy always says to use your inside voice when you're indoors."

"I know, and I will. I promise. Now, go back over there and finish coloring that pretty picture." I smiled as I kissed the top of her head.

"Look, man, I'm sorry I upset you, but Lily's a real nice girl, and she doesn't deserve to be treated rudely. She's never done anything to you."

I stared at him, sat back down on the couch, and threw back my beer. "You act like you've known her your whole life when it's only been two days. Do you want to date her or something? Are you trying to get my approval?" I asked.

"No, I'm not trying to get your approval, and I don't need it either. If I wanted to date Lily, I would ask her on a date, but I'm really into her friend, Gretchen."

I took the last sip of my beer as Maddie walked through the door. I got up from the couch and kissed her on the cheek.

"Hey, sis, do you need any help?"

"Nope, I already took the bags upstairs." She smiled.

We both walked over to the table where Charley was coloring and looked at her picture. "That's a pretty picture, Charley. Can I have it?" I asked.

"Sorry, Uncle Luke. This picture is for my new teacher tomorrow." She smiled.

"Ah, well, she's one lucky teacher to get such a pretty picture," I said.

Maddie and Charley cleaned up the crayons and paper then walked out the door. Charley stopped in the middle of the hallway and turned to look at me.

"Uncle Luke, are you going to come over tomorrow morning before I go to school?"

"You bet I am, peanut." I smiled at her as she waved goodbye.

I loved that little girl more than anything in my life.

***

Later that evening, Lucky came over and we headed to Bernie's. It was the bar my sister worked at during the day and some evenings, but it was also where me and the boys played a little music. We could draw in quite a crowd when Bernie, the owner, told people when we were playing. We weren't playing tonight. We were just having a few drinks and shooting some pool. I'd known Lucky and Sam since freshman year at college. The three of us were roommates. Lucky's a womanizer. He always had been, and he always would be. His real name is Thomas, but we started calling him Lucky when he scored with the hottest chick on our college campus. He knew just the right things to say to a woman, and they always fell right under his spell. After a few games of pool and a few beers, I was calling it a night. Lucky invited a few girls over to the apartment to play *his* version of strip poker. I rolled my eyes when the girls giggled when he said that.

We arrived back at the apartment and Lucky got out the cards. It was him, Sam, and two other girls playing. The third girl didn't want to play, and neither did I. I walked to the refrigerator and grabbed a beer. I took off the cap and flung it over to Sam as he put his hand up and caught it. I smiled and sat down on the couch. The girl introduced herself as Monica. I didn't really care what her name was, and I wanted to be left alone. Lucky got up from the table and turned on some music. Sam yelled at him to turn it down. I shot Sam a look because he never told anyone to turn down the music. He liked it loud. He tilted his head to the side, indicating it would be too loud for Lily. I rolled my eyes and went back to watching TV.

It wasn't long before Monica scooted closer to me and started running her finger up and down my arm. I looked at her. She was attractive, but she wasn't my type. She leaned in closer and whispered in my ear.

"I give great blow jobs if you're interested." She smiled as she slowly licked her lips.

I was drunk, and I wasn't going to have sex with her, so I took her up on her offer. It had been a while since I'd had one, and I was more than ready. I got up from the couch and motioned for her to follow me into the bedroom. As I shut the door, Monica got on her knees and unbuttoned my jeans. She slid them down to my ankles along with my boxers. She wrapped her mouth around my hard cock as I fisted her hair and moved her head up and down. I was just about to come when the door opened. I looked up and saw Lily standing there.

4

Lily

I rummaged through my closet, trying to find the black skirt that I wanted to wear tomorrow. I couldn't believe I was going to be teaching fourth grade for an entire year. The teacher that I replaced took a year off to take care of her terminally ill husband. I unpacked the last of the boxes and found my black skirt. Looking at the clock, it was midnight. I needed to take a shower because I felt dirty from unpacking. As I walked to the bathroom, I undressed, and turned the shower on. As I reached up to adjust the shower head, the pipe broke, and water started pouring everywhere. I screamed, then quickly reached down and turned the water off. I stood there in a fit of rage. It was late, I was dirty, and now, what the hell was I going to do? I had no choice. I had to ask Sam if I could use his shower. I knew he was up because I could hear the loud music through the paper-thin walls. I threw on a tank top and a pair of yoga pants then went next door. After several knocks, Sam finally opened the door.

"Lily, what's up? Is everything ok?"

"No, the shower head pipe in my shower just broke and I start my new job in about seven hours. Can I use your shower real quick?" I asked.

"Sure, come in. The bathroom's right down the hall." He smiled.

I walked into his apartment and quickly scanned for Luke. He was the last person I wanted to see right now. All I saw was some other guy and two half-naked girls. I looked at Sam and raised one eyebrow.

"Sorry, but we're playing strip poker," he said.

"None of my business, Sam," I said as I held up my hand.

Suddenly, standing before me, was the guy that was sitting at the table.

"Sammy, who's your friend?" Lucky asked.

"This is Lily. She just moved in next door."

"*Hello*, beautiful." He smiled as he softly kissed my hand. "I'm Lucky, and it's my pleasure to meet such a gorgeous woman."

"It's nice to meet you, Lucky," I said with a fake smile. I knew his kind, and I wasn't about to fall for it.

I excused myself and headed down the hall. I opened the door—to which I thought was the bathroom—and gasped when I saw Luke standing there, getting a blow job. I instantly shut the door and left the apartment. Sam came after me and asked what was wrong. I told him that I'd changed my mind and went back into my apartment, shut the door, and slid down until I was on the ground. I cupped my face in my hands and sat there. I was startled when there was a knock at the door. Getting up and looking out the peephole, I saw it was Luke. I opened the door, and he stood there in jeans and a t-shirt, holding a tool box in his hand. I couldn't even look at him after what I saw. I was so embarrassed.

"Sam said the pipe in your shower broke."

"Yeah, it did. What are you, the handyman?" I asked.

"As a matter of fact, I am. I'm the maintenance guy, and I need to take a look so that I can get whatever parts I need and come back tomorrow to fix it."

"Fine. Come in," I snarled as I stepped aside.

I couldn't stop staring at his ass as he walked down the hall. *What the hell's the matter with me?* I didn't want to look at him or any part of his body. I followed him into the bathroom as he set his tool box on the toilet.

"So, what the hell did you do to this?" he asked.

"I didn't do anything. I just went to adjust it, and it broke off."

"These things just don't break off that easily. You must've really grabbed it and yanked it hard."

He was making me angry with his attitude, and I thought about something on him that I was going to grab and yank really hard. I rolled my eyes as I stood there, leaning up against the sink.

"You know what, Mr. Handyman? You're right. It must be my superhuman strength that broke it."

He turned his head and looked at me. The corners of his mouth turned up into a small smile that grabbed my attention. I couldn't look at him anymore. I was getting turned on, and that was something that hadn't happened to me in a very long time.

I was starting to get annoyed with the way my body was reacting just at the mere sight of him, and the worst part was I couldn't get what I just saw out of my head.

"I'll be in the kitchen if you need me." I walked out of the bathroom.

I looked at the clock on the stove, and it was two a.m. I was practically in tears because I had to be in my classroom at seven a.m., but I still needed to clean myself up. Luke came walking out of the bathroom with his tool box.

"I'll get the parts that I need tomorrow and come back to fix it. Will you be home?" he asked as he looked at me and I didn't answer. "Lily, what's wrong?"

I turned towards the refrigerator and acted like I was getting a bottle of water so that he couldn't see the tears that were about to fall.

"Nothing's wrong. I'm just really tired. I start my new job in a few hours, and I feel disgusting from unpacking boxes all day. And to answer your question, no. I won't be home tomorrow; at least not until after three o'clock."

I heard him take a few steps closer to me from behind. "Hey, grab your things and take a quick shower at my place. By the way, I'm sorry for what you saw earlier."

I put my hand up to stop him. "Please, don't apologize. You did nothing wrong. It was my fault for walking in on you and your girlfriend."

"She's not my girlfriend," he said unexpectedly. "Come on. Time's ticking away, and you need a shower."

I turned around and looked at him. "Thank you, Luke. Let me grab my things."

He waited for me, and we walked to his apartment. He opened the door, and as I stepped inside, the only thing I saw were two completely naked girls sitting at the table while Sam and Lucky were fully dressed. Luke sighed and walked over to the table and gathered up the girl's clothing and threw it at them.

"Girls, it's been fun, but it's time to leave now."

"Hey, man, what the hell are you doing?" Lucky said as he stood up.

"Lily, the bathroom's on the left."

I started to walk to the bathroom, and I heard Luke tell Lucky the party's over and that he needed to leave as well. Lucky wasn't happy about it, but he did what Luke said. I shut and locked the door. I stepped into the shower and stood under the hot water and relaxed. As I was shampooing my hair, I heard the door open.

"It's just me. Don't freak out," Luke said.

I froze. "What the hell, Luke? Get out!" I yelled.

"You're not the only one who has to get up early. I just need to brush my teeth real quick."

"You can't wait until I'm out of the shower and back in my apartment?"

"No. I'm tired, and I want to go to bed. Besides, you women take long showers."

I heard him start brushing his teeth. I couldn't believe the nerve of him.

"The door was locked. How did you get in?" I asked.

"The lock's broke, so it wasn't locked."

I heard him turn the water off. "I'm going to bed. I'll be by your place to fix your shower tomorrow after you get home. Night," he said.

The door shut, and he was gone. I stepped out of the shower, dried off, threw my clothes on, grabbed my things, and headed towards the door. Sam was cleaning up the mess that was left in the kitchen.

"Lily, before you go," he said as he walked towards me. "I'm sorry for tonight, and for the things you saw."

"Don't be sorry, Sam. What you and Luke do is your business, not mine. You have nothing to apologize for." I smiled.

He leaned over and kissed the top of my head. "Sleep tight. I'm going to give Gretchen a call tomorrow. Could you please not mention what you saw here tonight?" he asked with a twisted face.

"Don't worry. I won't tell her a thing." I smiled and walked out the door.

***

I jolted out of bed at the sound of my alarm buzzing. I quickly turned off the irritating sound and looked at the time. It was five thirty. I didn't fall asleep until three thirty, and I was exhausted. I made my way to the bathroom and splashed cold water on my face to try and wake myself up. I stumbled into the kitchen, and made a pot of coffee. As the coffee brewed, I put on my makeup, straightened my blonde hair, and put on my clothes. After pouring some coffee into my travel mug, I grabbed my purse, my school bag, and opened the door to leave. As I was locking up, Luke's door opened and he came walking out. Our eyes met.

"Morning," he said.

"Good morning," I replied. "You're up early."

"I told you last night that you weren't the only one who had to be up," he said as he locked his door.

"Have a good day." I smiled.

"Yeah, you too," Luke said as he walked up the stairs.

On the way to the school, I couldn't help but wonder why he was up so early, and why he went upstairs. He said he didn't have a girlfriend. Well, he said *she* wasn't his girlfriend. I shook my head. He was no different than every other guy out there, except he was the hottest looking man that I'd ever seen. I couldn't stop thinking about the scar I saw on him, and I wondered where it came from. *Why was I thinking about Luke so much?* I couldn't do this. I was starting over, and I couldn't have any distractions. I pulled into the school parking lot and headed to my classroom. I walked through the door and stared around the room. This was going to be my second home for the next ten months. I smiled at that thought, and I set my things on my desk. My main focus had to be my students, not Luke.

I heard a soft knock on the door. As I turned to look, Chris Channing, Gretchen and Giselle's aunt, and the principal of the school, was walking towards me.

"Lily, it's been way too long. How are you?" she asked as she hugged me.

47

"I'm good, Chris. Thank you again for hiring me."

"You're welcome. You were the perfect candidate. Not only have I known you for the past twenty years, but I know how much you love children. Gretchen told me about your situation, and I just want to tell you that I'm sorry."

I looked away and started rearranging things on my desk. "Don't be sorry, Chris. I'm moving on and starting over. Things worked out for the best."

"They sure did," she said as she hugged me again. "Your students will be here any minute. If you need anything at all, call me."

"I will," I smiled as the bell rang, and a flock of children entered the classroom.

***

I spent most of the day getting to know the children and having them get to know me. We all had lunch together in the classroom, which they thought was cool. I wanted them not only to like me, but to trust me as well. I wanted them to feel safe every time they walked into the classroom. The end of the day approached, and the bell rang. In a matter of minutes, the classroom was empty. I walked around the room and straightened the desks. Grabbing my things, I turned off the light, and headed home. Once I arrived at the apartment building, I unlocked and opened the door, threw my bags onto the chair, and kicked off my heels. I sat down on the couch for a minute to relax when I heard a knock. I got up, looked through the peephole, and saw Luke standing there. I opened it and motioned for him to come in.

"Hi," I said.

"Hey," he said without even looking at me as he walked down the hall.

I rolled my eyes. I was extremely tired, and I was in no mood for his attitude.

I put the kettle on the stove for some tea. All I wanted right now was the comfort of my plush bed. As I was waiting for the water to heat up, I heard Luke yell from the bathroom.

"Shit!"

It sounded like a yell of pain, so I walked to the bathroom to see what had happened. He stood there holding his hand.

"Are you okay? What happened?" I asked.

"Nothing, just go!" he spat.

"Excuse me, mister, but this is my fucking bathroom, and I'll be in here if I want to be."

He looked up at me. "Do you always use that kind of language?"

"Yes, I do. Now let me take a look at your hand," I said as I lightly touched it.

He pulled away quickly. "No, it's fine. I don't need your help."

"Maybe you do or maybe you don't. You're hurt, and I need to see how bad it is. Now sit your goddamn ass on that toilet so I can take a look."

He looked at me with anger in his eyes. "You can come off as being really mean."

"Good, I'm glad you noticed. Now, give me your hand."

He held out his hand and I removed the blood-soaked tissue. I grabbed a washcloth from under the sink and wrapped it around his hand.

"Put pressure on that while I get the antiseptic and a Band-Aid. It doesn't look like it needs stitches."

I reached into the cabinet and got out the antiseptic and some cotton balls. I could see him staring at me out of the corner of my eye. I soaked the cotton ball with antiseptic and set it on the edge of the counter. I turned to him and took his hand. I didn't want to look at him because he had the most amazing brown eyes.

"Where are you from?" he asked out of nowhere.

"Why do you care?" I replied.

"I don't. I'm just trying to make small talk."

"Seattle."

"Is your family still there?"

"I don't have any family. They're dead."

I removed the washcloth and took a cotton ball from the edge of the counter. "This is going to sting, but I know that you're a big boy, and you can handle it." I dabbed his cut on the side of his hand with the antiseptic soaked cotton ball.

"Fuck!" he screamed and tried to pull his hand away.

"Do you always use that kind of language?" I asked.

"Only when someone's hurting me!" he exclaimed.

"Stop being a baby and man up."

"Don't tell me to man up!"

"Fine. Be a baby."

I put the Band-Aid on his hand. "There, all better. Now get back to fixing my shower."

He looked at me and got up from the toilet. "Thank you."

"You're welcome," I said as I walked out of the bathroom.

I took a teabag from the cupboard and made some tea. About thirty minutes later, Luke emerged from the bathroom.

"You're all set."

"Great. Thank you. Can I offer you a beer?" I asked, not sure why those words escaped my lips.

"No, I need to go. Enjoy the rest of your evening," he said as he walked out of my apartment.

5

Luke

I opened the door to my apartment and set my tool box by the closet. I looked at my watch, and it was almost time for Mrs. Clements to bring Charley home. I walked outside to wait for her. Charley took a dance class after school with her best friend, Allie. Allie's mom picked the girls up from school, took them to dance class, and then dropped Charley off at my place. When Maddie worked the day shift at the bar, she usually didn't get off work until six. She didn't work many nights, but when she did, Charley spent the night at my place.

"Hey, peanut, how was your first day of school?" I asked her as I carried her backpack inside.

"It was great. I'm hungry," she pouted.

"What do you want to eat?" I asked.

"Grilled cheese." She smiled.

"One grilled cheese sandwich coming right up," I said as I got out the pan. "Tell me about your day."

"I love my new teacher. She's so nice and super pretty."

"Is that so?" I asked. "What's her name?"

"Miss Gilmore."

I made Charley her grilled cheese sandwich and listened to her as she told me all about her day.

"Uncle Luke, what happened to your hand?" she asked as she looked at the Band-Aid.

"Yeah, Uncle Luke, what happened to your hand?" Sam asked as he walked through the door smiling.

"It's just a cut from fixing the shower next door. It's nothing to worry about. Do you have homework, Charley?" I asked.

"Nope. Miss Gilmore said we would all be too tired from our first day to concentrate on homework, so she didn't give us any."

"She sounds like a cool teacher," I smiled.

"She's really cool. You would like her."

I walked out of the kitchen as she said that and sat down on the couch. Sam opened a beer, handed it to me, and sat in the chair across from me.

"How did it go at Lily's?"

"It went fine, except I cut myself," I said.

"I invited Gretchen to go with us to the beach this weekend, and I think you should invite Lily."

I looked at Sam and sighed. "Your hang up with me and Lily is getting old. I'm not interested. If you want her to join us at the beach this weekend, ask her yourself."

"Fine, I will," he said as he pulled out his phone.

Charley came over and sat next to me. "Can I watch SpongeBob Squarepants?"

I put my arm around her, and she snuggled up against me. I turned on her show, and looked over at Sam as he started laughing.

"What is so funny?" I asked.

"Lily asked if you were going to the beach, and when I told her yes, she said no. You two are going to kill me."

I rolled my eyes. I couldn't stop thinking about how Lily told me that her family was dead. I couldn't imagine not having my family. I hadn't seen any guys coming around, so I was pretty sure she didn't have a boyfriend. Not that it mattered. I was just surprised that someone as beautiful as her didn't have one.

The door opened, and Maddie walked in.

"Mommy!" Charley exclaimed as she jumped up from the couch.

"Baby, how was school?" she asked as Charley jumped in her arms.

"Hey, Maddie," I said as I kissed her on the cheek. "How was work?"

"It was the same as every other day. I got hit on a few times. A couple of drunken guys grabbed my ass. You know; the usual."

"Yeah, well I better never see them grabbing your ass, otherwise I'll kick theirs," I said.

"Tell Uncle Luke and Uncle Sammy goodbye, Charley."

"Bye, Charley," Sam smiled from the couch.

"Bye, peanut," I said as I held out my fist to her.

"Later gator," we both said at the same time.

I walked over and sat back down on the couch. "Do you know anything about Lily's past?"

Sam shot me a look. "No. Why are you asking?"

"I don't know. It's just something she said earlier."

"What did she say?"

"I asked her where she was from and she said Seattle. I asked if her family lived there, but she said that she didn't have any family and that they were dead."

Sam looked at me and his mouth dropped. "Seriously?"

"Yeah, seriously, dude."

"Wow, poor Lily, to be all alone with no family. That's awful."

Sam got up from the chair to take a shower. He was taking Gretchen out on a date.

I grabbed an ice-cold beer from the fridge and sat back down on the couch. My phone beeped and there was a text message from Lucky.

"Dude, come to the bar tonight. There's some really hot chicks here and I scored us a gig for Saturday night."

I wasn't in the mood for the bar tonight.

"Sorry, Lucky, not tonight, and thanks for the gig on Saturday."

I got up from the couch and grabbed my guitar. I sat back down, and as I was going to begin to play, I heard music coming from the other side of the wall. Lily was playing her guitar. The song she was playing sounded familiar. As I strummed a few chords, the music from the other side of the wall stopped. I played a short tune and waited. Lily played it right back. I strummed another tune, something a little more difficult, and then I waited. A few seconds later, she played it back. I couldn't help but smile.

"Is that a smile I just saw on your face, Luke?" Sam said as he walked by.

"No, and where are you taking Gretchen?" I asked to change the subject.

"I'm taking her to a new restaurant for dinner and then maybe a movie after."

"Have a good time," I said as Sam headed out the door.

I strummed a few more chords and waited for Lily to strum back, but she never did. I decided to try and write a new song. It's been a year since I've written anything. Ever since…

6

Lily

"Hello," I said as I answered Gretchen's call.

"Guess what I'm doing tonight?"

"I don't know. Taking a bubble bath and shaving your legs?"

"No, Lily, stop it! I'm going on a date with Sam!"

"Ah, so he finally called you. That's great, Gretchen. I'm happy for you."

"Try it sometime, Lily. You might surprise yourself and like it."

"No thanks. I'm happy with my life as it is. I don't need a man to be complicating things. Have fun on your date with Sam. You better call me tomorrow and let me know how things went."

"I will, Lily. Try not to have too much fun in that apartment all by yourself."

"Goodbye, Gretchen."

"Goodbye, Lils."

I smiled as I hung up the phone and picked up my guitar. I could hear Luke trying to play something. He kept strumming and stopping. The little game we played just before Gretchen called was fun. He would play a tune and stop, and I would play it back. I couldn't help but wonder how his hand was doing. Something about him bothered me. On one hand, I couldn't stop thinking about him. On the other, I couldn't stand him. I got up and put my guitar back. I had a corner in my living room that sat empty, so I moved my guitar there. That guitar held a lot of memories for me. Some bad and some good.

***

The next morning, I stumbled out of bed, tired as hell, and made my way to the kitchen for some coffee. You'd think I'd be used to only getting a couple hours of sleep a night since it's been over a year. I poured a cup then headed to the bathroom for a shower. I stepped out of the shower and heard my phone beep. Grabbing it from my dresser, I noticed a text message from Sam.

"Good morning. I need to see you before I leave for work. Can I stop by?"

I smiled because he probably wanted to talk to me about his date with Gretchen. I replied back.

"Sure, the door's unlocked. Grab a cup of coffee, and I'll be right out. I'm getting dressed."

I quickly ran to the door and unlocked it then ran back into my bedroom. As I was putting on my black pants, I heard Sam come in.

"Hey, Lily, it's just me."

"Hey, Sam, I'll be right out!" I yelled.

I put on my shirt and walked out to the living room, rubbing my hair with a towel.

"You look very professional today." I smiled.

He was wearing a three-piece black suit with a light green shirt and matching tie. Needless to say, he looked hot.

"I have a meeting today with a big client, and he's the uptight. He's the 'everything needs to be professional', type of person."

"So, what brings you here for a visit this early in the morning?" I asked.

"Being a teacher, I knew you'd be up getting ready for work."

"Follow me to the bathroom. I need to start getting ready," I said.

Sam got up from the table and stood in the doorway of the bathroom while I put on my makeup.

"I had a great time with Gretchen last night. She's an amazing person." He smiled. "I think the four of us should go out."

"The four of us?" I asked as I put on my mascara.

"Gretchen, me, you, and Luke."

"I don't date," I said as I looked at my eyes in the mirror.

"I know you don't, and I'm really sorry to hear that."

I instantly looked at him. "Gretchen told you, didn't she?"

"Yes. She told me all about your ex and what happened at the church."

"Damn her. Just wait until I talk to her," I said in anger.

"Don't, Lily. She's worried about you. She told me that she's happy you moved to Santa Monica because then she can keep a closer eye on you. She doesn't want you to be lonely."

"I like being lonely. Did she say anything else?" I asked as I ran a brush through my damp hair.

"She told me that your family isn't dead and that they're still living in Seattle."

"My family's dead to me, Sam. What my sister and mother did is unforgivable. I want you to forget about that conversation, and don't ever mention it to anyone. Do you understand me? I'm starting my life over, and that's my story. I never plan on seeing either of them again."

"Okay. I'll forget about it, but I want you know that Luke isn't a bad guy like you think he is. He's hiding himself, just like you are."

"I don't care about Luke, Sam. I'm not interested in men, *period*. I don't care who they are. They're all lying, cheating bastards who break my heart over and over. I refuse to ever let it happen again."

He put his arm around me and held me tight. "I understand, and don't worry; your secret's safe with me."

"Thank you, Sam."

"I have to go or I'll be late. Have a good day with your students." He smiled as he turned and left the apartment.

"Have a good professional meeting!" I yelled from the bathroom.

As I was blow-drying my hair, I couldn't stop thinking about what Sam had said about Luke hiding himself. I didn't care about Luke or his life. I threw my hair up in a ponytail and headed out the door.

***

The students were wound up, but we had a productive day. I was sitting at my desk as the students were doing a writing assignment when Charley came up to me.

"Miss Gilmore," she said.

"Hi, Charley, what's up?" I asked.

"My uncle's taking me to the carnival Friday night," she said with a huge smile plastered on her face.

"Wow, what a nice uncle you have." I smiled back.

"He's the best! He takes care of me a lot while my mom's working. He helps me and my mom out since my daddy isn't around."

Hearing Charley say those words broke my heart. I knew what it was like not having your dad around.

"Your uncle sounds like he's an amazing person."

"He is, and I love him very much. I think you would like him, and he doesn't have a girlfriend. She died."

"Oh, Charley, I'm sorry to hear that. I'm sure that I'd like him."

The bell rang, and the end of the school day had arrived.

"Bye, Miss Gilmore." Charley smiled and waved.

"Bye, Charley. See you tomorrow."

The classroom emptied, so I walked around putting things away and straightening the desks. I grabbed my bags, got in the Explorer, and started driving down the road. As I was driving and listening to my favorite tunes, my car started to shake. I quickly pulled over onto the side of the road, and it stalled. I turned the key to try and start it, but it was dead. I sighed and got out my phone. I tried to call Gretchen and Giselle, but there was no answer. Shit—shit—shit! I said as I got out and leaned up against the side of the Explorer. I tried to call Sam, but he didn't answer either, so I left a message and told him where I was.

Thirty minutes had passed, and I was getting ready to start walking when a motorcycle pulled up behind me. I was a little nervous. He pulled off his helmet and looked at me. I couldn't help but smile as Luke got off his bike and started walking towards me.

"So, you're my knight and shining armor?" I asked.

"Something like that," he said. "Pop the hood so that I can take a look."

I popped the hood and stood next to Luke as he examined the engine. "Try and start it."

I got inside and turned the key—nothing. "Sorry, but it still doesn't want to start!" I yelled form the driver's seat.

Luke shut the hood and walked over to the driver's side window. "It's probably the alternator. You're going to have to get this towed."

"Great," I said as I put my forehead on the steering wheel.

"My buddy owns a garage not too far from here. I'll call him and have him come tow it."

"Thank you, Luke."

"No problem," he said as he walked away and made the phone call.

He walked over to me as I climbed out of the truck and handed me his helmet. "Here, put this on."

I looked at him confusion. "Why?"

"Because I don't want you on the back of my bike without one on."

I looked at him like he was crazy. "I'm not getting on the back of that thing. I hate motorcycles."

"Suit yourself. The guys won't be here for another two hours. If you want to sit in the hot sun, or the hot car, that's fine with me. I really don't care either way," he said as he walked away.

I sighed as I sat down on the ground, leaning up against my broken down Explorer. This was going to be the longest two hours of my life. Luke got on his bike and started it. He pulled up next to me and yelled over the roaring engine.

"Are you sure? This is your last chance!"

"I'm sure," I said.

He sped away and left me sitting there on the side of the road in the hot sun. I pulled my phone from my pocket, and it was dead. Of course it was. Could this day get any worse? A few minutes later, I heard the roaring engine of a motorcycle. I look up and saw Luke getting off his bike. He walked over to me and grabbed my arm.

"What the fuck do you think you're doing?!" I yelled as he pulled me off the ground.

"Taking you home, and watch your mouth," he said.

"I'm not getting on that thing, and you can't make me!" I said as he was dragging me to his bike.

He stopped dead in his tracks, turned around, and looked at me. "What is it that you're scared of, Lily?"

"Nothing," I said as I walked back to the Explorer. "Just leave me alone and go home, Luke."

I sat inside to try and escape him. He opened the passenger door and climbed in. I stared straight ahead and wouldn't look at him.

"Something about motorcycles has you freaked out. Tell me what it is, and maybe I can help you."

"You can't help," I said as my eyes started to tear. He wouldn't stop staring at me, and once again, he was making me feel uncomfortable.

"Please, just tell me, Lily," he whispered.

I sighed and took in a deep breath. "I was in a motorcycle accident with my dad when I was a child. I can still remember the pain as if it happened yesterday. I haven't been on a bike since, and I don't plan on starting now."

"I can understand that, but you'll be safe with me. I promise."

I turned my head towards him. There was something in his eyes that drew me into him. It was hot, and the thought of sitting here for the next two hours wasn't a pleasant one.

"Fine, I'll go," I said hesitantly. "But just to let you know, I may have an anxiety attack."

He reached over and touched my hand. I should've pulled back, but I couldn't. He tilted his head and smiled. "You'll be fine."

We both got out of the Explorer and walked over to his motorcycle. The memories of the accident started to flood my mind. He handed me the helmet and saw I was shaking. He clasped my shoulders.

"Take a deep breath. You'll be safe."

I took the helmet and put it on. There was something soothing about his voice. I trusted him, and I started to calm down. He straddled his bike and started it. Patting the seat behind him, he told me to get on. I climbed on and leaned forward, wrapping my arms around him as tight as I could. I closed my eyes as he took off down the road, and the only thing I felt was the wind against us and Luke's muscular form. He looked back for a second and asked me if I was okay. I told him I was. The sick feeling that I had a few minutes ago had passed, and it wasn't so bad riding with him. He made me feel safe.

We reached our apartment building and I let out a sigh of relief. When he pulled into a parking space, a car pulled up next to us. I looked over and saw my student, Charley, getting out of the car. Luke got off his bike as Charley ran up and hugged him. I took off my helmet.

"Miss Gilmore!" Charley's eyes lit up.

Luke looked at her. "This is Miss Gilmore. Your teacher?" he asked in shock.

"Yes, Uncle Luke, that's her." She smiled.

I looked at Charley with widened eyes. "This is your uncle that you've been telling me about?"

"Yes! It sure is!" Her smile widened.

A woman was walking over to us with a couple of bags in her hands. Luke immediately took them from her. She looked at me and held out her hand.

"Hi, Miss Gilmore. I'm Maddie, Charley's mom."

I smiled as I shook her hand. "It's nice to meet you. Please call me Lily."

"Miss Gilmore, why are you riding on my Uncle Luke's motorcycle?" Charley asked.

"Your teacher lives in the apartment next door to me. Her car broke down, so I gave her a ride home," Luke said.

"I had no idea you lived here, Lily," Maddie said. "Charley and I live in the apartments upstairs. My parents own the building."

"Uncle Luke, can Miss Gilmore come with us to the carnival on Friday?" Charley asked.

Luke looked at me, and I looked at him. I could tell he was uncomfortable.

"Thank you for inviting me, Charley, but I won't be able to make it," I said.

"Uncle Luke, tell her she can come," Charley whined.

"Yeah, you can join us. Maddie has to work at the bar Friday night so Charley's staying with me."

"Please, Miss Gilmore. Please," Charley begged.

How could I resist her? "Okay, Charley. I'll go." I smiled as I put my hand on her head.

We walked inside the building, and I said goodbye as the three of them headed upstairs to Maddie's apartment.

I opened the door and threw my things on the chair. I grabbed a bottle wine and poured some into a glass. As I stood against the kitchen counter, I remembered something Charley said about her uncle. She said he didn't have a girlfriend because she died. I was in deep thought when I was startled by a knock at the door. I looked out the peephole, and Luke was standing there.

"Hi." I smiled. "Come on in."

He walked inside. "I just wanted to tell you that I called my buddy's garage. They towed your Explorer and it'll be ready tomorrow afternoon."

"Thank you, Luke. I appreciate it. Do you want a glass of wine or a beer?" I asked.

Placing both his hands in his pockets, he spoke, "Nah, I need to get going," He opened the door and turned around. "I'm driving Charley to school in the morning. I can give you a ride if you don't already have one."

I tilted my head as my heartbeat started to pick up the pace. "Thank you, but I don't think the three of us will fit on your bike."

Luke chuckled. "We wouldn't take my bike. I have a vehicle."

"You do?"

"Yes, and my sister wouldn't let me take Charley on the bike anyway. She hates motorcycles."

"Thank you for your offer. I think my students would appreciate you making sure their teacher gets to work." I smiled.

"Okay then. I'll meet you here in the hall at six forty-five." He smiled back.

I took in a deep breath as he shut the door. Something was happening to me. That feeling was beginning to come back and it scared the shit out of me. I couldn't and wouldn't let myself go down that road again. I'm happier alone. I needed to be alone for my own sanity because I couldn't take more heartbreak. Just as I was getting caught up in my emotions, there was a knock at the door. I looked out the peephole, and saw Luke standing on the other side. I opened the door and stared at him.

"By the way, I'm Luke Matthews," he said as he held out his hand.

"It's nice to meet you, Luke Matthews. I'm Lily Gilmore," I replied as I shook his hand.

He turned and went back to his apartment. I shut the door, smiled, and headed for the shower.

7

Luke

I couldn't believe that Lily was Charley's teacher. I walked into the apartment and Sam was cooking dinner.

"What are you making, dude?" I asked him.

"I'm making chicken parmesan. Gretchen's coming over for dinner."

"Thanks for the notice, bro."

"Sorry. I was in meetings all day, and it was kind of a last minute thing. Did you go and pick up Lily?" he asked.

"Yeah. I had her car towed to Huey's Garage. It'll be ready tomorrow. Hey, did you know that she's Charley's school teacher?"

"I knew she was a teacher, but I had no idea she was Charley's. That's pretty cool. Don't you think?" he asked.

"I guess. I'm driving her and Charley to school in the morning. Maddie has to be at the bar early for a meeting. Lily's going with me and Charley to the carnival tomorrow. Why don't you and Gretchen come with us?"

Sam gave me a pointed look; his brow raised. "You asked her to go with you to the carnival?"

"No. Charley asked her to go."

"And she said yes?" Sam asked in a surprised tone.

"Yes, she did. She wasn't going to turn down Charley."

"That's great, Luke. Gretchen and I already have plans for tomorrow night though, sorry."

"Wow, you're really serious about this girl."

"I really like her, man. She's all I ever think about."

I walked over and put my hand on Sam's shoulder. "That's great. I'm really happy you found someone. I'm going to go up to Maddie's to give you and Gretchen some privacy."

"Thanks, man." He smiled.

I walked out the door and up to Maddie's apartment. Charley was playing video games, and Maddie was cooking dinner. I could tell something was wrong with Maddie, and it looked like she'd been crying.

"What's wrong, Maddie?" I asked.

"Nothing's wrong. It's the onions," she said.

"Daddy called," Charley spoke from the couch.

"Is that true?" I asked Maddie.

She nodded her head without saying a word. "What did the bastard want?!" I spat.

Maddie turned and looked at me. "Not in front of Charley, Luke."

I looked over at Charley who was lost in the world of video games.

"Then let's go into the other room. I want to know what that bastard wanted," I whispered.

We walked into Maddie's room. "All he said was that he's coming to town in a couple of weeks and that he wants to see Charley. I told him that he couldn't see her until he paid his child support, but he said I better watch it or he'll take me to court and sue me for full custody of her."

"Over my dead body," I spoke in anger.

"Calm down, Luke. I have a couple of weeks to think of a plan. Technically, I can't keep him from her. He's her father."

I shook my head as I walked out of the bedroom. Walking over to the couch, I took a seat next to Charley.

"Are you and mom okay?" she asked.

"Yeah. We're okay." I smiled as I kissed the top of her head.

After dinner, I went back to my apartment. Opening the door, I stepped inside and didn't see Sam or Gretchen. I didn't have to see them. I could hear them before I reached the hallway. I rolled my eyes and walked out of the apartment. I didn't need to sit and listen to them having sex. I stood in the hallway and thought about going to Bernie's, but I decided I wasn't up for it, especially since I was driving Lily and Charley to school tomorrow morning. I stood and stared at Lily's door. I couldn't stop thinking about her and the way she held onto me while on the motorcycle. She held on as if her life depended on it. She trusted me even though she was scared to death to get on that bike. I smiled for a moment and thought about knocking on her door. Then decided it wasn't a good idea, so I went back inside my apartment, took my guitar from the stand, and sat down on the couch, playing a few chords as loud as I could to let Sam know I was home.

***

I slammed my hand down on the beeping alarm clock. I was so damn tired from being kept awake all night while Sam and Gretchen acted like they'd never had sex before. I stumbled out of bed and threw on a pair jeans and my black t-shirt. I ran the brush through my hair and went to the bathroom to brush my teeth. Gretchen was in the kitchen, pouring coffee.

"Good morning. You must be Luke," Gretchen said as she held out her hand.

"Yeah, and you must be Gretchen." I shook her hand.

I looked around and didn't see Sam. "Where's Sam?" I asked as I poured my coffee into my to-go cup.

"He ran to get some bagels. He'll be back soon."

I looked at the clock at it was six forty.

"I have to go. It was nice meeting you, Gretchen," I said as I walked out the door and up the stairs to get Charley. Just as I reached the top step, she was coming out of her apartment.

"Morning, Uncle Luke." She smiled.

"Morning, peanut." I patted the top of her head. "Do you have everything you need?"

"Yes, Uncle Luke." She sighed.

We walked down the stairs as Lily was coming out of her apartment. "Perfect timing!" She smiled as she held up her coffee cup.

"This is so cool that I get to drive my teacher to school!" Charley shrieked.

Lily looked nice. Oh hell, she looked beautiful. Every time I looked at her, I felt like I'd met her before. Her long, blonde hair was straight, and she was wearing a long cream-colored skirt with a light pink top and high heels. Damn, I wish my teachers looked like that when I was growing up. She was going to give those boys their first hard-ons. When she smiled, her bluish-gray eyes lit up.

"Good morning you two," Lily said.

"Morning," I spoke back.

"Good morning, Miss Gilmore," Charley said as she took Lily's hand and led her to the Jeep.

Charley climbed into the back as Lily sat in the passenger side.

"A Jeep Wrangler fits you. I like it better than that motorcycle you ride."

"Thanks, but I like my bike, so you'll get used to it." I winked.

"Keep dreaming." She smiled.

When I pulled into the school parking lot, Charley got out and leaned over to kiss me on the cheek. "Bye, Uncle Luke." She waved.

"Bye, peanut. Have a good day."

Lily got out of the car and slung her bag over her shoulder. "Thanks for the ride, Luke. Have a good day," she said as she started to walk away.

"Hey, Lily!" I yelled out.

She stopped, turned around, and looked at me. "I can pick you up at the end of the day and take you to the garage to get your car."

"Sounds good. I'll see you later." She smiled.

I caught myself staring at her as she walked into the school. For the first time in over a year, a woman made me smile. Sam was right. Lily was a nice girl—a *very* nice girl—and I couldn't stop thinking about her. I found myself thinking of her in ways that I hadn't thought about since...

8

Lily

I sat quietly at my desk while the students were having their daily reading time. I was trying to concentrate on grading papers, but the only thing on my mind was Luke Matthews. *Why does he have to be so damn sexy? Why does the universe have to light up every time he smiles? Why does he have to have such a great body? Why does he have to live next door?*

I found myself thinking about him more and more; that was something I didn't bargain for when I moved to Santa Monica. I was distracted by the chiming of my cell phone. I looked over at the screen and saw a message from Giselle.

"Gretchen had a date last night with Sam, but she never came home. I guess she got a piece of that hot man!"

"Lucky girl," I replied back.

"Do you want to meet up for dinner and drinks tonight?" Giselle asked.

"I can't. I'm going with Luke and Charley to the carnival."

"Who's Charley?"

"She's Luke's niece who also happens to be one of my students."

"We have some catching up to do. Call me later, and let's set up dinner."

"I will. Bye."

I immediately sent Gretchen a text message.

"Did you have sex with Sam?" I asked.

A few minutes later, she replied, *"Yes I did. It was wonderful, Lily. He's a GOD in bed."*

I smiled at her reply. *"I'm glad you had fun. Are you still at his place?"*

"Yeah, I'm getting ready to leave. I have a photo shoot across town in an hour."

"Is Luke there?" I asked.

"No. He's not. Why are you asking?"

"I was just wondering. I have to go. Reading time is over."

I wondered why Luke didn't tell me that Gretchen stayed the night. After all, she was my best friend. The rest of the day went quickly, and before I knew it, the bell rang, and the children scurried out of the classroom. As I stood by the door saying goodbye to the students, Maddie walked in.

"Hi, Maddie." I smiled.

"Mommy!" Charley exclaimed as she came running from the other side of the room.

"I saw Luke outside. He's taking you to pick up your car?" she asked.

"Yes." I nodded my head.

"That's great. It's good to see that Luke's helping you."

I thought that was an odd thing to say and I wondered what she meant by it. My mind went back to what Charley had said about Luke's girlfriend dying.

"Bye, Miss Gilmore. I'll see you later!" Charley smiled.

"Bye, Charley. I'm looking forward to it."

"Have a good time tonight, Lily," Maddie said as she took Charley by the hand and left the classroom.

I grabbed my bags and headed to the parking lot. I smiled when I saw Luke's Jeep parked in front and Luke sitting in it with his Ray Bans on. I felt a rush of sensation down below. I hated myself for that. He turned to me and smiled as I climbed inside.

"Did you have a good day?" he asked.

"I did. Thank you for asking. How about you?"

"I fixed a couple of toilets, a leaky sink, and changed a light bulb for the woman in 4B."

"I didn't know you changed light bulbs." I smirked.

"I can do just about anything."

"So, if I needed my light bulb changed, then you'd change it for me?" I couldn't believe what I just said. *What the hell was the matter with me?*

Luke looked over at me as the corners of his mouth turned upwards. "Just call me and I'll be over in a flash. I can change anything you want."

"How can I call you if I don't have your number?" *Oh my god, I have no control over my mouth. Why was this happening? This wasn't me.*

We were stopped at a light. "Give me your phone," he said as he held out his hand.

I looked at him strangely then placed my phone in his hand. He typed in his number and handed it back to me.

"There, now you have my number. If you need anything fixed, call me," he said as he took off from the light.

As we were driving to the garage to pick up my Explorer, a song came on the radio that was all too familiar to me. Luke reached over and turned it up. I looked the other way. It was one of my dad's songs.

"I love this song," Luke said. "Do you know it?"

"I've heard it a few times," I said as I looked down at my phone.

When we finally reached the garage, Luke parked the Jeep and we both got out.

"Hey, Huey," he said as they fist-bumped each other.

"Hey, Luke. We need to hit the bar sometime, man."

"I know. It's been a while. This is Lily. Lily, this is Huey."

"It's nice to meet you, Huey," I spoke as I held out my hand.

"It's nice to meet you too, Lily. Your truck's all fixed and ready to go."

I paid Huey what I owed and thanked him as he led me to where the Explorer was parked. Luke followed close behind.

I got inside and turned the key. Luke walked over, and I rolled down the window.

"I'll follow you home just in case it breaks down again."

"Thank you. I appreciate it." I smiled.

He turned away and I couldn't help but stare at his fine ass as he walked back to his Jeep. It didn't matter what side of him you saw, front or back, he was still sexy as hell.

***

I drove home, and Luke followed behind me. We pulled into the parking spaces next to each other and walked inside the building.

"What time should I be ready tonight?" I asked.

"Charley will be at my place around seven. So, we'll pick you up then."

"Sounds great, and thanks again for your help," I said as I slid my key into the lock.

"No problem. I'll see you in a couple of hours." He entered his apartment and shut the door.

I threw my bags on the kitchen counter and walked to the bathroom for a quick shower. I had no idea what I was going to wear. I was standing in my room, in a towel, when I heard a knock on the door.

Shit, I thought. I looked out the peephole and saw Giselle standing there. I unlocked it and opened the door, standing behind it. Giselle walked in and looked at me.

"I bet you were wishing I was Luke right now." She smiled.

"Very funny," I said. "What brings you over?"

Giselle followed me to the bedroom. "I had an appointment not too far from here and I just thought I'd stop by. What's going on with you and Luke anyway?"

"Nothing. We're just friends. Why do you think something's going on?"

"I don't know. Wishful thinking, I guess." She smiled. "Do you even find him attractive?"

I pulled out my jean shorts from the drawer and put them on. "Of course I find him attractive. Have you seen his ass? You'd have to be blind not to see that."

"Well, at least you find him hot; that's a start," she said as she sat on the bed.

"You know my past, and you know I won't go down that road again. I'm happy the way I am."

"Lily, stop trying to convince yourself. You're twenty-six years old, and you've vowed to stay single and not date guys for the rest of your life. Sorry, honey, but it's not going to happen unless you join the convent."

"Very funny, Giselle," I said as I put on my black tank top. I picked up my brush from the dresser and starting running it through my hair. "Should I wear my hair up?" I asked as I looked in the mirror.

"Why does it matter? It's not like you're trying to impress anyone."

I shot her a look and walked into the bathroom to brush my teeth. Giselle followed behind me.

"You know I love you, right?" she asked. "I just want you to be happy and not become some old cat lady who keeps herself locked up with her twelve cats."

I laughed as I rinsed my mouth and spat in the sink. "I don't even have a cat."

"Not yet, you don't. But you've been talking about maybe getting one."

I smiled and smacked her on the arm as I left the bathroom. I grabbed my black cowboy boots from the closet and put them on. I twirled around the living room.

"What do you think?" I asked.

"I think you look hot, and Luke isn't going to know what hit him when he sees you." She smiled. "There's nothing sexier to a man than short jean shorts, tank tops, and cowboy boots."

I tilted my head. "How do you know that?" I asked.

"I dated a cowboy once."

"Oh yeah, that creepy guy from Montana that wouldn't let you take your boots off during sex and wanted you to ride him on a bull."

"Yep, that's the one." She laughed.

Suddenly, there was a knock at the door. The second I opened it, Luke looked me up and down.

"What did I tell you?" Giselle whispered in my ear as she walked by me. "Have fun everyone, and Lily, make sure you call me tomorrow."

"Hi, Charley," I said as I patted her head. "Hi, Luke." I smiled.

"Are you ready to go?" he asked.

"I sure am. Just let me grab my purse and camera."

I turned around and headed towards my bedroom. I could feel his eyes staring at me as I walked away. You know that feeling you get when you know someone's looking at you? That's the feeling I had. I grabbed my purse, put my camera around my neck, and walked back to the living room.

"You look really pretty, Miss Gilmore," Charley said. "Uncle Luke, doesn't she look pretty?" Charley asked as she tugged on his pant leg.

"Yes, Charley, Miss Gilmore does look pretty," Luke said in embarrassment.

Charley looked at me and winked. I needed to watch out for this little girl. We climbed into Luke's Jeep and headed for the carnival.

"Nice camera. I take it you like to take pictures," he said.

"Yeah, I love taking pictures. Photography has always been a passion of mine. Someday, I'd love to work for a big magazine."

"You mean like National Geographic or something like that?" He smiled as he looked over at me.

I nodded my head. "Yeah, something like that." I smiled back.

***

Charley's eyes lit up the moment she saw the lights.

"I can't wait to get inside!" she said with excitement as she grabbed onto our hands and dragged us through the parking lot.

Luke looked over at me and smiled. We got to the gate, and I pulled out my wallet to pay for my ticket.

"I got your ticket," he said.

"I can buy my own ticket, Luke."

"Charley invited you, so I'm buying your ticket."

We stepped up to the window, and he purchased three wristbands. I tried to give him my money, but he wouldn't take it.

"If I let you buy my ticket, then this becomes a date. I don't do dates," I said to him.

He stared at me for a minute. "I can assure you that this isn't a date. I don't do dates either."

"Will you two stop it and *hurry up*," Charley said with an attitude.

"I'll make you a deal," Luke said. "You can buy the food."

"Deal," I spoke as I held out my hand to him and we shook on it.

We both held one of Charley's hands as we walked around the carnival. The lights were bright, and the music coming from the games was loudly blaring through the speakers. Charley saw a ride she wanted to go on, so we waited in line.

"Do you watch Charley a lot?" I asked.

"Yeah. I try to help Maddie out as much as I can. It's hard being a single parent."

"I'm sure it is."

"What about your parents?"

"They help out a lot. Right now, they're on a month long cruise."

"They own the apartments?" I asked.

"Yes. They've owned those apartments for over twenty years. I remember them buying the building when I was seven years old. It's where Maddie and I spent most of our childhood. What about you?" he asked.

I didn't want to talk about my childhood or my family. It wasn't a topic that I was comfortable with. The only thing I ever wanted was a normal, happy childhood. I can thank Mommy and Daddy for not giving me that. I felt horrible for having to lie to Luke about my family, but I didn't want him to know about how horrible they were. I didn't want to be judged for their actions. And as far as I was concerned, my family was dead.

"I grew up in Seattle with my parents and my sister. They died a couple of years ago in an accident."

Luke looked at me, and I could see the empathy in his eyes. "I'm sorry."

"Thank you. I don't like to talk about it," I said so he wouldn't ask me any other questions.

Luke nodded his head. We finally arrived to the front of the line, and Charley got on the ride. We stood there, waving to her as the car she was sitting in sped by us.

"She's a great little girl." I smiled.

"She's the best," Luke said. "She's a huge part of my life, and I would do anything to protect her."

The ride ended, and Charley got off. She grabbed onto our hands once again and led us over to the games.

"Miss Gilmore, do you like to play games?" she asked as she looked up at me.

"I love to play games, Charley."

"So does my Uncle Luke." She winked.

I couldn't help but laugh. "Charley, when we're not in school, you can call me Lily."

"Really?!" she asked in excitement.

Luke looked over at me and laughed. "Just remember though, she's Miss Gilmore during school hours," he said.

"Okay, I'll remember," she said as she led us to the game that had the huge, stuffed purple cat hanging from the tent. "I want that cat, Uncle Luke," she begged.

I laughed as we approached the milk bottle toss. There was no question that Luke was going to win that cat for Charley. He paid the guy behind the booth as he handed him three baseballs.

He told Luke to stand behind the line. I looked at him and frowned.

"That seems pretty far back," I said.

"Nah, it's fine. I used to play some baseball in high school. I can do this." He smiled.

Luke threw the first ball and knocked down the milk bottles. There was something about watching him throw those balls that made my heart beat faster. I was scared, because I suddenly saw him as almost perfect. As promised, he won Charley her cat.

"Here," he said as he handed me the baseball. "Try it."

I shook my head. "No, I can't throw. I'd just embarrass myself."

"Just try it for fun." He smiled.

I sighed as I stepped behind the line and threw the ball. I almost hit the man behind the counter. Good thing he ducked when he did. Luke and Charley started laughing. Suddenly, Luke was behind me, and he grabbed my hand.

"Here, let me help you," he said as he continued laughing.

He brought my hand up over my head and counted to three. His touch was amazing, and my impulses were starting to go crazy. My heart was rapidly beating, and the sensation deep below was back. I closed my eyes for a moment. On the third count, he helped me throw the ball. Needless to say, I knocked down all the milk bottles. I jumped up and down, clapping my hands as Charley was cheering with excitement, and Luke was smiling at me. The carnie told me to pick which animal I wanted, so I picked the smaller version of Charley's cat.

"Look, now we match," I said as I held my cat next to Charley's. "Can you do me a favor and hold it for me while I take some pictures."

"Sure I can!" she said with excitement.

I brought my camera up and started taking pictures of Charley walking in front of us. I would call her name, and she would turn her head right before I pushed the button.

"Why photography?" Luke curiously asked.

"I love to capture people in a way you normally wouldn't see them when they're standing in front of you. Pictures capture true emotions. You know how people say that 'a person's eyes are the window into their soul'?"

"Yeah."

"That's how I feel about pictures. I feel photographs capture the true nature of a person at that moment. The people don't just become images, they become stories. If you know what I mean."

"Yeah, I think I do." Luke smiled as he looked at me.

"I see the world differently through the lens of a camera." I smiled.

I felt comfortable talking to Luke. Too comfortable in fact, and it was scaring the shit out of me.

9

Charley wanted to go on the Ferris wheel. In fact, she wanted all of us to go together. I hated Ferris wheels because I was afraid of heights, and the thought of being stuck at the top scared the shit out of me.

"Come on, Uncle Luke and Lily. Let's go on the Ferris wheel!" Charley squealed in excitement.

"Okay, Charley. We're coming." Luke smiled as he tried to catch up with her.

"You two go ahead. I'll watch from the sidelines."

"You don't like Ferris wheels, do you?" Luke asked with a small grin on his face.

"No. I don't. I'm scared of heights."

We got up to the gate and Luke grabbed my hand. I looked at him as he smiled at me.

"Luke, what are you doing?" I asked in panicked tone as he pulled me through the gate.

"Face your fears, Lily. It's the only way you'll get over them."

"Luke Matthews, I'm not getting on that Ferris wheel," I said as I tried to loosen the tight grip he had on my hand.

"Just like you weren't getting on my bike?" he asked.

He stopped pulling me, turned around, and our eyes met. "You'll be safe. I promise."

Just like with the motorcycle, I trusted him. I took in a deep breath as the three of us climbed into the seat of the Ferris wheel.

"Lily, since you're scared, you can sit next to Uncle Luke," Charley said.

I sat in-between Luke and Charley. The ride started to move and I gripped the bar so tight that my knuckles turned white. My heartbeat quickened as my panic grew. I closed my eyes, wishing that the ride would end before it even began. I felt Luke take my hand.

"Take slow, deep breaths, Lily," he whispered as he gave my hand a gentle squeeze.

The touch of his warm hand soothed me as my racing heart began to slow down and a sense of calm slowly washed over me.

"Now open your eyes. You can get some great pictures," he said.

I slowly opened my eyes to see Charley staring at me.

"Are you okay, Lily?" she asked.

"I'm fine, sweetie."

The time had come for the ride to end, and of course, we stopped at the top. I gasped. Luke looked over at me and smiled.

"Look at the world through your camera lens. It'll calm you down."

I brought my camera up to my face and began taking pictures of the bright lights and the people down below. Luke was right. For a minute, I forgot we were stopped at the top because I was focused on getting the best pictures. Before I knew it, we were back on the bottom, and it was time to get off the ride. Luke took my hand and helped me out of the seat.

"I'm hungry," Charley announced.

"Me too, peanut," Luke said as he picked her up to give her a piggyback ride.

Charley was giggling. I wanted to capture the sweetness and innocence of this moment, so I began snapping pictures of the two of them. We stopped at a stand where they sold burgers, hot dogs, and fries. Charley ate a hot dog, while Luke and I ate hamburgers. We were sitting down at the wooden table eating, when Luke and Charley started throwing French fries at each other and laughing.

"You both need to stop." I laughed at them.

Luke picked up a fry, threw it at me, and smiled. I looked at him and smirked as I threw one back. After our food fight had ended, I glanced at my watch and saw that it was late, and Charley looked exhausted. Luke picked her up and carried her to the Jeep while I carried her oversized cat. He set her down and buckled her in. Being with him tonight and seeing him with Charley told me he would be an amazing father. It was just one more thing about him that seemed to be making him perfect.

We arrived back at the apartment building and I held the door while Luke carried Charley into his bedroom and laid her in his bed. Luke walked out of the bedroom and I whispered good night to Charley. She opened her eyes and gently took my hand.

"I haven't seen Uncle Luke so happy in a long time," she whispered.

I smiled and kissed her gently on her forehead. "I had a great time too."

Sam and Gretchen were sitting on the couch, watching a movie, when I walked back to the living room.

"Hey, you guys, did you have fun?" Sam whispered as not to disturb Charley.

"Yeah. We had a great time," Luke said as he walked into the kitchen.

"It was a lot of fun," I agreed.

Gretchen looked at me and winked. I rolled my eyes at her.

"Call me tomorrow," she whispered.

As I headed towards the door, I heard Luke ask Sam to keep an eye on Charley while he walked me home.

"One foot out the door and I'm already home." I laughed.

"You can never be too careful in these parts." He smiled.

I inserted the key into the lock. "Would you like to come in for some adult drinks?" I asked.

"You mean I can have something alcoholic?" he asked jokingly.

I laughed and nodded my head. "Come on in and have a beer with me. I think after tonight, we deserve one."

Luke followed me in as I walked to the refrigerator and grabbed two beers. After handing Luke his and opening mine, I held my bottle up.

"Here's to a wonderful evening spent in good company and facing my fears of the Ferris wheel."

Luke threw his head back and laughed. "I'll drink to that," he said as our beer bottles came together.

I was leaning against the refrigerator while he was leaning up against the counter across from me. It was one of those awkward moments when neither person was sure what to say next, so I just went for it.

"Let's go sit on the couch while we finish our beer."

"Um, okay," Luke said as he followed behind me.

I sat with my back against the arm of the couch so I was facing him. I brought my leg up and tucked it underneath me. Suddenly, I had felt the urge to pee.

"I'll be right back." I smiled.

Luke smiled back and took another drink of his beer. A few moments later, when I walked back into the living room, I saw him standing in front of my guitar.

"Hey," I said as I put my hands in my pocket. I knew he was going to figure it out soon— if he hadn't already.

"This guitar of yours, there was only one made in the whole world and it belonged to Johnny Gil—" He stopped before he could get my last name out. After pausing for a moment, he continued. "The guitar was handmade by an old man who lived in a small village in Southeast Asia. It was most known for the initials, L.G., that was engraved into the frets. No one could figure out what it stood for."

He turned around and looked at me. The expression on his face was pure shock. "The initials stand for Lily Gilmore. Don't they?" he asked.

I took in a deep breath. "Yes, the initials are mine. He had that guitar made one week after I was born," I said as tears started to fill my eyes. I quickly looked up at the ceiling. There was no way I was going to let Luke see me cry.

"Wow, I had no idea that you're the daughter of Johnny Gilmore. He's a legend." He smiled. "The way he merged the sounds of the late 70's and early 80's was amazing. He's a musical genius. He created a sound that no one could duplicate, and everyone said it was because of *this* guitar."

I was getting pissed off with the way he idolized my father. He may have been a musical genius, but nobody knew the way he lived his life like I did. Luke's phone went off, so he pulled it from his pocket and then looked up at me.

"I have to go. Sam and Gretchen are leaving, and I need to get back to Charley. Thanks for the beer," he said as he headed towards the door. He stopped as he put his hand on the knob and looked at me. "Come to the beach with us tomorrow."

I didn't know what to say at that moment. *Did I want to go? Was he only asking me because now he knew who my father was? Are we really friends?* I started to question everything about our time spent together and he put me on the spot.

"Sure, I'll go. It sounds like fun."

"Great. I'll see you tomorrow then." He smiled.

After locking the door behind him, I pressed my forehead against it, immediately regretting my decision. *I can't let this happen again.*

10

Luke

Charley was sleeping peacefully as I carefully opened the door and peeked into the room. Closing the door as silently as I could, I grabbed a pillow and a blanket from the hall closet, set them on the couch, sat down, and ran my hands through my hair. I couldn't believe that Lily was Johnny Gilmore's daughter. I remembered her father having passed away about two years ago, but I didn't recall hearing anything about her mother or sister, so I decided to grab my laptop. I did some online searching, and because her parents were divorced for the past ten years, I couldn't find anything on them until an article popped up that caught my attention. The headline read: *'80's Musical Legend's Daughter Calls off Wedding'*. I clicked on the headline to bring up the article.

"Lily Gilmore, daughter of 80's musical legend, Johnny Gilmore, calls off wedding after she caught her fiancé having relations with her sister, in the church, on their wedding day. Sources say Miss Gilmore caused quite a scene outside the church, climbed into a limousine and then hasn't been seen since…"

I looked at the date of the article, and it was dated a little over a year ago. At that moment, it had occurred to me that she lied to me about her family. The only person in her family that had passed away was her father, whereas her mother and sister were still alive. I set my laptop on the coffee table and laid myself down on the couch with my hands behind my head. *Why would she lie to me?* I couldn't understand her motive and I was pissed. There was one thing in my life that I hated most and would not tolerate—people who lie.

***

I awoke to the feeling of tapping on my shoulder. I opened one eye and saw Charley standing over me, smiling.

"Wake up. I'm hungry," she said.

"Okay. Okay. I'm getting up."

I sat up on the couch and rubbed my eyes. "What time is it, Charley?"

She looked at the clock in the kitchen. "It's seven o'clock."

"May I ask why you're up so early?"

"Uncle Luke, it's not early for a kid my age."

I couldn't help but smile as I gave her a kiss on the top of her head. "What do you want for breakfast?"

"I want your smiley pancakes." She smiled.

I walked into the kitchen and took out everything I needed to make pancakes. Charley loved the way I made them. Her favorite part was when I use chocolate chips for the eyes and whipped cream for the smile.

"Don't forget the eyes, Uncle Luke!" she shouted from the couch.

"Don't worry, Charley, I won't."

The pancakes were cooking on the griddle when Sam walked through the door.

"Damn, Luke, those smell good."

"Want some?"

"Yeah, I'm starving. Gretchen had a photo shoot this morning, so we didn't get to eat."

I poured more batter onto the hot griddle.

"Hey, don't forget to make them smiley," Sam said as he turned and looked at Charley.

Charley looked at him and giggled. I rolled my eyes. Sam walked into the kitchen and started a pot of coffee.

"I pulled up an article last night about Lily."

"Are you stalking her or something?" he asked.

"No. Do you know who her father was?"

I could tell by the way Sam looked at me that he already knew.

"You asshole. You knew and didn't tell me?"

"Uncle Luke, language!" Charley yelled from the couch.

"Sorry, peanut. Please, don't tell your mom."

"The article said that she caught her fiancé with her sister on the day of their wedding."

"Yeah, I only found that out from Gretchen," Sam said as he poured some coffee into his cup and sat on the bar stool. "I asked Lily about it, but she got really pissed and told me to forget that I even knew about it."

"You asked her about it?" I said as I took the pancakes off the griddle. "Why would you do that?"

"Because I think you two would make a great couple and I wanted to get her feel about dating."

"Bro, leave it alone. Jesus Christ, I already told you that I'm not interested in dating anyone."

"Uncle Luke, I'm pretty sure J.C. is a bad word when used that way," Charley said as she sat down at the table.

"I'm sorry, Charley." I sighed as I set down the plate of pancakes in front of her.

Sam got up from the bar stool and sat at the table across from Charley. "Dude, what the hel—heck did you do my pancakes? They're frowning cakes," he said with a pout.

I rolled my eyes and poured myself a cup of coffee. Just as I was about to sit down, Maddie walked into the apartment.

"Good morning, baby," she said as she walked over and kissed Charley on the head. "Good morning, guys."

"Hey, Charley, would you mind if Sam took you home while I talk to your mom for a few minutes?"

Charley looked at Sam and tilted her head. "Will you give me a piggyback ride upstairs?"

"You bet I will. Hop on, little girl, and we'll giddy-up outta here."

Charley climbed on Sam's back and giggled. As soon as the door shut, Maddie asked me what was going on.

"Lily's the daughter of Johnny Gilmore," I said.

"What? As in Johnny Gilmore, the musician?"

"Yeah, and she lied to me about something."

"What did she lie about?" Maddie asked as she poured more coffee into our cups.

"She told me that her family was killed a couple of years ago in an accident, but I did some research. The only person who died in her family was her father, and I remember that day. The reports said he had a massive heart attack. Her mom and sister are still alive and living in Seattle." I grabbed my laptop, set it on the table, and brought up the article I saw last night. "Here, read this," I said as I turned my laptop towards Maddie.

"Wow, poor girl." She looked up at me. "She obviously had her reasons for telling you her family's dead. I know that if I had a sister and caught her having sex with my fiancé, I would never talk to her again. But to find them on her wedding day, in the church! Cut her some slack, Luke, you don't know the whole story."

I stood there for a few moments, pondering what Maddie had said. "You're right, sis. Thanks."

"You're falling for her, aren't you?" Maddie asked as she put her hand on my shoulder.

"No. We're just friends," I replied.

"It's okay, Luke. Don't fight what's natural," she said as she walked out the door.

I sighed and started cleaning up the kitchen.

11

Lily

I lay there in bed, staring at window as the sunlight filtered through the sides of the blinds. It was going to be another beautiful day, but I wasn't sure if I wanted to go to the beach. After last night, I wasn't sure of anything anymore. I knew for a fact that I was falling for Luke. His brown eyes stared at me intently when I talked. His sculpted face and chiseled chin was perfection, as was his perfectly shaped lips that I've found myself wanting to touch. It's the way he lit up the room when he smiled, and his perfect body; a body that was strong and that I knew could protect me. I fantasized about running my hands across his chest and down to his forbidden area…

Snapping out of my fantasy, I threw back the covers and jumped out of bed. I did a little stomping dance because I'm angry with myself for thinking about him that way. I refuse to give my heart away. It's mine, and it's my job to keep it safe. It was tucked away deep inside, and I wouldn't let it come out. It wouldn't be able to withstand any more pain. After I threw my hissy fit, I picked up my phone and sent a text message to Luke.

"Something came up so I won't be able to go to the beach today. Sorry, maybe next time."

I waited for a response, but I didn't get one. Maybe he was pissed at me for not telling him who my father was or maybe he just didn't care whether I went or not. Whatever the reason, I didn't care. I couldn't care. I wouldn't care.

Walking into the bathroom, I brushed my teeth and threw my hair up into a ponytail. I put on my bikini because I decided that, when everyone left for the beach, I was going to lay out by the pool. After throwing on my jean shorts and a tank top, I grabbed my phone from the nightstand. When I saw I still hadn't received a message from Luke, I sighed and walked into the living room. The beer bottles from last night were still on the coffee table. As I was walking over to pick them up, there was a knock at the door. I looked out the peephole and Luke was standing on the other side. My heart started racing as I turned the lock and opened the door.

"Good morning," I said.

"Morning," he replied. "Can I come in?"

"Oh sure," I said as I stepped out of the way. "What's up?" I could feel something was off.

"Grab your things. You're coming to the beach," he said.

"Didn't you get my text? I told you something came up."

"I got it, and I don't believe you, so grab your things, and let's go. The gang is probably already there."

"I don't appreciate you being so bossy," I snapped.

He stared at me with his beautiful brown eyes that were making me weak in the knees. I had to turn away because I was starting to melt right in front of him. I walked over and picked up the beer bottles. As I walked passed him, he reached out and lightly grabbed my arm.

"I know you probably think things are weird now because of last night, but they're not. You said that you would come to the beach with us. I don't want you changing your mind over something that isn't true. Things are fine, Lily."

I stood there for a moment before looking at him. I could hear the sincerity in his voice. He let go of my arm, and I set the bottles on the counter.

"Let me go get my things. I'll be right back," I said as I headed towards my bedroom. I grabbed my bag that was already packed for the pool, grabbed my camera, and then I slid into my flip-flops.

"Okay, I'm ready."

Luke looked at me and smiled. When we left the apartment, I walked towards the spot where he parked his Jeep, but his Jeep was gone. I looked behind me, and Luke was sitting on his motorcycle with a big grin across his face.

"Oh no! Once was enough. I'm *not* getting on that bike again!"

Luke started it up and rode over to me. "Come on, Lily. Hop on," he said as he handed me his helmet.

"Let's take the Explorer!" I yelled.

"Hop on, Lily. Let's not keep everyone waiting."

I rolled my eyes, grabbed the helmet from his hands, and put it on. Climbing on behind him, I put my bag across my shoulder and wrapped my arms around him.

Here we go again.

***

The beach was crowded. I took off the helmet and handed it to Luke as I got off the bike. My heart was still racing from the nerves and excitement.

"Now, that wasn't so bad, was it?" he asked.

I looked at him and smirked as I made my way through the parking lot. When I reached the end of the sidewalk, I stopped to take off my flip-flops. The minute my toes hit the warm sand, I felt serene. Luke and I walked across the sand and over to where Sam and a group of people were sitting around. Lucky jumped up when he saw me.

"Hello, beautiful," he said as he lightly kissed my hand.

As I smiled at him, I could see Luke giving him a dirty look out of the corner of my eye. I said hi to Sam and Luke introduced me to the rest of his friends.

"Isn't Gretchen here?" I asked Sam.

"She'll be here in about an hour. She had a photo shoot this morning."

I gave him a small smile. They already sounded like a real couple, and it made me happy that Gretchen found someone. I couldn't ask for a better man for her. Lucky put his arm around me and started walking me away from the others.

"Every time I look at you, I feel like I've died and gone to Heaven. You're a real angel in disguise, aren't you? I just know that we could make beautiful, angelic music together. How about we give it a try?"

I looked at Luke and winked at him. He could tell I wasn't falling for Lucky's bullshit lines.

"You know Lucky," I said, pausing to turn around and face him. "Every time I look at you, I feel like I've died and gone to hell, so please do me a favor and back the fuck off so that I can go on with my day." I smiled politely.

He looked at me for a moment with knitted eyebrows. Extending his hand to me, he said, "You are one awesome chick! Friends?"

I smiled and shook his hand. "Friends," I said.

Sam and Luke both busted out laughing. I looked over at Luke as he was shaking his head at me.

"What do you guys want to do?!" Luke yelled to everyone.

"I think I'm just going to lay in the sun for a while," I said as I took off my top and shorts, revealing my bikini underneath.

"Hot damn!" Sam squealed as he ran towards me, picked me up, and ran to the water.

I yelled at him to put me down, but he just laughed and said he would, but not until we cooled off. We hit the water and he carried me out until the water stopped at our chest.

"Sam! You just wait!"

He was smiling at me, and suddenly, out of nowhere, someone had a tight grip around my waist and pulled me under the water. My heart started racing, but within moments, I was released and returned to the surface. When I turned around, Luke was inches from my face, smiling.

"You asshole! You scared the shit out of me!" I said as I splashed him.

"Watch your mouth, and I couldn't resist! Please tell me you're not mad."

How the hell could I be mad at that face? He was having fun, and I'm all up for crazy, wild fun—at least I used to be.

"I'm not mad."

"Good. Then let's get out of the water," he said as we swam back to shore.

Sam was standing at the shoreline with two towels. "Here, dry off, and let's play some volleyball."

I saw Gretchen waving to me as she sat in the sand, so I ran over to her.

"Look at you miss sexy thing in that teeny weeny bikini! You've gone and gave all the boys a boner!" she said in her fake southern accent.

I threw my towel at her and sat down. Putting my arm around her, I laid my head on her shoulder. "I'm glad you're here."

"Looks like you and Luke were having some fun in the water."

"He found out last night about Johnny." I sighed.

"What did he say?"

"He was shocked, but then he raved about him like he was some sort of God."

"Lily, he was a God to a lot of people, and one of them happens to be Luke. How weird is that? You move here to start a new life, and you live next door to a twenty-seven-year-old guy who worships your dad."

I lifted my head and gave her a dirty look.

"I'm just saying."

Sam walked over and asked Gretchen if she wanted to play volleyball. She jumped at the chance. Little did the boys know she was the captain of her volleyball team and star player. She grabbed my hand and told me to come on, but I really just wanted to lay back in the sun and relax for a while, so I told her that I'd play later. I looked around, and Luke was off to the side, talking to a group of people, and the volleyball game was about ready to start. I decided to wander the beach and take some pictures, so I put on my jean shorts, grabbed my camera from the bag, and headed down the beach. The sun was bright, the sand was warm, and the beach was filled with people enjoying a beautiful Saturday. I heard someone call my name. When I turned around, Luke was running up behind me.

"Hey, where are you off to?" he asked as he caught up with me.

"I was just wandering around, taking some pictures." I smiled.

"I know this great little area that has the best view that's perfect for taking pictures. Come on, follow me."

I followed him about half a mile down the beach. When we reached the area, I looked around. It was a cove with large boulders around one side, forming a small wall. There were a few sailboats in the water, but overall, there wasn't anyone else around.

"If you climb those rocks over there, you'll be able to get some great pictures looking out into the ocean," Luke said.

I smiled as we walked over to the area. Luke climbed up first and then held his hand out to me. "I don't want you to fall. These rocks are tricky and you could slip."

I took his warm, strong hand, and he helped me up onto the rock. We climbed a couple more until we were at the top. Luke was right; this was a beautiful place to take pictures. I took my camera and began clicking. Luke was staring out into the water as I turned towards him and took his picture.

"I think I took enough pictures from this spot."

Luke took my hand as we carefully stepped down onto each rock. Only when we reached the sand, did he let go.

"This is a quiet spot," I said as I sat down.

"I come here when I need to think."

"Think about what?" I asked.

"Life," he replied as he stared out at the water. "There's something that I want to ask you."

I suddenly became nervous and I had a sick feeling in my stomach. "Okay, ask away."

"Why did you lie to me about your mom and sister being deceased?"

I felt a knot in my throat. *Did I owe him an explanation? Was I obligated to tell him everything?* I stood up and grabbed my camera. "They're dead to me," I said as I walked away from him. He instantly jumped up and followed me.

"Lily, wait!"

He caught up with me and lightly grabbed my arm. "Please, don't walk away from me."

I sighed and stood there. Luke let go of my arm, and our eyes locked onto each other. I shook my head and pursed my lips. The last thing I wanted to do was dredge up the past, but I didn't think I had much of a choice.

"My mother and sister did horrible things, and as far as I'm concerned, they're dead to me."

"I read the article about you and your ex-fiancé. I'm sorry that happened."

I took in a deep breath as I looked down. "Hunter's an asshole, and my sister's a whore. My mother knew they were fucking behind my back for a long time, but she didn't say a word to me about it. She was going to let me marry that cheating bastard and ruin my life. Just because she stayed in a marriage where her husband did nothing but cheat, doesn't mean everyone else wants that life. I hate them for what they did!"

Tears started to fall down my face. Luke stepped closer, and before I knew it, his arms were around me, embracing me, and letting me know everything was all right. My heart started racing. His arms were so strong. I wanted to push him away, but I couldn't muster up the strength to try. My head was telling me to run, but my heart was saying it was okay.

"I had no idea that your mom knew. I'm sorry, Lily."

I broke our embrace and looked at him. "Thank you, Luke. I moved here to start a new life and to forget about them as well as everything that happened. I'll tell you more sometime over *several* drinks." I laughed.

Luke laughed and put his arm around me. "Come on, let's head back to the gang. They're probably starting rumors about us."

12

LUKE

As we walked back to the part of the beach where everyone had been playing volleyball, I couldn't stop thinking about holding Lily. It felt right, and it scared me to think of us being more than just friends. My feelings were growing for her, and holding her the way I did to comfort her, intensified those feelings. Her warm skin against mine felt incredible and it stirred up emotions that I hadn't had in a long time. We reached our friends as the volleyball game was ending. I saw Sam walk over to Gretchen and kiss her on the lips.

"Break it up you two, or go get a room." I smiled.

"Well, well, well, if it isn't Mr. Matthews and Miss Gilmore. Where did the two of you go off to?" Sam asked with a smirk on his face.

"I showed Lily the cove. She wanted to take some pictures."

Sam gave me a strange look, and I knew why. He was surprised because that cove was where I practically lived after the accident. I shrugged my shoulders and walked away. It felt right taking Lily there. I wanted her to get some great pictures.

"Let's cook some lunch!" I yelled to everyone.

I started the grill, and Sam got out the hot dogs and hamburgers. I put them on and stood there, watching them cook.

"I'm proud of you, man," Sam said.

"No big deal, bro. Leave it alone."

He patted me on the back and smiled. Lucky came walking over and stood next to me while I grilled the food.

"Dude, don't forget about our gig tonight."

"I haven't forgotten."

"What gig?" Lily asked as she walked up.

Lucky put his arm around her. "Lukey boy didn't tell you that we have a band, and that we occasionally play at Bernie's?"

"No. He didn't tell me," she replied as she shot me a look.

"To be honest, I really didn't think about it," I said in my defense.

"Tell me you'll be joining us tonight and listening to the lovely Luke sing his heart out?" Lucky smirked.

"You sing?" Lily asked.

Shit, I wanted to kill Lucky. "A little." I smiled.

"We'll have to talk about this later. I see Giselle coming," Lily said as she walked away.

"Hot damn! Another hottie coming my way. Later, man," Lucky said as he went to check out Giselle.

I rolled my eyes and continued to grill the food. Moments later, Lily came up beside me with a plate in her hand. "I thought you might need this."

"Thanks." I took it from her and put the hot dogs and hamburgers on it. We walked over to the picnic table, and as I set the plate down next to the other food, the gang started lining up, so I walked back to grill some more. Lily followed me.

"Go eat," I said.

"I will. I want to wait for you." She smiled. "I want to know more about this band you have."

"It's no big deal. Bernie's is the bar Maddie works at. I play guitar and sing a couple of songs every once in a while. Sam plays on the keyboard, and Lucky's the drummer."

"That's cool. I'm surprised you never mentioned it."

"I guess I didn't think about it," I said.

"What's your band's name?" Lily asked.

I froze because I didn't want to explain it. I wasn't ready to open that door and walk down that road with her.

"Well?"

I took in a deep breath. "The band's called 'Love In Between'."

"Cool name. How did you come up with it?"

"You know what, Lily, you really should go eat. Don't wait for me."

"Oh, okay." She walked away.

I could tell by the look on her face that I had hurt her feelings, so I turned around and watched her walk back to the table. Now, I felt like shit. Damn it. I didn't want to hurt her feelings, but I just couldn't talk about anything to do with Callie. It still hurt too much.

I finished grilling the second round of hamburgers and hot dogs and walked over to the table. I sat down and stared at Lily as she sat in the sand across from my friend, Jasper, who was playing guitar. They were talking, and then he handed her his guitar. I watched her as she strummed each chord. She looked amazing with a guitar. As I sat there, watching her, Gretchen came over, grabbed a hot dog and sat down next to me.

"She's pretty amazing with the guitar. She gets it from her father," Gretchen said.

"I've only heard her play a couple of times."

"Well, I'll ask her to play later. I know you don't want to hear this, but I'm saying it anyway. Sam told me about the accident and Callie, and I'm really sorry for your loss. I was there with Lily when she found out about Hunter and Brynn. I saw the look of pain and betrayal on her face, and I was there the whole night, holding her and telling her that everything was going to be okay. I've never seen someone so hurt in my life, that is, until I met you."

I turned and looked at her. "What the hell is that supposed to mean?" I asked.

"It means that the first time I saw you, I saw the same look on your face that I see on Lily's every day. She puts up a good front, but deep inside, she's dying, and not only because of what Hunter did, but because of her family, including her father. I see that in you."

I turned away. I didn't want to hear anymore, and I wasn't in the mood to get lectured. I got enough of that from my mom and Maddie. Gretchen got up and left the table. I looked over to where Lily was sitting, but she was gone, so I got up and walked over to Sam.

"Hey, bro, have you seen Lily?"

"Yeah, she's over there in the water." Sam pointed.

"Thanks, man."

I walked to the shoreline. "Want some company?!" I yelled out to her.

"Sure!" she shouted back.

I stepped into the water and swam over to where she was. "I'm sorry about earlier."

"Don't be."

"No. I was an asshole. It's just that I don't want to talk about certain things."

"I get it, Luke. I'm the queen of not wanting to talk about things. Please don't worry about it."

I gave her a smile. Every time I saw her, I found myself smiling.

"I want you to come to the bar tonight," I blurted out.

"I'd love to. Thank you for inviting me."

We swam back to the shore, and Lily looked over at me.

"I think I'm going to ask Giselle to drive me home."

"If you're ready to leave, I'll take you."

"No, you stay and enjoy yourself."

"I'm taking you home, Lily. End of discussion."

She shook her head at me and grabbed her bag.

13

Lily

I climbed onto the back of Luke's bike and wrapped my arms him, making sure to close my eyes as he took off out of the parking lot. It was getting easier to ride with him, and I didn't feel as scared anymore. He told me that I'd be safe with him, and that's how he made me feel.

We reached the building, Luke parked his bike, and we both climbed off.

"Aren't you going back to the beach?" I asked as I handed him his helmet.

"Nah, I think I'm going to practice some songs for tonight."

As we walked to our apartments and inserted our keys into the lock, we both turned and looked at each other.

"See you later," he said.

"Yeah, see you later." I smiled.

I walked into my apartment and threw my keys onto the counter; then I went into the bathroom and started the shower. Looking at myself in the mirror, my hair was a hot mess, not only from the water, but from Luke's motorcycle helmet. I stepped into the shower and washed the salt and sand off my body. After spending a ridiculous amount of time in there, I turned the shower off and stepped out only to hear my phone chiming. I grabbed a towel and wrapped it around me as I walked over to my bag to get my phone. There was a text message from Giselle.

"Brace yourself darling, I just got a call from your mom."

I gasped, and my eyes grew wide.

"What the hell did she say?"

"She said she misses you dearly, and she wants to speak with you. She's trying to track you down. I told her that I haven't talked to you in months, and that the last time I did, you were in Portland."

"Thanks, Giselle."

"You're welcome. I'll see you tonight at the bar."

"You're going?"

"Yep, Lucky invited me. He's so sexy, Lily!"

Oh God, I didn't know how to respond to that. Giselle and Lucky are total opposites. I messaged her back.

"Okay, see you later."

I felt sick to my stomach. *Why the hell would my mom be trying to track me down?* I knew why, because I'm her daughter, and even though she's dead to me, I'm not dead to her. I needed to go lay down, so I walked into the bedroom and climbed onto my bed. When I settled underneath the covers, I heard Luke playing his guitar from the other side of the wall. Laying down on my side and tucking my hands underneath my pillow, I lay there and listened as Luke strummed the chords of his guitar. The sound was soothing, and it reminded me of the times when my dad would sit at the end of my bed, play his guitar, and sing me to sleep.

***

I was standing alone in the main entrance of the dark church. Looking down at my wedding dress, it suddenly turned black. My heart began pounding in my chest as I began to panic. I slowly made my way down the dark halls. As I approached the main part of the church, the white bows that sat upon the pews had turned black. I looked up at the altar and saw that the several arrangements of white calla lilies were also black. *What's going on? Where is everybody?* I started calling Hunter's name. I needed to find him. As I approached a small room by the kitchen, I heard noises coming from it, so I extended my hand and reached for the doorknob. Suddenly, I heard a voice behind me.

"Don't open that door, pumpkin."

I turned around to the familiar voice, and I saw my father standing there, shaking his head.

"Daddy, someone's in there. They can explain what's happening."

"Don't do it, Lily. Don't open that door!" he screamed.

Suddenly, he disappeared. I slowly turned the knob and opened the door. Hunter was standing there, naked, with a naked woman pinned up against the wall. I couldn't understand what was going on. Hunter turned his head, and the woman looked at me. That woman was my sister, Brynn, and the two of them were smiling at me. I put my hand over my mouth and looked to the corner of the small room only to find my mother standing there, pointing and laughing at me. I slammed the door shut and ran down the long hallway that kept getting longer and longer. I couldn't breathe, and I started screaming. Tears were falling from my eyes so fast that everything became blurry, and I could no longer see, so I dropped to my knees...

* * *

"Wake up, Lily. Wake up. You're having a bad dream."

My eyes flew open, and Luke was standing over me with his hands clasping my shoulders. I couldn't catch my breath, and my face was soaked with tears. I just lay there and stared at him, trying to focus on what just happened. He sat down on the edge of the bed.

"Are you okay?" he asked as he wiped the tears from my face.

"I'm fine. How did you get in here?" I asked as I sat up.

"I'm the maintenance man, remember?" He smiled. "I heard you screaming, so I came right over. I thought you were in trouble."

I pushed my hair back with my hands and took in a deep breath. "I had a bad dream, that's all."

"Do you want to talk about it?"

"No, I just want to forget it," I said as I looked down.

Luke put his arms around me and pulled me into him. I wrapped my arms around him and buried my face in his neck. His scent was captivating, and his arms were strong as he sheltered me. I wanted to run my lips softly against his skin. I was lost in him and in the moment. I pushed back and looked at him.

"Do you always treat your neighbors like this?" I asked.

"Only the beautiful ones." He smiled.

The butterflies in my stomach awoke and started fluttering around as we stared into each other's eyes. He took his finger and ran it along my jaw line, then over my lips. My heart was racing. I knew what was coming, and I braced myself for it. Luke leaned into me and tilted his head as he softly brushed his lips against mine. He put his hands on each side of my face as our kiss deepened. I parted my lips, allowing access for his tongue to enter my mouth and meet with mine. He stopped and put his forehead against mine while still holding my face in his hands.

"I'm sorry," he whispered.

"Don't be," I whispered back.

He got up from the bed. "I'll see you later at the bar."

"Yeah, see you later."

I put my fingers on my lips, recalling that breathtaking moment. There was feeling and magic in the way he kissed me and I'd never felt anything like it before, not even with Hunter. I heard music coming from the other side of the wall, and I could tell Luke regretted kissing me. *How am I going to face him tonight at the bar?* There was also the issue with my mother. I walked to my closet and pondered about what to wear. I pulled out my black strapless sundress, slipped it on, and looked at myself in the full-length mirror. I couldn't stop thinking about Luke. The moment he kissed me, I wanted more of him. My life was starting to unravel right before my eyes, but

I needed to stay in control. I wouldn't let anyone hold power over my emotions or feelings again.

I ran the flat iron through my hair as I looked in the mirror. All I saw was a broken girl who had trust and daddy issues. Suddenly, my phone rang, and Gretchen was calling me.

"Hello," I answered.

"Hey, Lils. Sam is going with Luke to the bar to set up the equipment. Do you want me to pick you up so that we can drive together?"

"What about Giselle?"

"She sent me a text to tell me she's going with Lucky. They left the beach together, and I don't know where they went. That situation is weird."

"Sure, we can drive together."

"Great, I'll be over in two seconds. Bye."

I looked at my phone in confusion. Then it hit me, she must be at Luke's. I put the finishing touches on my hair as Gretchen came strutting in the bathroom.

"You look great, Lily." She smiled.

"Thanks, so do you."

"Sam and I just had the most amazing sex!"

I sighed as I walked out of the bathroom and into my bedroom. "TMI, Gretchen."

"Did something happen between you and Luke?" she asked as she sat on the bed.

"No, why do you ask?"

"I don't know. When Sam and I got back to the apartment, he looked more depressed than usual."

"I don't know what his problem is, but I don't need it," I said as I slid on my silver bracelet.

Gretchen jumped up from the bed. "Something did happen! You better tell me right now, Lily Gilmore!"

"We shared a small kiss, but he regretted it and left. There's nothing more to tell, and I don't want to talk about it again."

Gretchen came up behind me and put her arms around my neck. "He's badly wounded, Lily, and he doesn't know how to heal. Sam said Luke's pretty much isolated himself since the accident."

"I'm sorry about that, and I feel really bad for him, but I'm not the person to put him back together again. I'm broken too, and I have my own issues. I don't need to take on someone else's."

"Wow, Lils. That's deep. But tell me this, what's more perfect than two broken people trying to heal each other?"

"Let it go, Gretchen. I'm done with guys, and I don't want to talk about it anymore. Let's go now because I need a drink."

"I know you when you get like this, and you better stay away from the vodka," she warned as she grabbed her keys.

14

Luke

"Dude, come on, get out of the shower already," I said as I pounded on the bathroom door. "You're worse than a girl!"

"I'll be out in a minute!" Sam yelled.

I couldn't get my mind off of Lily, and I couldn't believe I kissed her. Her soft lips against mine were intoxicating, and it left me wanting to explore more of her. *She probably thinks I'm a jerk, and this will probably ruin our friendship. How could I be so stupid? I haven't kissed a girl since Callie.*

"Bro, what's up?" Sam said as he stood in the doorway of my bedroom.

"Nothing, I'm just thinking about some things."

"I could tell you were in deep thought the way you were just standing there. Are you okay?"

"Yeah, I'm fine. I kissed Lily," I blurted out.

"What! Seriously, man?"

"Don't make it a bigger deal than it already is. I'm sure she hates me now, and I'm positive I ruined our friendship," I said as I walked out of the bedroom.

"You didn't ruin anything, Luke. I can tell Lily likes you and maybe kissing her was what you needed to do to let her know you're interested in her. And don't say you're not, because I know you," he said as he pointed at me.

"I can't stop my feelings, but I can stop my actions. I find that when I'm with Lily, I think less and less about Callie, and that's not right, man."

Sam walked over to me and put his hand on my shoulder. "Luke, you loved Callie, and what you had was great, but she's gone, and you have to start accepting that. Do you think Callie would want you to live in misery and not move on? Wouldn't you want Callie to find someone who'd make her happy and take care of her the way you did? Dude, come on, you need to let go."

"You think it's so easy," I said as I wiped away a tear that fell down my face. I grabbed my keys from counter. "Let's go," I said as I walked out the door, out of the building, and climbed into the Jeep.

***

As we walked into Bernie's, I saw Lily sitting at the bar. Gretchen jumped up and ran over to hug Sam. I didn't know what to say to Lily. I already apologized for kissing her. She turned around and looked at me as I gave her a small smile before walking over to the stage to get things set up. Shortly after, Lucky came strolling in with his arm around Giselle.

"Feeling good tonight, boys." Lucky strutted over with a big smile across his face.

I looked at him and rolled my eyes. "Let me guess, you got laid."

"That's right, Lukey boy," he said as he slapped me on the back. "You should try it some time."

I ignored him because he was Lucky, and that was how he was. When we got the stage set up, the bar had already filled up since Bernie had advertised that we'd be playing tonight. I kept looking over at Lily, but she wouldn't look at me. She kept her back turned and drank her beer. I took a deep breath, and I walked over and sat on the bar stool next to her.

"Hey," I said.

She picked up her beer, took a sip, and looked at me. "Hey."

Candi, the bartender, walked over to where we were sitting. "The usual, Luke?"

"The usual." I smiled.

Lily sat there and stared at her beer bottle.

"I'm sorry about earlier," I said.

"Sorry about what?" She smiled as she looked at me.

"Um, when I crossed the line and kissed you."

She tilted her head and slowly shook it. "I'm sorry, Luke, but I don't recall you kissing me."

I grinned because that was her way of telling me that everything was cool between us. I held up my beer bottle as she held up hers, and we lightly tapped them together.

"I have to get on stage now."

"Good luck." She smiled.

15

Lily

I sat there while Luke walked to the stage. He was still apologizing for our kiss. I could tell he felt awkward about it, so I had to turn it into nothing, even though it was something to me. It was something real that stirred up desire and passion from within. Something I wouldn't so easily be able to forget. I was in deep thought, holding the beer bottle between both my hands, when I heard his voice. I closed my eyes for a moment because it was breathtaking. As I turned around to face the stage, I saw him standing there, in his stonewashed jeans and brown boots. His navy blue shirt was tight and emphasized his muscular, ripped body. He was sexy as hell, and I couldn't stop thinking about how much I wanted him to kiss me again. I needed another drink, so I motioned for Candi, and I ordered a shot of vodka. The beer just wasn't doing it, and I needed to forget about Luke, the kiss, and my mother. I threw back the shot that Candi set down in front of me, and I ordered another. I listened intently as he sang his song. The words haunted me.

"Sleep, baby, sleep

Peace is just a dream away

Let it go and release your fears

For tomorrow's another day."

I grabbed the shot glass out of Candi's hand before she could set it down. After Luke finished his song and sang a few more, I started to feel the effects of the alcohol. Giselle and Gretchen walked over and sat down at the bar next to me.

"Why didn't you sit with us at the table?" Giselle asked.

"I was already sitting here and I didn't feel like getting up."

"Are you okay, Lily?" Gretchen asked.

"Sure. Everything's just dandy. My mom, who's dead to me, is trying to track me down. The boy next door kissed me, then apologized and left me sitting on the bed, looking like an idiot. I found my fiancé and my sister fucking in a closet on my wedding day, and best of all, my mother knew they were seeing each other for a long time. Cheers to my awesome fucking life," I said as I held up my beer bottle.

"What's going on?" Luke said as he walked up behind me.

"Hey, Luke, great show," Giselle and Gretchen said at the same time.

Sam and Lucky walked over, grabbed their girls, and kissed them. I rolled my eyes and turned back around towards the bar.

"Let's dance," Giselle said as she grabbed Lucky's hand.

"Awesome idea! Come on, Lily," Gretchen said.

"You go ahead. I'll join you in a while."

"Come on. Let's go sit at a table and talk," Luke said as he lightly touched my arm.

I got up from the stool, grabbed my beer bottle, and walked with Luke over to a table.

"You were really amazing. I want you know that." I smiled.

"Thanks." He smiled as he looked down in embarrassment.

A waitress, named Deb, came over to the table and set down two napkins. "Great performance as always, Luke. You want the usual?"

"Thanks, Deb. Get me a beer and whatever Lily wants."

"What can I get you, sweetie?" Deb asked.

"Two shots of vodka and make them doubles, please."

"Two shots of vodka and a beer coming right up." She smiled.

"Switching over to the hard liquor?" Luke asked.

"I need it tonight," I said.

"Why's that?"

"I really don't want to get into it."

Suddenly, two girls approached the table. I recognized one of them; she was the one giving Luke a blow job that night I walked in on them.

"Hi, Luke." She smiled. "You were *so* awesome tonight."

"Thanks." He smiled.

"Would you like to get together later and maybe talk or something?" she asked.

"No, not tonight."

Deb walked over with our drinks and just in time. She set the vodka down in front of me and handed Luke his beer. I slammed the first shot and then the second.

"Aw, come on. I promise that you'll have a really good time," she whined.

"Back off. He said *no*! Now, take your little slutty asses and get away from my table!" I yelled.

Luke looked at me in surprise as he drank his beer.

"Who the hell are you?" she asked.

I got up out of my seat. "I'm someone who's trying to have a conversation here, but instead, I'm being bothered by some little groupie who thinks she's going to get laid."

Luke stood up and lightly grabbed my arm. "Lily, sit down."

I jerked my arm away. "Don't touch me!" I snapped.

Giselle and Gretchen came running over to the table with Sam and Lucky following behind.

"Go down the street. I'm sure there's a very profitable corner with your name on it. If you're going to blow random strangers, than you might as well get paid for it."

"Bitch!" she snapped as she turned on her heels and walked away.

Giselle clasped my shoulders, and Gretchen picked up the shot glass and smelled it.

"Shit, she's drinking vodka."

Luke looked at me and then at Gretchen. "Is that bad or something?" he asked.

"Yeah, it is," Giselle answered.

"Lily tends to get mean and violent when she drinks vodka. It's the only alcohol that affects her that way. She can drink anything else, get drunk, and have fun, but vodka turns her into a different person," Gretchen answered.

"Oh, fuck off! I can drink whatever the hell I want. Who are you? My mother?"

Luke leaned over the table. "Watch your mouth."

I leaned over until I was inches from his face. "Fuck you too! I want everyone to just leave me the hell alone!" I exclaimed as I got up from my seat.

Anger washed over his face. He got up from his seat and followed me to the bar. "You aren't drinking anymore tonight."

"I'm going to the restroom. I'll be right back," I said.

I just wanted to go home. At this point, I was drunk, and I didn't feel good, so I left the bar and started walking down the street. It wasn't too long after when I heard Luke calling my name.

"Are you crazy? You told me you were going to the bathroom. Why did you leave, Lily?"

I stopped, and as I turned around, I started to stumble, but he caught me. "I just want to be left alone. I want *you* to leave me alone, Luke."

We were by a dark alley with only a dimmed light post to provide some lighting. Luke pushed me up against the brick and pinned my hands with his to the wall. "I don't want to leave you alone, Lily."

We stared into each other's eyes before he leaned forward and forcefully pushed his lips against mine, forcing my lips to part. He kissed me as if he wanted to devour me. Our tongues were tangled as the alluring scent of him engulfed my senses. I felt helpless, and I couldn't move because he was too strong. My heart was racing. Moments later, he broke our kiss and stared at me.

"I hope you don't remember this tomorrow," he whispered.

Luke let go of my hands and picked me up. He carried me to his Jeep, set me in the passenger seat, pulled the seatbelt over me, and buckled it. I closed my eyes and fell asleep.

***

My eyes flew open, and I looked around my bedroom. Looking down, I noticed that I was still in my dress from last night. Over to the right, the clock read eight a.m. I put my hand on my head as it felt like there was someone inside, pounding it with a sledgehammer. I felt sick, and I was still a little dizzy. I couldn't remember how I got home or in my bed. Stumbling out of bed, I walked into the bathroom and looked at myself in the mirror at the mascara that was smeared underneath my red eyes. I started the bath and poured some bubbles under the stream of running water. After climbing into the tub, I laid myself back. The last thing I remembered about last night was Luke's band performing. I ran my fingers across my lips, remembering the dream I had about him kissing me and how real it felt. I closed my eyes to try and soothe my pounding head, but it didn't help. After a thirty minute soak, I got out of the bathtub and threw on a fuchsia cotton sundress. I ran a brush through my hair and piled it on top of my head in a messy bun; then I stumbled back into the bathroom for some Motrin. As I pulled out the bottle, I noticed it was empty. I sighed. As I made my way to the kitchen, I was startled by a knock on the door. I walked over, looked out the peephole, and saw Luke standing there with coffee in his hands.

"Good morning. I've come with coffee, which I'm sure you need." He smiled as he held up two cups.

"You don't by any chance have some Motrin, do you?" I asked.

He handed me a coffee cup, reached inside the pocket of his shorts, then pulled out a bottle, shaking it in front of me.

"You may come in," I said as I stepped out of the way.

I took the bottle from him and set it on the counter. As I grabbed a bottle of water from the fridge, I caught him staring at me.

"What? I know I look like a hot mess, but you don't have to make it so obvious."

He laughed. "You do look like a hot mess, but I like it. It's very becoming on you."

I sighed as I took three pills out of the bottle and shoved them in my mouth, chasing them down with water.

"I bet you say that to all the girls."

"Only the ones I like." He smiled.

"So, how did you know I was up?" I asked.

"I heard you run the bath water."

"Oh, that's nice. Do you also hear it when I'm getting myself off?"

An expression of shock overtook his face and he didn't know what to say.

"I'm joking, Luke."

He shook his head and grinned at me. He was sexy in his long khaki shorts and tight red t-shirt.

"I apologize for anything I may have done or said last night. The last thing I remember is watching you perform," I said as I motioned for us to sit down on the couch.

"That's the last thing you remember?"

"Yes, so please enlighten me on my activities so that I can decide whether or not to show my face at Bernie's again."

"Well, you told some girl to find a street corner and get paid for giving blow jobs. You told Gretchen and Giselle to fuck off, and then you told me to do the same. After that, you said you were going to the bathroom, but instead, you went out the front door and I had to chase after you."

"Oh," I gulped. "I'm sorry. It was the vodka. I'm sure Giselle and Gretchen told you how I get when I drink it."

"Yes, they did. If you know how you get then why do you drink it?"

"It soothes me, and after the news I got yesterday, I needed it."

"What news? Did it have anything to do with that nightmare you had?"

I took in a deep breath before I answered him. "I think it did. Giselle called after you dropped me off, told me that my mother had contacted her, and that she was looking for me. It upset me, and when I went to lay down for a while, it must have manifested into that nightmare."

"Please tell me about your nightmare. I know you'd rather not, but I want to hear about it."

I heard the sincerity in his voice, and that he truly wanted to hear about my dream, so I took in a deep breath and told him everything. Luke reached out, taking both my hands and interlaced our fingers. His touch made my heart flutter.

"That's horrible, Lily." He pulled me into him. "You shouldn't be having nightmares like that. I'm sorry."

He leaned back against the arm of the couch, almost in a laying position and I was snuggled against his chest. He let go of my hands and wrapped his arms around me as if he was keeping me safe. I could feel the rapid beating of his heart; a similar beat that matched mine. As he began stroking my hair, I tilted my head to see him smiling down at me, and the words suddenly flew out of my mouth before I could stop them, "Kiss me."

Luke hesitated. "Are you sure?"

"I'm positive. Unless you don't want to."

"Believe me, I want to."

"Then shut up and do it."

He slowly brought his lips down to mine and kissed me softly. After a short moment, he stopped and looked at me while gently running the back of his hand across my cheek. I smiled.

That was all he needed to be convinced I wanted him as much as he wanted me.

16

Luke

Her lips were soft, and her tongue was smooth. I softly kissed her, nipping at her bottom lip and watching her smile as I did it. Our tongues gave way and accepted each other instantly. I was hard, and I knew she could feel it pressing against her as she moved up and positioned herself perfectly on top of me. I fisted her hair as she held my face in-between her hands. Our breathing was rapid, and our hearts pounded at the same pace. I wanted to be inside her and feel her skin against mine. I removed the clip that held up her hair and let it fall over her shoulders. She was a sexy, beautiful person, and I needed and wanted more of her. My hands traveled down the back of her dress and over her ass. I caressed every bare spot until I reached her thong. I ran my hands up and down her back as we kissed deeply and passionately. It felt incredible to be underneath her, but I wasn't sure if this was the right time. I wanted us to make love for the right reasons. I didn't want to be a one-night stand with her, and I was sure she didn't want to be one with me, so I broke our kiss and looked into her eyes. She had awoken something in me—something that's been dead for a year.

"What have you done to me, Lily?" I asked her as I ran my fingers through her hair.

"The same thing you've done to me," she responded.

"As much as I want you right now, I think we should wait."

Lily looked at me and nodded her head. Pulling her into me, I held her tight.

"I'm scared. I don't know where this is going. There's so much I don't know about you, and there's so much you don't know about me. I don't want us to have sex on a whim and end up regretting it later. That's not who I am, Lily, and I need you to trust me."

She whispered in my ear, "I do trust you, and I agree with you."

I tightened my arms around her, knowing that this woman before me was truly perfect. She slowly got off of me and sat up on the couch. Sitting up next to her, I ran my finger along her shoulder, making small circles.

"Will you go on a date with me tonight?"

"I don't do dates." She smiled.

"I don't either, but I thought maybe tonight we could both make an exception." I smiled back.

She took my finger from her shoulder and tenderly kissed it.

"I think maybe I could make an exception this one time."

"Me too." I grinned.

I got up from the couch. "I'm going to go now, before it gets any hotter in here," I said as I pointed to the door.

Lily got up and followed me. "Maybe I should call my maintenance guy over so he can cool me off."

"Somehow, I think your maintenance guy will make you sweat." I smiled as I leaned into her and kissed her lips. "I'll pick you up at six o'clock. We'll go to dinner and then figure it out from there."

"That sounds great. I'll be ready." She smiled as she closed the door.

***

"Dude, where the hell were you?" Sam asked as I walked through the door.

"I was over at Lily's," I replied and headed towards my bedroom.

Sam followed behind me. "Bro, your hair's all messed up. Did you have sex with her?!"

"No, we didn't have sex. We almost did, but I stopped it."

"Dude, are you crazy? Why did you stop it?"

"Maybe I am, but I'm not thinking with my dick. I'm thinking with my head and my heart, and I want to—no, I need to know her better. I have too much hurt going on and so does Lily. Neither of us needs to just have a sympathy fuck just for the sake of it."

"I get it, and I'm proud of you," Sam said.

"I asked her out on a date tonight. I'm going to take her to dinner and then I think I'll take her to the cove so we can really talk to each other without anyone else around."

I heard the door open and little footsteps running around the apartment. I walked out of my bedroom and saw Charley in the kitchen. "How's my favorite niece?"

"Uncle Luke!" she exclaimed as she ran to me and hugged my legs. "I'm your only niece, silly."

I kissed her on the head as Maddie walked over to me. "Hey, do you think you can watch Charley for a few hours while I go out with some friends?"

I looked at her, and she could tell something was up. Immediately, Sam spoke up. "Your brother isn't available tonight, but I am, and I would be more than happy to look after Charley for you."

"Not available?" Maddie asked as she looked at me in surprise.

Sam walked over to her and whispered in her ear, "Luke has a date with Lily tonight."

Maddie put her hand over her mouth. "Oh my God, yay!" she exclaimed.

Charley walked up to Sam. "What are your plans for tonight, Uncle Sammy?"

He bent down and looked at Charley square in the eye. "Well, little one, if you must know, Gretchen's coming over, and we're going to grab some chicken fingers and fries for dinner, then we're going to go for ice cream and maybe play a little miniature golf."

Charley's eyes widened. "Can I come?"

"You sure can!"

"Thanks, man. I owe you," I said to him.

Maddie motioned for me to follow her into my room. "I'm so happy for you. I can't believe you actually asked her out."

"Me neither, but both of us still have a lot of personal issues that we need to work out."

Maddie hugged me. "It'll be okay, Luke. You're a great guy, and from what I can tell, Lily's a great girl. Charley loves her."

We walked back to the living room, and Maddie kissed Charley goodbye.

"Thank you, Sam. It's a school night, so I'll be back by nine o'clock."

"We'll be here waiting." He smiled.

"Uncle Luke, where are you going that you can't watch me?" Charley asked.

"I'm going on a date with Lily."

A beautiful smile graced her face. "I hope you have fun."

"We will, peanut. Make sure you give Uncle Sammy a hard time."

"Stop being silly, Uncle Luke." She giggled.

17

Lily

I was on cloud nine. Luke left me breathless with that kiss, and for the first time in a very long time, I was happy. Nothing was on my mind except Luke and our upcoming date. I stood at my closet and stared at the clothes hanging on the rack. Picking up my phone, I sent Luke a text message.

"Hi, casual or dressy?"

"Hi right back. Which do you prefer?"

"Casual?"

"Casual it is then. Actually, it was always casual."

I smiled and replied, *"Good. See you soon!"* I heard a soft knock on the wall.

"Did you just knock on the wall?"

"Yes."

"LOL, why?"

"I just wanted you to know that I'm right on the other side if you need anything."

"Thank you, but I need to go or I won't be ready when you come to pick me up."

"Pick you up? Why don't you pick me up?"

"You asked me out, remember?"

"Of course I do, but that doesn't mean you can't pick me up."

I laughed. *"Fine, I'll pick you up."*

"Good. I'll be waiting."

I smiled and shook my head as I pulled out a pair of black Capri pants. The floral print maxi dress I bought was hanging there, with the tag still attached. I haven't had the chance to wear it yet, so I put the pants back and pulled out the dress—it was casual enough. I picked up my phone and sent another text message to Luke.

"Are we taking your motorcycle?"

"Do you want to?"

"Not really. I needed to make sure because I want to wear this dress I bought."

"I thought this was casual."

"It is causal. It's a casual dress."

"Then maybe we'll take my bike. I'd like to see you get on it in that dress."

I smiled as I bit my bottom lip. *"Bye, Luke."*

"Bye, Lily."

I took the tag off and slipped it on—it was *perfect*. Walking into the bathroom, I decided to wear my hair wavy. By the time I was done putting the last wave in, it was already time to leave. I slipped on my flip-flops, grabbed my purse, and walked next door to Luke's. I knocked on the door and gasped when he opened it. He was wearing dark jeans with a white, button down cotton shirt that he left untucked. Once again, he took my breath away. He smiled at me, grabbed my hand, and turned me around.

"You look amazing," he said.

I smiled as he pulled me into him, and we shared a small kiss. "You're looking pretty sexy yourself, Mr. Matthews."

"I try." He winked.

He shut and locked the door before heading to his Jeep.

"Do you like Mexican food?" he asked.

"I love Mexican food." I smiled.

"Good." He smiled back.

I found myself no longer being nervous around him. He was such an easy going guy, and he made me feel safe, unlike the first time I met him when I thought he was an ass. We pulled into the restaurant and got out of the Jeep. As Luke grabbed my hand, I looked at him and smiled as we made our way to the entrance. We decided to sit outside on the patio for dinner and I ordered a margarita while Luke ordered a beer. We talked a little bit about Charley, and he asked me how I got into teaching, so I told him how much I loved kids. Just as we finished our drinks, he touched on a taboo subject—my family.

"What was it like growing up with Johnny Gilmore?"

"You want to know the truth?"

"Of course I do," he said as he gave me a weird look.

"It was like living in a whore house."

He didn't have a chance to respond because the waitress brought over our food. I took a bite of my taco as he stared at me.

"I'm sorry, Lily."

"Don't be, you didn't know. We can talk more about it later."

***

We walked hand in hand back to his Jeep, and Luke opened the door for me. Before I climbed in, he cupped my chin in his hand and softly kissed me on the lips.

"I've wanted to do that since we got here." He smiled.

"I've been waiting for you to do it," I said as I bit my bottom lip.

We climbed into the Jeep, and he drove us to the cove.

"I thought this would be the perfect place for us to be alone and talk."

"It's the perfect place," I said as he led me to the secluded area.

I sat in the sand as he built a small bonfire. The atmosphere was beautiful, and there was no other place I wanted to be but here with him.

"So, you wanted to know about life with Johnny Gilmore, right?" I asked.

He stopped what he was doing and looked at me. "If you don't want to talk about it, I'll understand."

"My father was a manwhore that slept with any woman who glanced his way. My mother knew about it and threatened to divorce him if he didn't stop. He promised her that he would, so to try and keep her from finding out, he would use me and my sister as an excuse. He called it 'daddy-daughter day'. Once a week, he'd take me and my sister somewhere fun; then we'd end up at one of his whores' house, and he'd make us sit on the couch while he went and fucked her in the bedroom. He would tell us that she was a friend that needed something fixed. This went on for years. Sometimes, at night, he'd ask me if I wanted to go for ice cream, and he'd make me sit in the car, alone and in the dark, and wait for him while he went inside someone's house. I'll never forget the feeling of being so scared."

Luke finished building the bonfire and walked over to me. He sat behind me and put his arms around my waist, pulling me into him.

"Wow, I really had no idea. What an asshole. Didn't you ever tell your mom what he was doing?"

"Johnny said that mom wouldn't understand, and that she'd leave us, and he didn't want me being responsible for breaking up the family. He said it was our little secret, and that I'd be rewarded in the end."

"What the hell did he mean by that?" Luke asked.

"When he died a couple of years ago, I found out there was a bank account in my name that he started when I was a kid. I guess that's what he meant. He did have his good moments. He taught me to play the guitar, he sang special songs to me, and he left me a great deal of money, but I would've rather had a father who was home and faithful to his wife instead of all that money. I remember many Christmases where he'd be there in the mornings and then he'd have to leave. He would tell my mom that he and the boys had to practice, but we knew he was going to see one of his whores. I don't know what I would have done if it wasn't for Giselle and Gretchen. I practically lived at their house just to experience some normalcy."

Luke tightened his arms around me as I laid my head back on his chest. "So it's hard for me to hear people idolizing him because he was a shitty father who could have been so much better."

"I'm sure he loved you."

"I know he loved me. He told me every chance he could, but those were just words."

Luke rested his chin on my shoulder. "Why didn't your mom leave him?"

"She was afraid of being alone. She convinced herself that he loved her more than all the other women. That they were just distractions, and at the end of the day, he always came home to her."

"That's crazy," he said as he lightly squeezed me.

"She's crazy. Look at how she was going to let me marry Hunter so that I'd live the life she did."

Luke pushed my hair to the side and began kissing my neck. I smiled as I tilted my head.

"Keep that up, and you'll be sorry."

"Somehow, I don't think I'll be sorry," he whispered.

I closed my eyes and I could feel his erection pressing against the small of my back. I wanted him, but I was scared. It had been over year since I last had sex, and I was afraid I wouldn't be any good for him. As I brought my hands up to his head and ran my fingers through his hair, he let out a light groan and turned me so that I was laying on my back, in the soft sand. He lowered himself on top of me as his lips found their way to mine. His kiss was soft and alluring, and his actions were gentle and slow. His hands traveled to my breasts as he gently squeezed them through the fabric of my dress. Our breathing was rapid, and our hearts were beating fast. He reached his hand under my dress and up to my thong, cupping my ass as he let out a moan of excitement. Pushing the edge of my panties to the side, he dipped a finger inside me. I let out a light moan and arched my back as a feeling of pleasure took over me.

"Do you want me to stop?" he whispered as he kissed my lips.

"No, I don't ever want you to stop."

He groaned as he inserted another finger. I was already wet and getting ready to come.

He softly rubbed my clit in small circles as his fingers moved in and out of me fluently.

"Luke, I'm going to come. Don't stop, please."

"I won't stop. I want to feel you come with my fingers inside you."

This man knew what he was doing, and I wanted more of him. I wanted to feel every inch of him inside me. My body shook as I climaxed, and every tingling nerve in my body heightened. The flickering light of the fire showed off his beautiful smile as he brought me to orgasm. I moaned quietly even though I wanted to scream from the pleasure, but I was afraid someone would hear me.

Luke didn't say a word. He just stared at me and smiled as he gently removed his fingers.

"I want to have sex with you," I whispered.

He took the back of his hand and gently stroked my cheek.

"We aren't going to have sex, Lily. We're going to make love, and it's going to be beautiful, but not tonight and not here."

I couldn't speak. I was lost in his stare and his words.

"We should get going. You have school tomorrow, and I have a broken garbage disposal that needs to be fixed."

I let out a light laugh. I didn't want our night to end. Luke stood up and put the bonfire out. Moments later, he took my hand and helped me up from the sand then he pulled me into him and kissed me. I smiled as we held each other and danced for a minute.

We climbed into the Jeep, and I sat there, thinking about how he never told me a thing about his ex-fiancée or the accident. I wanted to know everything about him. I sighed, and he reached over, taking my hand.

"Is everything alright?" he asked.

I looked over at him and smiled. "Everything's perfectly fine."

18

Luke

When we arrived home, I walked around and helped Lily out of the Jeep. I couldn't stop thinking about what happened and how much she enjoyed it. Feeling the inside of her was incredible, and hearing her moan as I gave her pleasure was heart-stopping. My feelings for her were strong—stronger than I'd ever imagined. I needed her in ways I didn't understand. Every time she smiled at me, I grew weaker.

"Please come in and have a beer," she said.

I couldn't resist her and the tone she used.

"That'd be great." I smiled.

She threw her keys on the counter, and I pulled out my phone to see if I had any messages. The only one was from Sam's phone.

"Have fun with Lily, Uncle Luke."

I laughed and looked at Lily as she grabbed two beers from the fridge. She handed me one, then we both sat down on the couch.

"You haven't told me anything about you. All I know is that you're the maintenance man, you love my father, and you're in a band."

Eventually, I needed to tell her about Callie and the accident. It wasn't fair to her that I haven't spoken about it yet. I looked at her and took in a deep breath.

"I was the quarterback of the high school football team, and Callie was the lead cheerleader. We met senior year when her dad was transferred here from Ohio. We both felt an instant attraction, and we had dated up until the accident."

Lily reached over and grabbed my hand. She could see the tears beginning to fill my eyes. It was still too hard to talk about.

"You don't have to talk about it anymore. I understand how hard it is."

I leaned forward and grabbed her, pulling her into a warm embrace. I needed to feel the comfort of her being in my arms. I drank most of my beer and looked at the clock; it was midnight.

"You need to get some sleep. You have to be up early for work, and I don't want you to be tired," I spoke as I got up from the couch.

"I don't sleep anyway," she said.

I set the beer bottle on the counter and turned to look at her. "What do you mean you don't sleep?"

"I can't sleep more than a couple of hours a night."

I walked over to her and pushed her hair behind her ear. "Have you talked to someone about this?"

She took my hand and kissed my palm. "No, not yet."

"How long has this been going on?"

"Since the whole church ordeal."

"That was over a year ago, Lily!" I exclaimed. "How the hell do you function on only a couple hours of sleep?"

"I don't know. I'm used to it, I guess."

Kissing her head, I wrapped my arms around her, she held on tight.

"I'm staying here tonight to make sure you sleep."

"If you're staying here, then you're going to have to make love to me," she said as she stared into my eyes.

"Lily," I whispered as I tilted my head and gently kissed her lips.

I couldn't refuse her. She wanted me to make love to her just as bad as I wanted to. I slowly took down the straps of her dress, letting it fall to the ground, revealing her lace bra and thong. Her body was amazing, and I instantly became hard. I took her face in my hands. "I don't have a condom. I'll have to go get one."

"You don't need one. I'm on the pill, and I'm clean. I haven't had sex in over a year," she whispered as she stroked my cheek.

"I haven't had sex since the accident, and I'm also clean, so I don't want you to worry." I smiled.

"I'm not worried." She lifted my shirt over my head.

As I picked her up and kissed her passionately, I set her up against the wall. She tightly wrapped her legs around my waist. I was holding her by her perfectly tight ass as my lips traveled down to her neck. I've never wanted anything so bad in my life, but I had to slow down. I wanted this moment to be as perfect as she was. I stared into her beautiful eyes as she stared into mine.

"I'm nervous," she whispered.

"So am I." I smiled as I carried her to the bedroom and sat her on the bed.

I kicked off my shoes, unbuttoned my jeans, and took them off. I unhooked her bra, exposing her beautifully shaped breasts and hardened nipples. She laid herself back on the bed as I took off my boxers. Hovering over her perfect body, I kissed her tenderly on her breasts. She let out a soft moan when I took her hard nipple in my mouth and lightly tugged on it. Her back arched in excitement, wanting more. I moved my hand down her torso until I reached the edge of her thong, then I grabbed it and slid it off her body. I could feel how wet she was when I touched her, so I slid my finger in and out of her, feeling her warmth. She was ready for me, and she had me throbbing.

19

Lily

I gasped when Luke took off his boxers. He was incredibly big and very well endowed. I silently thanked God, but I really didn't expect anything less considering his perfect body. As he erotically sucked my nipples, I reached my hand down and took a hold of his hard cock. Running my hand down the entire length of him gave me chills. As I stroked him up and down, a moan escaped the back of his throat.

"God, Lily, you're amazing," he moaned as he continued to explore each breast.

My skin was on fire, and I needed him more than I needed air. He brought his mouth up to mine, kissed me passionately, and then whispered in my ear.

"I want to make you come with my mouth before I make passionate love to you."

I gasped as his tongue traveled down to my body. His breath was hot as he began licking the inner edges of my thigh before moving to my swollen lips. I was already on the verge of an orgasm. He reached his hands up and cupped my breasts. He aroused me more than I'd ever been aroused before. His mouth moved swiftly over my swollen, wet area that so desperately throbbed for him, and he moved his tongue in small circles around my clit. Placing my hands on each side of his head, I breathlessly called out his name as my body released itself to him. He softly kissed the sensitive area as he smiled before his lips made their way back to my mine.

"You're so beautiful, Lily," he said as he took his cock and placed it between my legs.

"You're amazing, and I want you inside me," I whispered.

He slowly pushed himself into me, inch by inch. He was so hard, and he felt incredible.

"God, Lily, you're so tight. Are you okay?" he asked.

"Yes, Luke. Please don't stop!" I exclaimed as I dug my nails into his back.

He smiled and pushed himself deeper inside me. I wrapped my legs around him as he cupped my ass with both hands and gently squeezed. He slowly moved in and out of me as we stared into each other's eyes. This was the most beautiful moment I've ever experienced. His thrusting became rapid and brought my body to the heightened state of another orgasm.

"Lily, come with me," he moaned as he pushed himself into me one last time before filling my insides with him come.

Watching the look on his face as he came was the sexiest thing I'd ever seen. He collapsed on me and held me tight, our bodies melting together, and our hearts racing at the speed of light. I'd just had the best sex of my life and I wasn't sure if my body would recover. He lifted himself up on his elbows and pushed my hair back with one hand.

"Are you all right?" He chuckled.

"I'm fantastic. How about you?"

"I'm great. No, better than great."

I giggled as I ran my hands through his hair. He glanced over at the clock; it was three a.m.

"You need to get up in a couple of hours."

"I know. Don't worry about it, I'll be fine. Will you stay here with me?" I asked as he climbed off of me and got out of bed.

"Of course I'll stay here. There's no place else that I'd rather be. I want to wake up with you in my arms."

We climbed under the covers and Luke wrapped his strong arms around me, pulling me in as close as he could.

"You feel good naked," he said as he softly kissed my back.

"So do you." I quivered.

"Good night, Lily."

"Good night, Luke."

***

I opened my eyes as the buzzing sound of the alarm began, increasing in sound with each buzz. I reached over and turned it off while still wrapped up in Luke arms. I tried to get up as slowly as possible because I didn't want to wake him up. As soon as I moved, his arms tightened their grip around me.

"Don't leave this bed. Call in and tell them you're sick. I'm not letting you go."

I laughed as I turned and looked at him. "I have to go. I have a class to teach, and remember, your niece is part of that class."

He sighed as he kissed me. "Fine, but I'm joining you in the shower."

"I was hoping you would." I winked.

He grabbed me, turned me on my back, and started tickling me. I laughed and screamed at the same time. Suddenly, there was knock on the wall. Luke stopped, looked at me, and we both started laughing. Luke didn't knock back, he banged on the wall.

"Dude, it's called payback!"

Luke got up and took my hand as we stepped into shower, having sex before starting our morning.

I looked at the clock on my phone as I threw my hair up. Luke walked up behind me as I stood there in my bra and panties.

"I made you some coffee," he said as his hands traveled up my sides, and his lips met with my neck.

"Thank you, and you need to stop, or I'm going to be late." I turned around, kissed him on the lips, and then made my way to the bedroom to get dressed.

Luke followed and stood in the doorway of my bedroom, leaning up against it with one arm while holding his coffee cup in his hand.

"I want to see you tonight."

"I want to see you too," I said as I put on my heels and stopped in front of him.

"Kiss me and I'll let you through." He smiled.

I smiled as my lips met his. I wanted to leave him with more than just a kiss, so I stuck my hand down the front of his jeans and grabbed his semi-hard cock. He moaned. "Lily, how could you?"

"How can't I? You're too damn irresistible," I said as I lifted his arm and walked through.

I heard him chuckle as he followed behind me. I grabbed my bags, my keys, and my coffee cup from the counter. Luke opened the door, and we both walked out.

"Have a good day," he said as he kissed me.

"Uncle Luke!" Charley exclaimed.

He broke our kiss and looked at her as she ran down the rest of the stairs to him. "Hey, peanut."

"I saw you two kissing." She smiled. "Did you spend the night?" she asked.

Luke looked panicked as we both looked at each other. "No, of course not. Lily had something that she needed fixed."

Maddie stood behind Charley and smiled at me.

"Let me drive Charley to school for you," I spoke.

"That's okay, Lily. You don't have to do that."

"I want to. I'm going there anyway, and I'm already running late," I said as I looked at Luke.

"Mommy, please!" Charley squealed.

"Okay," she said as she gave Charley a kiss goodbye. "Thank you, Lily."

"No problem." I smiled as I took Charley's hand.

"Bye, Mommy. Bye, Uncle Luke." She waved as we walked out the building.

20

Luke

"Would you like to join me for some coffee? I know you're *dying* to talk to me."

"Yes, I do want coffee, and yes, I'm dying to talk to you." Maddie smiled as she followed me into my apartment.

I walked into the kitchen and poured the last of the coffee in a cup. Just as I handed the cup to Maddie, Sam walked out of his bedroom, straightening his tie. He walked over and fist-bumped me.

"Thanks for keeping me awake all night," he said as he picked up the empty coffee pot and looked at it.

"No problem, man."

"As happy as I am that you finally gave in and had sex with the hot girl next door, I have to go to a meeting. We'll talk about it later, dude. Love you, Maddie," Sam said as he walked out the door.

"Love you back, Sammy." She smiled, and then turned to me. "The only thing I want to know is if you're okay."

"I'm fine, Maddie," I said as I started another pot of coffee.

"You've been depressed for over a year, Luke. You haven't made any attempt to meet or date anyone, and now all of a sudden, you're spending the night with the girl next door."

"That's because the right girl never crossed my path. I didn't think I'd ever fall for anyone after Callie. She was my life, my whole world, and you know that. But since Lily moved in, I started seeing things differently. She makes me smile, Maddie. No one has been able to do that in a very long time."

"I know, and I'm happy for you. I just don't want you or her to get hurt. You both have endured enough pain. Mom and Dad are going to love her. You know they'll want a family dinner as soon as they get back from their cruise, right?"

"I know, and I want Lily to meet them." I kissed Maddie on the top of her head and walked to the bedroom to change. I had work that needed to be done.

***

I couldn't stop thinking about Lily and our night together. I didn't plan on making love to her quite yet, but she wanted me to, and who was I to deny her. I needed to tell her about Callie and the accident. I was actually surprised she didn't ask about my scar last night. My phone beeped with a reminder about the job I needed to do. I snapped out of my thoughts and back into reality; then I grabbed my tool box and headed upstairs to Mrs. Lopez's apartment to fix her garbage disposal.

"You have that look, Luke," Mrs. Lopez said.

"What look would that be, Mrs. Lopez?" I asked as I tightened the pipe under her kitchen sink.

"The look of love."

I chuckled. "Is that so? How can you tell?"

"I can see it in your eyes. They have a new life about them. Who is she?"

I crawled out from under the sink and threw my wrench in the tool box. "I'm not in love, but I have met someone that I really like." I smiled.

"Ah ha! I knew it!" she exclaimed. I sure hope it's that cute little blonde that just moved in next door to you."

"As a matter of fact, it is, and her name's Lily," I said as I took the bottle of water she held out me.

"I'm happy for you, Luke. I know you've had a rough year, and you deserve true happiness."

I closed my tool box and picked it up from the floor. "Thanks for the water, Mrs. Lopez. Everything's working perfectly now. Just call me if you need me," I said as I walked out the door.

I walked back into my apartment, set my tool box down, then sat on the couch. I missed Lily already. She was always on my mind, and it was driving me crazy, so I decided to send her a text message.

"How about dinner tonight at your place? We can cook together."

"That sounds great! I don't cook though."

"I'll teach you. We can go to the store together when you get home."

"All right, I can't wait."

"Me neither."

***

As I was watching TV, and thinking about how slow the day was going, there was a knock on the door. As soon as I opened it, Lily threw her arms around me and kissed me. I pulled her into the apartment, kicked the door closed with the heel of my shoe, and pinned her up against the closet door as I kissed her passionately. After a moment, she broke our kiss and smiled at me.

"I missed you," she said out of breath.

"I missed you too, and I couldn't wait for you to get home," I responded as my lips made their way behind her ear.

The door opened, and Sam walked in. "Really? You do know there's a bedroom down the hall over there, right?" he said.

Lily and I laughed as I shook my head at Sam.

"Seriously, dude. I don't want to come home and find the two of you having sex on the couch, because I may have to join in."

I smacked him on the back of the head as I walked by. "That's not even funny, bro," I said as I pointed at him.

"Lily thinks it's funny. Look at her; she's laughing."

"Babe, don't humor him, please."

Sam was laughing as he walked to his room.

"Are you ready to leave?" I asked as I walked over to her and ran the back of my hand softly across her cheek. She nodded her head, so we headed out the apartment and walked to the Jeep.

"What are we making?" Lily asked as I pushed the cart through the grocery store.

"I thought maybe we can cook some spaghetti with a homemade sauce, salad, and bread."

"You make homemade sauce?"

"I sure do, and Charley loves it. My mom never cooked alone; she always made us cook as a family from the time we were six years old."

Lily hooked her arm around mine and laid her head on my shoulder. "Your mom sounds amazing. My mom never cooked. She had her chef do all the cooking, and we rarely ate as a family."

My heart ached for her when she told me that. I leaned over and kissed her head. "Come on, let's get what we need and get out of here."

While we were walking through the store, I saw Bernie.

"Hey, Luke," he said as he looked at Lily.

"Hey, Bernie, how was Florida?" I asked him.

"Florida was great, and I'm getting closer to retirement. Who's this beautiful woman on your arm?"

"This is Lily Gilmore. Lily, meet Bernie, the owner of Bernie's Bar."

Lily shook Bernie's hand, and he smiled at her.

"I'm going to take a stab in the dark here, but you wouldn't happen to be Johnny Gilmore's daughter, would you?"

"Yes, Johnny was my father." She smiled.

"I knew it!" Bernie exclaimed. "Look at you, all grown up. Your dad used to play in my bar when he was in Santa Monica, and he used to show me pictures of you. He was a brilliant musician. I'm sorry to hear about his death."

"Thank you," Lily said. "He was a great musician."

"Hey, Luke, we need to sit down and discuss what you want to do with the bar. This last trip to Florida pushed me closer to selling, and the next time I go, I'm not coming back."

"I know, and I have to give it some more thought. I'll call you."

"Don't take too long, son, I have others who are interested. It was nice to meet you, Lily. Luke, I'll talk to you soon," he said as he walked away.

Lily looked at me as I sighed. "What was all that about?" she asked.

"We'll talk about it over dinner."

21

Lily

Luke opened the bottle of wine as I took two glasses from the cupboard. He started making the sauce, and I started on something a little more simple—the salad.

"How was your day at work?" he asked.

"It was good, and my students were very well-behaved today."

"Did Charley say anything to you about us?" he asked as he began to chop the onions.

"No. Though she did smile at me a lot." I laughed.

"She's a great little girl. I hope to have a daughter like her someday."

I stopped my knife halfway through the tomato when Luke said that. A sick feeling in my stomach instantly developed because the talk of family terrified me, but I proceeded to talk about it anyway.

"How many kids would you like to have?" I asked like an idiot.

"I don't know. Four kids would be nice, I guess."

"Four!" I gasped.

Luke chuckled as he put the onions in the sauce. "What's wrong with four kids?"

"Nothing's wrong with four kids. I'm just surprised you want so many."

"Cal—forget it. I'm sorry I brought it up," he said.

I could see the sadness in his face as he turned to the stove and stirred the sauce. I put down the knife and wrapped my arms around his waist.

"Don't ever be sorry. You need to talk about her, Luke, and I don't ever want you to feel as though you can't or shouldn't."

He put down the spoon and turned to face me.

"It just doesn't feel right to talk about her like that, and I don't want to hurt you."

"You wouldn't hurt me. She was a huge part of your life for many years, and I want to know about her."

Luke softly brushed his lips against mine. "You're amazing, do you know that?"

"I've been told a few times." I smiled.

He hugged me and went back to making the sauce as I finished slicing the tomatoes for the salad.

"On the night of the accident, we were on our way home from a trip," he began to speak. "We were stopped at a red light a few streets away from here. When the light turned green, and I began to go through the intersection, another car ran the red light and crashed into us, hitting Callie's side. Our car spun out of control and another car hit my side." Luke paused for a moment. "I'll never forget the sound of both crashes, the sounds of the squealing tires, the brightness of the headlights as both cars headed towards us, and Callie screaming my name before I blacked out. I'd woken up in the hospital three days later without any recollection of the accident at that moment. My parents had told me that Callie had died, and that's when everything came rushing back to me."

I gulped as I heard him tell the story and my eyes couldn't help but fill with tears. He wouldn't look at me, and I knew if I tried to comfort him in any way, he would lose it, so I quickly changed the subject.

"Have I told you how much of an asshole Hunter is?"

Luke looked over at me and started to laugh. "What?"

"He's an asshole, plain and simple. He's an uptight, cock sucking, piece of shit, and I truly despise him. Did I ever tell you that he color coordinated his underwear with his clothes?"

"Seriously?" Luke asked.

"I'm dead serious, and not only did he do that, but he also kept a divider in his drawer for his socks. What guy does that? Oh, and the best part, he has pants that he'll only wear on certain days of the week."

Luke was laughing and shaking his head. "What the hell did you ever see in that guy?"

I had to stop and think about that for a moment because I honestly didn't know.

"He wasn't hot, that's for sure. He was cute in a *boyish* way. I think it was because he's a charmer, and he charmed his way into my life, like the lying piece of shit he is."

Luke walked over to me, put his hands on my hips, and kissed me on the forehead. "Watch your mouth." He smiled.

"Sorry," I said as I looked up at him.

I grabbed two plates from the cupboard, some silverware out of the drawer, and set the table for dinner. I heard the beep of my phone indicating there was a text message.

"Your phone went off, babe," he said.

I walked over to the counter and picked it up. The message was from Giselle.

"I'm off to Seattle for a modeling job and Lucky's coming with me. I just thought you and Luke would want to know."

I knitted my eyebrows and quickly replied.

"What the hell's going on with the two of you? Are you a couple or something?"

"We're two adults who are having fun—without a commitment."

"All right, if you say so," I replied.

Luke set the spaghetti on the table. "What's wrong? You look confused."

"I am confused. I'm confused about this whole Lucky and Giselle thing. She's going to Seattle on a modeling job, and he's going with her. Don't you think that's weird?"

"Lily, Lucky's weird. You should know that by now." He chuckled.

I sat down at the table as Luke put some spaghetti on my plate. "Eat up."

I took a bite as he watched me. "Luke, this is the best spaghetti I've ever had."

"You're not just saying that spare my feelings, are you?"

"Of course not! The sauce is truly amazing."

I left a long piece of spaghetti hanging from my mouth as I motioned with my finger for him to come closer. He smiled and leaned across the table, taking the other end of the spaghetti in his mouth and followed it until his lips reached mine. He licked my lips with his tongue and then inserted it in my mouth. We got up from our seats as we continued to share a kiss. He slowly put his hands up my shirt, pulling the cups to my bra down and feeling my hardened nipples. I reached my hand down to his hard cock and stroked it through the fabric of his jeans. Getting lost in the hotness of the moment, our kiss became more passionate with a little bit of roughness until we were interrupted by a knock on the door.

"Uncle Luke, are you in there making your famous spaghetti?"

We both broke our kiss and looked at each other. Luke's eyes were wide.

"What the hell?" he whispered. "Um, yes, Charley, I am!" he yelled across the room.

I started laughing as Luke had to sit back in his chair to hide his erection until it had gone down. I walked over to the door and opened it.

"Hey, sweetie!" I smiled. "Would you like to come in and have some of your Uncle Luke's famous spaghetti?"

"I sure would!" she exclaimed.

Charley walked in and sat down next to Luke at the table. "Hi, Uncle Luke," she said as she kissed him on the cheek.

"Hi, peanut. How did you know I was making spaghetti?"

"Mommy and I just came back from the store, and I could smell it in the hallway, but the smell was stronger coming from Lily's door."

Luke and I both laughed as I set a plate in front of Charley. I put some spaghetti on it with some bread, and she sat there and ate it. Luke looked at me and smirked.

"So, are you two dating or what?" Charley blurted out with a mouthful of spaghetti.

Luke and I shared a glance at each other. "Yeah, you could say that we're dating." He winked at me.

"I knew it!" Charley giggled. "I can't wait to tell my friends that my teacher and my uncle are dating."

Luke pulled his ringing phone from his pocket. It was Maddie calling to ask him to send Charley home.

"Your mom wants you home as soon as you're finished eating, peanut."

"Why?" she whined.

"I think it's because you have homework to do." I smiled at her.

"Oh yeah, I forgot." She giggled.

Luke looked over at her and whispered, "Your teacher is mean."

"I am not!" I exclaimed as I pick up some plain noodles and threw them at him across the table.

"Oh, you want a food fight, do you?" He laughed as he reached in the spaghetti bowl, grabbed a handful, and threw them at me.

"Charley, get under the table!" I said.

She started laughing and ducked under the table. I reached my hand in the salad bowl and threw what I'd grabbed at Luke. He looked at me and sighed as he brushed the lettuce out of his hair. I started laughing uncontrollably until he put some butter on a knife, flung it at me, and it stuck to my forehead. He couldn't help but laugh as he took out his phone and started taking pictures. I took my finger and wiped the butter off as I seductively brought my finger to my mouth and started sucking it. Luke put his phone down and looked at me.

"Come on, Charley, it's time to go home and do your homework."

"Ok," she said with an exaggerated sigh.

Luke looked at me and whispered, "Stay right where you are."

He took Charley by the hand and walked her back up to her apartment. I already knew what was going to happen the minute he returned.

22

Luke

I ran Charley up to her apartment so that I could get back to Lily. The way she sucked her finger made me hot for her, and there was no time to waste. We were already interrupted by Charley earlier, and I wanted to avoid any further interruptions. I walked into Lily's apartment, but she wasn't sitting at the table, so I followed her trail of clothes that led to the bathroom. She was lying in a bubble-filled tub, waiting for me. I leaned up against the door with my arms folded, smiling at her.

"What are you waiting for?" she asked seductively.

"I'm waiting for an invitation to join you, and I thought I told you not to move."

"Get your hot, naked ass in this tub, right now!" she demanded.

I kicked off my shoes, took off my shirt, and removed my jeans and boxers. Lily moved forward as I stepped into the tub behind her, pulling her naked, wet body into me.

"I thought this would be better. We do need to wash off from our little food fight."

I began kissing her neck as she tilted her head to the side. "This was a very good idea."

Lily took the soap and started washing my arms that were holding her against me. I took it from her hands and began to soap her breast. She moved her body against mine as my erection pressed against the small of her back.

"You feel so good like this," I whispered as the water sloshed back and forth. She let out a moan as I inserted my finger inside her. "I don't think we're going to last too long in this tub. I want to be inside of you, right now."

She moved up as I climbed out of the bathtub and grabbed an extra-large towel she had sitting on the toilet. I held out my hand, helped her out from the tub, and wrapped us both in the towel, holding her closely as she buried her face into my chest. I picked her up and set her on the bathroom counter. Her smile grew as my tongue traveled down her damp body and below where she ached for me. As my mouth sucked, and my tongue licked every inch of her, Lily ran her fingers through my hair, pulling and tugging as she enjoyed my movements. Standing up, I thrust myself inside her. I reached under her and grabbed a hold of her ass as I moved in and out of her. Her legs wrapped around me. She was so warm inside, and it made me want to come fast.

"Faster, Luke, faster!" she yelled as her nails dug into my back.

"Ah, baby, you're going to make me come already," I said as I pushed deeper inside her.

I felt her swelling around my cock, and I was going to explode any second. Suddenly, she let out a loud moan as we both came at the same time. I held her face in my hands, kissed her softly on the lips, and stared into her eyes.

"Can we consider us a couple?"

"I don't do boyfriends," she said.

"I don't do girlfriends, but I thought maybe we could make another exception."

"I guess I can make another exception for you." She smiled.

I picked her up from the counter and carried her to the bedroom.

***

I woke up as Lily got in the shower, and I made a pot of coffee. Grabbing my phone off the counter, I saw I had several missed calls from my mom. The voicemail indicator lit up, so I punched in my code and listened to her message.

"Hi, Luke, it's Mom. Your father and I are back from our cruise, and we're having a family dinner this Friday night at six o'clock. Your sister told me that you've met someone very special, but she won't tell me anything else, so bring her with you. I'm dying to meet her. I love you, Luke. Bye."

I poured some coffee in a cup, took it in the bathroom, and handed it to Lily as she was getting ready for work.

"My mom called last night and left a message. She's having a family dinner this Friday night, and she's dying to meet you. Maddie told her about us."

"That sounds great. I'd love to meet your family." She smiled.

"Would you like to go to Bernie's tonight?" I asked her.

"Sure, that sounds fun. We never did talk about that last night."

I walked over to her and moved my hands under the towel she had wrapped around her and placed them on her small hips.

"That's because we were too busy making love all night," I whispered as I nibbled on her ear.

She smiled, turning her head and meeting her lips with mine. I could kiss her all day. She put her hands on my chest and broke our kiss.

"I'm going to be late if we don't stop."

"I know, and I'm sorry. Finish getting dressed. You have approximately fifteen minutes before you have to leave."

"Thanks for the warning," she said as she began brushing her teeth.

I heard a knock on the door and wondered who would be at here so early in the morning. I opened it and saw Sam standing there, holding a brown bag in my face.

"Bagels for the two lovebirds."

"Come on in, man. Thank you."

Sam stepped inside the apartment as I took the bag from him.

"Lily and I are going to Bernie's tonight. Do you and Gretchen want to join us?" I asked.

"That sounds good. I'll ask her."

"Want some coffee?" I asked Sam as I walked over and poured some in a cup for myself.

"Nah, I have to get going soon. Are you free to grab a burger at the burger bar this afternoon?"

"Sure, I'll meet you there around one."

Lily came out of the bedroom, looking smoking hot. *We were going to have to role play in bed.* The thought started getting me hard.

"Good morning, Lily. You're looking as beautiful as always." Sam smiled.

"Good morning, Sam, and thank you," she replied as she kissed him on the cheek.

"Hot damn! I've been kissed by two beautiful women already this morning," he said as he spun around and put his hand on the doorknob.

"Later, bro. I'll see you later for that burger."

"Later, dude. Bye, Lily," Sam said as he waved and left the apartment.

I poured the rest of the coffee in her to-go cup and handed it to her as I walked her to her Explorer. I opened the door and wrapped my arms around her.

"Have a good day, babe," I spoke as I kissed her lips.

"You too." She smiled.

***

"Two burgers, medium, with everything and a side of fries," the waitress said as she set our food in front of us.

"I'm taking Lily to family dinner Friday night."

"Wow! That's a big step taking a girl home to meet the family. I haven't done that with Gretchen yet. I love how I was right that you and Lily would make a great couple. You are a couple, right?"

I nodded my head as I took a bite of my burger. "Yep, we made it official last night."

"Dude, that's awesome." Sam smiled as he fist-bumped me.

When we finished our lunch, Sam went back to work, and I headed to Bernie's to talk to Maddie. I walked in the bar and took my usual seat.

"Hey, Luke. What brings you in here today?" Maddie asked.

"I know you talked to Mom last night. I listened to her message this morning, and she knew about Lily."

"I may have mentioned that you've met someone and that she's really special. I hope you're not mad."

"No, I'm not mad at all. It actually bought me some time before the million questions Mom's going to be asking me about her."

Maddie set a beer down in front on me.

"Luke, my boy, tell me you're here to give me your decision?" Bernie said as he came from the storage room with a box in his hands.

"Not yet, Bernie, but I promise you'll have my answer by the end of the week," I replied.

"You're actually thinking about buying the bar again?" Maddie leaned over the counter and asked.

"Yeah, I'm thinking about it, but I want to talk to Lily about it first. We were supposed to talk about it last night, but we kind of got distracted by a bathtub, a countertop, and a bed."

"Whoa, stop right there!" Maddie said as she put her hand up.

I finished my beer and got up from the stool. "Later, Bernie. Lily and I will be in tonight. See ya, sis," I said as I kissed her on the cheek.

23

Lily

I grabbed my bags and headed to the Explorer. Once I got inside, I inserted the key—nothing. The fucking thing wouldn't start. I took in a deep breath and calmly turned the key—nothing. "Damn—damn—damn it!" I yelled as I slammed my hands against the steering wheel. I pulled out my phone and dialed Luke. *Please answer, please answer,* I thought to myself.

"Hey, babe, are you on your way home?"

"I never made it out of the parking lot. My truck won't start!"

"Sit tight. I'll be there shortly."

"Thank you, I—I'll be here!"

I couldn't believe what almost came out of my mouth. Just then, a text message came through from Gretchen.

"Sam and I will be joining you at Bernie's tonight. Make sure you have your dancing shoes on because we're going to get down and dirty!"

I laughed as I replied, *"Alright, but we have to get the guys to dance with us. If Luke dances, he's perfect. I love a man who can dance!"*

I looked up and saw Luke pulling into the parking lot. I let out a sigh of relief when he was in his Jeep and not on his bike. Pulling up next to me, he smiled, and I gave him a small wave and a smile in return. I was so happy to see him. I got out of the Explorer as he got out of his Jeep, and I hugged him tight.

"I missed you," I said.

"I missed you too. Now let's see if we can get your truck running."

I popped the hood and stood next to him as he fumbled with some wires. I was totally turned on by how sexy he looked, trying to fix my truck.

"Go try to start it."

I sat in the truck and turned the key—nothing. I got out and walked over to Luke as he was on the phone with the mechanic. After he hung up, he shut the hood of my truck and put his hands on my hips.

"They're on their way to tow your truck back to the garage."

I sighed. "I need a new ride."

"The good news is that I get to drive you to and from work tomorrow." He smiled.

"There's no school tomorrow. The district's closed."

"That's great! So I guess that means you don't have to be home early tonight."

"Nope, I can stay out late because it's not a school night." I smiled.

We walked over to Luke's Jeep, and he opened the door for me. I climbed in and we drove back to the apartment building. We pulled up as Maddie and Charley were getting out of the car.

"Uncle Luke, Lily, guess what? My daddy's coming to visit in a few days!"

I could see the tears in Maddie's eyes as Luke looked at her. She looked away.

"Lily, take Charley to your apartment. I want to talk to my sister for a minute."

I took Charley's hand and led her inside the building. I began to worry about the conversation Luke was going to have with Maddie. Obviously, no one liked Charley's father. After a few minutes, they walked into my apartment and Maddie took Charley home. Luke opened my refrigerator and grabbed a bottle of beer. He opened it and flung the cap across the counter.

"Do you want to talk about it?" I asked as I stood there with my arms folded.

"He hasn't seen Charley in three years. He hasn't paid child support, and he hasn't sent her any gifts; nothing. The only thing the bastard's done is made a few phone calls, talked to her for a couple of minutes, and made up excuses as to why he can't visit her. Now, he's coming here after three years and expects to take her for a weekend."

I walked over to where Luke was standing. "He's her father."

"Don't give me that bullshit, Lily! The only thing that attaches that title to him is his DNA. He's no father to that little girl!"

I could see the pain in his eyes, and I knew he was more of a father to Charley than anyone. I watched him as he threw back his beer. Wrapping my arms around him, I held him tight.

"He's a drunk and a drug addict, Lily. There's no way I'm letting him take her. He can visit her at Maddie's, with me sitting there."

"I'm sorry, but Charley seems really excited to see him."

"I know, and that's the sad part. She doesn't even know what he's like. She hasn't seen him since she was six years old."

"Come on, let's not worry about this now. Let's go to Bernie's and have a good time. Speaking of Bernie, we never discussed what you two were talking about yesterday," I said as I looked up at him.

He took his thumb and softly stroked my cheek. "You're so beautiful," he whispered.

I smiled as I put my hand on his face. "You're beautiful too, Luke, inside and out. The way you take care of Charley is amazing. You treat her like she's your own daughter and that's what I love about you."

He took my hand from his face and pressed his lips against my palm while staring into my eyes. "I'm falling in love with you, Lily."

My pulse started racing. Chills ran up and down my spine as he spoke those words to me. There was no denying that I was falling in love with him. He consumed my every thought, and I craved his touch all the time. I brought my face closer as I kissed his lips.

"I'm falling in love with you too, Luke."

Picking me up, he buried his face into my neck as I wrapped my legs tightly around him. He didn't say anything; he didn't need to. We both knew as we were holding each other that our love was growing, and whether we wanted it or not, there was no stopping what was happening between us. After carrying me to the bedroom, he stood me up in front of the bed. His fingers deftly unbuttoned my shirt as he slid it off my shoulders, letting it fall to the ground. He unhooked my bra, letting it fall from my breasts as he ran his fingers over my puckered nipples. I was mesmerized by him as he stared into my eyes while he undressed me. He took down my skirt, exposing my thong, and then he cupped my ass in his hands and squeezed it while taking in a sharp breath.

"I can never get enough of you. I can feel your body begging for me," he said as he placed his hand between my legs. He inserted his finger and kissed me gently. Everything he did was gentle and slow. I wanted to reach out and grab him, but he wouldn't let me. He took my hand and placed it on my clit, making me rub it in circles as he bent down and erotically kissed every inch of my throbbing sheath while my body trembled, and I had one of the best orgasms of my life. Moments later, he brought his mouth up to mine.

"I want you to taste what I taste every time we make love," he whispered.

His hand reached around to the back of my neck, and he held me steady while he kissed me passionately, sucking my tongue and nipping my bottom lip. "I need you, babe. I need you so bad it hurts."

As he broke our kiss, he turned me around and laid me on the bed, hovering over me and softly kissing my back. I could feel his hard cock rubbing against my ass and up the small of my back. A low groan turned louder as he pushed himself inside me. He moved in and out of me, making me come with him as he reached under me and rubbed my swollen clit. After lowering himself on top of me, he brought his mouth to my ear and whispered, "Don't ever leave me."

I felt a knot in my throat, finding it hard to catch my breath. He just asked me never to leave him, which meant things were moving faster than the speed of light. I turned my head to the side and kissed his lips as I smiled. He got up and went into the bathroom, and I lay there, pondering his words. A few minutes later, he emerged and walked over to where his boxers and jeans laid on the floor.

"I've been thinking about buying Bernie's bar," he said as he put his boxers on and sat on the edge of the bed.

I sat up and wrapped one arm around his neck.

"That's wonderful, Luke. How long have you been thinking about doing that?"

He took my hand and interlaced our fingers. "It's something I've always dreamed of doing, ever since I was a kid. Callie and I talked about it all the time. She encouraged me to go for it, and when I finally decided to take that leap, the accident happened and changed everything."

As I kissed his shoulder, he stroked my arm. "Luke, you should still buy it."

"It's not that simple, Lily."

I heard my cell phone ringing, so Luke told me to go answer it. I got up from the bed, walked over to the dresser, and saw Gretchen was calling.

"Hey, Gretch, what's up?"

"Are the two of you going to have sex the rest of the night or are you coming to the bar?"

"Are you already there?" I asked.

"No, we're standing outside your apartment, waiting for you."

"Oh!" I said. "Give us a minute. The door's unlocked, come in and make yourselves comfortable."

"Okay," she said as she ended the call.

Luke looked at me, and I could see that the tears and sadness that filled his eyes were gone. "I didn't realize what time it was."

"They can wait," I said as I pulled my black dress from the closet.

"If you wear that, you're going to have me fucking you in the bathroom at the bar."

I giggled as I slipped it on. "I dare you." I smiled.

"Dude and dudette, let's go!" Sam yelled from across the room.

"Shut it, man! We're coming!" Luke yelled back.

"I bet you are!" he exclaimed.

We looked at each other and started laughing. Luke got dressed, and we walked into the living room. Gretchen looked at me, got up from the couch, and grabbed my arm, leading me into the bathroom.

"You have sex hair. You can't go to the bar with sex hair."

I sighed as I took the brush, ran it through my hair, and touched up my makeup. "How's that?" I asked her as I turned around.

"Much better." She smiled.

We walked into the living room, grabbed our guys, and headed to Bernie's.

24

"Four beers, Candi," Luke said as he walked past the bar, and the four of us sat at a table.

"What's going on with your sister and Lucky?" I asked Gretchen as I grabbed her hand.

"I don't know. She said it's weird because he's not her type at all, yet she can't stop fucking him."

I twisted my face at her as Candi brought the beers to the table.

"It looks like it's a full house tonight, Luke. Maybe you should be up on that stage, playing your guitar and singing us a song." Candi smiled.

"I'd love to, Candi, but I didn't bring my guitar."

"Maybe *you* didn't bring it, but *I* did." Sam chuckled.

Luke shot him a look. "You brought my guitar, man?"

"Yeah, it's in the back of the Jeep. I put it in there in case you needed it." Sam replied.

"Great!" Candi grinned. "Thirty minutes, Luke. Get ready to knock the socks off this crowd."

Luke looked over at me as he took a swig of his beer. "How about you get up on that stage and play what your daddy taught you?"

"No way!" I exclaimed as I took a sip of my beer.

I didn't know if he was joking or not, but there was no way in hell I was getting up on that stage and playing the guitar.

"Come on, Lily. You have a beautiful voice." Luke smiled.

"Since when have you heard me sing?"

"Through the wall. You sing almost every night before you go to bed—at least you did before I started sleeping over."

"Damn it, I have to move. Those walls are too thin."

Luke laughed, pulled me from my chair, and hugged me. "You aren't going anywhere," he said.

Sam went out to the Jeep, grabbed Luke's guitar, and handed it to him as Candi announced Luke's performance from the stage. I smiled at him and kissed him for good luck. He winked at me, walked to the stage, and sat on the bar stool Candi provided for him. Luke adjusted the microphone and said hello as everyone in the bar clapped. His smile captivated me like it always did, and the way he held his guitar and strummed a few chords for a sound check, pulled me in. Candi set another beer down in front of me, leaned over, and whispered in my ear as she looked across at the stage.

"Luke's a great guy. It's good to see him smile again."

My eyes wouldn't leave him as he sat up on the stage, and I stared straight ahead as I replied, "He is a wonderful guy. Sometimes, I think he's too good to be true."

Candi patted my shoulder and walked away. I took a sip of my fresh, cold beer and listened as Luke sang a song.

The moment he finished his song, Luke spoke to the crowd. "I've met a very special lady. She's very talented, and I think you'd all like her. Ladies and gentlemen, I'd like to introduce Lily Gilmore."

My stomach dropped, and my heart started racing. There was no doubt in my mind that I was going to kill him, but that would have to wait because people were cheering and clapping for me. Gretchen pushed me up on the stage. I stood there and faced the cheering crowd.

Luke stood up, handed me his guitar, and whispered in my ear, "You can punish me later."

I shot him a look and sat down on the stool with his guitar in hand. Luke made his way off the stage and back to the table. I stared out in the crowd, remembering the night my father did the same thing to me. Closing my eyes, I took in a deep breath and started playing a song that I wrote shortly after my father's death.

"You were taken away

By the love and alcohol you liked to play

I love you are just words

If there's no action, it can't be meant

You told me you loved me, and I was heaven sent.

Love in Between

You left a cut so deep in my heart
There's no escaping who you are
But I'm your daughter, and I'm your star
You left me alone and full of scars.

There were more important things to you
Then the family that you once knew
You always told me to shine bright
And that I was your shining light.

You left a cut so deep in my heart
There's no escaping who you are
But I'm your daughter, and I'm your star
You left me alone and full of scars.

You said you'd always be with me
Even when I needed you most
You're just a phone call away
Over on the East Coast.

I'm done crying now, and I've said goodbye

I'll remember you always until I die

I hope you can hear me from wherever you are

This song is for you, from your daughter, your star."

While the people in the bar clapped and whistled, I strummed the last chord. Standing up, I smiled and thanked them as Sam walked up on stage and took Luke's guitar. He kissed me on the cheek and smiled. Luke got up from the table and stood in the middle of the bar, waiting for me to walk off the stage and into his arms. When I climbed down to meet him, his arms tightly wrapped around me.

"Babe, that was beautiful. Are you all right?"

"I'm fine, Luke," I said as I looked up at him.

"I didn't know you wrote songs. I thought you just sang and played random ones or the ones your father taught you."

"I write a song here and there." I smiled.

He cupped my face in his hands and kissed my lips. Gretchen walked up to us, broke our kiss, and hugged me.

"I've never heard that song before, Lily. What the fuck, girl, why didn't you ever sing it to me?" She started to tear up.

"It's just a song that I kept to myself."

"Just a song you kept to yourself? You just sang it in front of a shitload of people!" she exclaimed.

"Consider it my debut."

Suddenly, our favorite song, Blurred Lines by Robin Thicke, started playing, and Gretchen grabbed my hand, pulling me to the dance floor. We started moving our hips back and forth. Moments later, I felt two hands clasp my waist. As I turned around, Luke was smiling at me, moving his hands up and down my body while dancing to the music. Our bodies kept the same rhythm as we swayed our hips back and forth. As we stared into each other's eyes while we danced, Luke never stopped smiling, and neither did I. When the song ended, Luke put his arm around me, kissed me, and then led us back to the table. Sam held his hand up for a high five.

"You rocked that song, girl. I'm so proud of you, and I didn't know you could sing," he said.

"Thank you, Sam." I smiled.

Luke sat in his chair and put his arm around me. Scanning the crowd, I saw the two girls that had been at Luke's apartment, standing in the corner, staring at us. A few moments later, they left the corner and started walking over to our table. I looked at the girl who so graciously gave Luke a blow job and said, "Keep walking." Then I smiled and threw my beer back. Gretchen spit out her beer, unable to contain her laughter as Luke shook his head.

***

Barely making it through my apartment door, Luke already had my dress pulled up as he worked on tearing off my thong. Our passionate kiss couldn't be broken as we were both engrossed in the moment. This time, I pinned Luke up against the door as I unbuttoned his jeans and took them down, along with his boxers. He threw his head back and moaned as I took his hard cock in my mouth. No longer able to control his movements, his hands fisted my hair as my tongue ran around the tip and my hands moved in sync up and down his shaft. His moan grew louder as I started sucking and he moved his hips back and forth.

"Oh God, Lily. I'm going to come!" he exclaimed.

Suddenly, a warm, salty liquid filled my mouth. I've never swallowed before. In fact, I never sucked a guy off until they came before. Usually, I stop and finish them off with my hand, but with Luke, I didn't want to stop. I didn't know what to do, and I didn't want to seem rude and ruin the moment by running to the kitchen sink and spitting it out, so I just swallowed it. Luke pulled me up and pushed back my hair.

"You're unbelievable." He smiled.

"Correction, you're unbelievable," I replied.

He carried me to the bedroom, wrapped me tightly in his arms, made love to me, and for the first time in over a year, I slept soundly through the night.

25

Luke

I spent more time at Lily's place than I did my own. Sam and I worked out a system that if I'm staying at Lily's for the night, then Gretchen would stay at our place. Another morning had come, and Lily was getting ready for work. As I made the coffee, I sent a text message to Sam, asking if he could bring over some eggs. I was in my boxers, so I went into the bedroom and threw on my jeans. Hearing a knock on the door, I left the button and zipper of my jeans undone. I walked over, opened it, and, froze when I saw Charley standing there. She was looking me up and down, noticing I was half-naked. It's not the first time she's seen me like this, but it's the first time this happened at Lily's.

"Charley, what are you doing here?" I tried to smile casually.

"Why aren't you dressed? Did you spend the night?"

I took in a deep breath. "Peanut, what can I do for you?"

Lily emerged from the hallway, saw Charley, and looked at me.

"Hey, Charley, come on in," she said.

She ducked under my arm and walked into the apartment. "Are you coming to my grandma's family dinner tonight?" she asked Lily.

"I sure am!"

Charley glanced over at me as I came from the bedroom with my jeans buttoned and a t-shirt on.

"You didn't have to get dressed on my account," she said.

Lily busted out laughing, and I shot her a look. "Peanut, don't you have to go to school?"

"Yeah, but I was just—."

"You were just leaving." I laughed as I picked her up, threw her over my shoulder, and took her back up to her apartment. When I dropped Charlie off with Maddie, I walked back to Lily's apartment, and Sam walked over and handed me a carton of eggs.

"Dude, I sent you a text like twenty minutes ago."

"Sorry, but Gretchen had me tied up." He winked.

"Thanks, man," I said as I grabbed the eggs and walked inside Lily's apartment.

Lily was sitting at the table, eating a bowl of cereal and drinking her coffee.

"Babe, I was going to make you some eggs."

"Thank you, but I'm fine eating my cereal. Besides, I don't have time for eggs," she said as she looked at her watch.

I poured a cup of coffee and leaned against the counter as I stared at her. I couldn't believe this loving, beautiful girl was mine. I never thought I would say those words again after Callie, but with Lily, it's so easy.

She looked over at me and smiled. "Do you know how sexy you look, leaning up against that counter?"

"Why don't you show me?" I smirked.

"Don't tempt me, Luke. As it is, I'm running late, again," she said as she put her bowl in the sink.

She turned to me and put her hands on my chest. "I have to go, because if I'm late, Charley will start spreading some horrible rumor about us."

I chuckled, kissed her lips, and hugged her goodbye. "Have a good day, babe. I'll miss you."

"I'll miss you too," she said as she kissed me one last time.

***

I walked into my apartment to find Gretchen cleaning up the kitchen.

"Morning, Luke."

"Morning, Gretchen," I responded as I headed towards my bedroom.

As I was gathering my laundry, Gretchen stood in the doorway.

"I need to talk to you about something."

"Shoot."

"Giselle called me. Her and Lucky ran into Lily's mother in Seattle. With that being said, Lucky accidentally told her that Lily lives here."

"Shit, that's not good, right?"

"No, it's not, because if she or Brynn come here, there's no telling what might happen."

"Maybe Lily and her mom should have a talk. Family is really important, and I would hate for Lily to completely lose hers over what her mother didn't tell her. It was for the best that things worked out the way they did or else I never would have met her."

"You don't understand, Luke. Lily's life has never been normal. She's told you about her father's affairs and his alcohol and drug use, right?"

I turned around and looked at her as I carried the basket of dirty clothes to the living room.

"I knew he had multiple affairs and he drank, but she never mentioned anything about drugs."

"He did every drug out there and then some. I remember going over Lily's house one day, and her dad was snorting coke right off the kitchen table."

"Shit, that's terrible," I shook my head as I poured two cups of coffee.

"It really is, Luke. She's made up her mind to remove herself from her family, and I think we need to do whatever we can to protect her. I don't want her to get hurt again. I love her too much to see her go through that pain. She's a good person and doesn't deserve it."

"I love her too, and I will protect her in every possible way. I don't want you to worry." I smiled.

Gretchen grabbed her things and left the apartment. I was really bothered by the fact Lucky said something to Lily's mother, but he didn't know what was going on, so I couldn't really blame him. I decided not to tell Lily about what Gretchen told me because I didn't want her worrying about it, especially tonight, at my family's dinner. As I was excited to bring Lily home to meet my parents, I decided to send flowers to my two favorite women. I grabbed my phone and called the local florist. I had a nice arrangement sent to my mother for the dinner table, and I sent Lily a dozen red roses with a card that read:

"Beautiful flowers for a beautiful woman.

I'm missing you already.

Love always, Luke."

It was a beautiful day so I decided to go outside and work on some songs. I took my laundry to the laundry room, threw it in the washer, grabbed a notepad, pen, and my guitar, and headed over to the pool. As I sat in the chair and set my phone down on the table beside me, I looked up at the sky as the sun went behind a cloud; one of the very few clouds that filtered the sky. I thought about the conversation Gretchen and I had about Lily's family as I grabbed my pen and started writing down the words that came to my mind:

Even the clouds will say

There's nowhere we can get away from everything

There's nowhere we can practice positivity

I strummed the C and F chords to find the perfect tune, and then my mind went back to the first time Lily and I met. She didn't put up with my bullshit when I was an ass to her, because I could only focus on myself and my problems.

When all I see is me

So let's drop, let's stop this teenage rivalry

I strummed the C, F, and G chords to produce a tune that fit the words to this song I was writing. Lily's heart had been broken, not only by her father and her mother, but also by her ex-fiancé and her sister, and it killed me to see her cry.

And every heart will break

There's just no way to keep it safe from anything

If the only thing that makes it break is somebody

Please don't give it to me

'Cause seeing you cry makes me want to leave

But losing you scares the shit out of me

My phone rang, and Lily's beautiful picture lit up my screen. I smiled as I answered, "Hey, beautiful."

"I just received some beautiful red roses from a really sexy guy named Luke. You don't know him by any chance, do you?"

"Can't say I do, but when I find him, I'm going to kick his ass for sending my girl flowers."

"They're beautiful, Luke. Thank you. My students are very excited, and they keep making kissy noises at me. Charley came up to my desk and said they better be from you." She laughed.

I chuckled. "I'm glad you like them, babe."

"As you can hear, my class is out of control. I miss you, and I'll see you later."

"Bye, Lily."

"Bye, Luke."

I smiled as I set my phone down. *Were things moving too fast?* I wasn't sure, but the only thing I knew for certain was that she was the first woman to catch my attention and make me feel something since the accident. I played the chords again and added a couple of more lines before Mrs. Kramer called me to come fix her leaky toilet.

I'd sail the ocean blue

Or I'd fly a rocket to the moon

But I'm good for nothing without you

I got up from my seat, headed back to the apartment, grabbed my tool box, and fixed Mrs. Kramer's toilet.

26

Lily

I set the vase of roses that Luke sent me on the counter as I thought about what I was going to wear to his family's house. I was starting to get nervous because I haven't met anyone's family in a very long time. I always worried they wouldn't like me or found something wrong with me. I wondered where Luke was, usually he was waiting for me when I got home. Looking out my window, I noticed his motorcycle wasn't there, so I grabbed my phone and sent him a text message.

"Where's my knight in shining armor?"

A few moments later, a message came through.

"I'm at the store, babe. I had something that I needed to pick up. I'll be over shortly."

"See you soon," I replied back.

I walked into my bedroom and opened the closet door. I wanted to look perfect for his family, and I didn't want them to be able to see the destruction that had been left inside me thanks to my family. I took off my work clothes and stood in front of the open closet in my bra and panties. Suddenly, a voice came from behind me, startling me from my thoughts.

"Well, isn't this a sight for sore eyes," Luke said as he leaned up against the doorway with his hands behind his back.

"Shit, Luke, you scared me," I said as I turned around and looked at him.

"Sorry, babe, but what do you expect when you're standing there in nothing but your bra and that delicious lace thong."

I smiled as I walked over to him.

"What are you hiding behind your back?" I asked as I ran my finger down the front of his shirt. His top lip curled as he looked at me and brought his hands forward, revealing a helmet.

"Surprise!" he said.

I put my hands over my mouth in shock. "Luke!"

"I know, you probably hate me right now for this, but you should have your own helmet if you're going to be riding on my bike."

"I don't hate you at all. I love it!" I exclaimed as I took it from his hands.

The helmet was black with white lilies all over it, and it had my name engraved on the side. I reached up and kissed Luke's smiling lips. "Thank you, baby. I love it."

He took the helmet from my hands, put it on my head, and then placed his hands on my hips. "God, you're so sexy."

I walked over to my full-length mirror that sat in the corner of my bedroom. I couldn't help but burst out laughing as I stood there and examined myself in nothing but my bra, panties, and a motorcycle helmet.

"Why are you laughing?" Luke asked as he walked over to me.

"I look ridiculous like this."

As he cupped my ass, he grinned. "I seriously want to fuck you with that helmet on."

I instantly removed the helmet, turned around, and smacked Luke on chest.

"You're crazy! I'm not having sex with that on!" I exclaimed.

Luke sighed. "Fine, leave it off then," he said as he pushed me down on the bed and smiled.

***

I looked out the window of Luke's Jeep as we drove down the street to his parents' house. The streets were lined with trees and huge houses with well-manicured lawns. Luke reached over and took my hand.

"Please tell me you're not nervous."

"Why would I be nervous? I'm only meeting my boyfriend's parents for the first time," I said as I looked over at him.

"You're a smart-ass." Luke laughed as he brought my hand to his lips and gently kissed it.

As he pulled into the driveway, I admired the vast amount of palm trees that stood in front of the beige color, two-story home. I took in a deep breath before Luke got out of his Jeep and walked around to open the door for me.

"Close your eyes and breathe, Lily," he said as he helped me from the Jeep. "There's nothing to be nervous about. My family is as easy going as they come, and they're going to love you."

I nodded my head and smiled as we walked up the driveway to the front door. As Luke put his hand on the handle and pushed the door open, Charley came running over to us.

"Uncle Luke, Lily!" she exclaimed as Luke scooped her up in his arms.

"Long time no see, peanut," he said as he tapped her on the nose.

"Grandma, Grandpa, and Mommy are in the kitchen," she said.

"Well, let's go see them and introduce Lily." Luke smiled.

We walked down the hallway, and I could hear the rapid beating of my heart. As we approached the kitchen, Luke put Charley down and walked over to his mom.

"Luke, you're here!" she exclaimed as she hugged him tight. "Thank you for the beautiful flower arrangement."

Maddie walked over to me and gave me a hug. "Don't be nervous," she whispered.

Luke broke his hug from his mom and turned to his dad who patted him on the back as the two of them hugged each other. "Mom, Dad, I'd like you to meet Lily Gilmore." Luke smiled as he held out his hand for mine.

"Oh, Lily, It's wonderful to meet you! You can call me Annie," she said as she hugged me tight.

"It's nice to meet you as well. I've heard so much about you."

"It better be all good, or Luke will be in trouble," Annie said as she shot Luke a look.

"Of course it's all good." I smiled.

Luke's father held his arms out. "It's nice to meet you, Lily. You can call me Tom."

"It's nice to meet you, Tom." I smiled.

Luke walked over, smiled, and put his arm around me. "They love you already," he whispered.

I stood in front of the island and admired the granite counter tops that sat amongst the cherry cabinets, which matched the cherry wood floors. I couldn't help but be reminded of the kitchen in my childhood home. The resemblance was incredible.

"Come on everyone, let's start cooking dinner!" Annie exclaimed.

"What are we having, Mom?" Luke asked.

"We're making Chicken Marsala tonight, and I have everyone's job assigned," she said as she pulled a white piece of paper from her pocket. "Tom, you're in charge of pounding out the chicken breasts. Luke, you're in charge of making the coating for the chicken, and Lily, you're in charge of slicing the mushrooms. Maddie, you're in charge of making the salad, and I will make the potatoes."

"Grandma, what about me?" Charley frowned.

"You, my dear grandbaby, are in charge of helping me with the potatoes. Once I slice them, I need you to place them in the dish."

Luke and I took our place at the counter where all the ingredients were laid out. I took the mushrooms and started slicing them while Luke prepared the coating for the chicken. Being a part of this gave me an incredible feeling. Annie was a breath of fresh air. She stood about 5'2" with a petite stature. Her chestnut colored, mid-length hair, softly framed her face. Her eyes were a deep brown, and her smile reminded me of Luke's. From what I could already tell, her personality was bubbly and full of life. She was a real family person, and I took comfort in the fact that, for this night, I could be a part of it.

"I really like how your mom does this with dinner," I said to Luke.

"It's okay now, but it was kind of annoying growing up. Imagine your friends calling you to hang out and you telling them you can't because you have to cook dinner with your mom. I was teased a lot."

"Aw, poor baby," I said as I put a mushroom in his mouth.

Annie put the potatoes in the oven as Luke handed Tom the coated chicken and put it in the skillet. Tom was a handsome man who stood about six feet tall with a muscular build. His short, sandy brown hair and hazel eyes reminded me a great deal of Luke.

"Okay everyone, the potatoes are in the oven, the chicken is in the skillet, the salad is made, and now you can rest until it's ready!" Annie exclaimed.

Luke went to the refrigerator, grabbed two bottles of beer, twisted the caps off, and handed one to me. "Come on, babe, let me show you the house."

He took me on a tour and up to his old bedroom. The blue walls were lined at the top with a football border. In fact, everything in his room was football themed, right down to the lamp that sat upon the dresser. A twin bed sat in the corner of the room with a blue comforter and matching pillow. There were pictures on the wall of Luke and his family. I scanned the room to see if there were any pictures of Callie, but there weren't. My eyes traveled to the closet door where a poster of my father hung. He was sitting on a stool with his guitar. I walked over to where it hung and stared into his eyes. Tears started to fill my eyes as Luke came up behind me and wrapped his arms around me.

"I'm sorry, Lily. I forgot it was still hanging up," he said as he kissed my head.

"It's fine," I said as I wiped my eye. The anger I thought I'd buried when my father died began to emerge.

"Wait until I show you the backyard," Luke said as he walked me out of the bedroom.

Just as we were going to look at the backyard, Annie announced that dinner was ready. Everyone took their seat in the dining room, but before Luke sat down, he poured some wine in everyone's wine glass. He walked over to where Charley was sitting and pretended like he was going to fill her glass.

"Uncle Luke, I can't drink wine. I'm not old enough." She giggled.

"I'm so sorry, Madame, I thought you were at least the age of twenty-five."

I smiled as Charley laughed at him. To see him with her tugged at my heart strings. You could see and feel the love when he's around her. Luke looked at me and winked.

"Lily, tell us about your family. What do your mom and dad do? Do you have any siblings?" Annie asked innocently.

"Mom, not now," Luke interrupted.

"Luke, don't be silly, I want to know all about Lily."

At that moment, Charley decided to chime in. "Uncle Luke spent the night at Lily's. He answered her door this morning only wearing a pair of jeans and his hair was messy, like he just got out of bed."

"Charley!" Maddie exclaimed.

Luke shot her a look across the table.

"Well, I'm sure Lily had him over for coffee," Annie said.

"I saw them kissing in the hallway the other day, and he sent her pretty red roses today." She smiled.

"Peanut, you need to be quiet and eat your dinner or I'm eating your dessert."

"No you're not!" she whined.

"Watch me!"

"Mom, tell him to stop it!" she whined.

"For goodness sake, the two of you need to stop and eat your dinner," Annie said.

I leaned over to Annie and whispered to her, "I'll tell you about my family after dinner. I really don't want to do it in front of Charley."

She patted my hand and smiled. "I understand."

Dinner turned out great. The atmosphere was something I'd always dreamed of. The Matthews were a tight-knit family who would do anything for each other. This was the kind of family I'd craved my whole life. I helped clean up the table as Charley, Luke, and Tom went outside in the backyard per Annie's orders. Charley came running into the kitchen, asking if she could change into her bathing suit and go swimming. Luke walked over to me and put his hands on my hips.

"Do you want to go swimming with us?" he asked as he put his forehead on mine.

"I'm going to hang back with your mom and dad so we can get to know each other better. You go and swim with Charley. I'll be watching." I smiled.

As Luke leaned in to kiss me, there was a knock on the door. Suddenly, we heard a familiar voice.

"Hey, Mrs. Matthews, how was your cruise?" Sam's voice echoed through the hallway.

"Sam's here?" I asked as I looked at Luke confused.

"Sam is mom's second son, and she always invites him, but I thought he said he had plans tonight with Gretchen."

Sam walked into the kitchen, gave Luke a high-five, and kissed me on the cheek.

"I thought you couldn't make it tonight, man," Luke said.

"Gretchen got called on a last minute photo shoot. The model they had got sick at the last minute, so they needed a replacement."

Charley came running down the stairs in her pink, frilly bathing suit and ran straight to Sam.

"Uncle Sammy, are you going to go swimming with us?!" she excitedly asked.

"You bet I am!"

Sam and Luke changed into their bathing suits and took Charley into the pool. I sat on the patio with Annie, Tom, and Maddie as we talked and drank margaritas.

***

Annie and Tom's backyard was simply breathtaking. The beauty of the stone patio and perfectly placed palm trees gave way to the infinity shaped pool and hot tub that sat next to it. There was a built-in grill over to the side and a large glass patio set that sat in the middle. Exquisite flowers were planted in stone pots, surrounding the space, and the in-ground lights began lighting up the area as the sun had set, and dusk was setting in.

"So, tell me about your family," Annie said.

I smiled lightly because I knew it was inevitable. If Luke and I were going to continue our relationship, then they would need to know everything about me.

"My father was Johnny Gilmore," I said as I took in a deep breath and let out a long sigh.

Tom looked at me and cocked his head. "*The* Johnny Gilmore? As in Johnny Gilmore, the musician?"

I nodded my head as I took a sip of my margarita. "Yep, that's the one."

Annie put her hand on my knee. "I'm so sorry for your loss. I remember reading about your father's massive heart attack in the papers. He was so young; what a shame."

I lowered my head as I moved my straw back and forth, banging the ice cubes against the glass. "Well, I'm sure all the alcohol he drank and all the drugs he did, didn't help."

"He was a brilliant musician, and that's what you should remember him for." Tom winked at me. "Do you play the guitar, Lily?" he asked.

"Yes, I do. Johnny began teaching me when I was four years old."

"You'll have to play for us sometime. We'd love to hear you play." Annie smiled.

I looked straight ahead at the massive in-ground pool where Luke and Sam were swimming with Charley. There was laughter and a lot of splashing going on.

"Maddie told us that you just moved to Santa Monica. Where were you living before?" Annie asked.

"I grew up in Seattle, but I spent the last year living in Portland. I needed a fresh start and leaving Seattle was the only way to get it. I moved here because I was offered a year-long substitute teaching job."

Annie reached over and grabbed my hand. "May I ask why you wanted a fresh start?"

I looked at her and Tom and pursed my lips together. I took a sip of my margarita and sighed. They were great people, and I found them very easy to talk to—as if I'd known them my whole life. I felt connected to them and I found comfort in them, just like I did in Luke.

"I caught my ex-fiancé cheating on me, in the church on our wedding day."

Annie gasped as she squeezed my hand. "Lily, I'm so sorry."

"The worst part is that my mother knew about it, and I guess it had been going on behind my back for a long time, but she was going to let me marry him anyway."

Annie tilted her head to the side and frowned as she listened to my words.

"Lily, you poor girl. I just want to reach over and hug you right now, but I don't want Luke to think something's wrong, so I'll hug you later." She smiled.

Tom looked at me and held up his glass. "You got dealt a raw deal in life, Lily, but look at it this way, you never would have met my son, and we wouldn't be in the presence of excellent company right now."

"Now, I'll drink to that," Annie said as she tapped both of our glasses.

Luke got out of the pool, grabbed a towel, and walked over to where we were sitting. "What are you toasting to without me?" he asked.

"We're just toasting your beautiful girlfriend." Tom winked at me.

Now I know where Luke gets all his winking from. I smiled as Luke leaned over and kissed me with his cold, wet lips. Maddie came out of the house with two more margaritas, and she handed one to me.

"I'll be right back, babe. I'm going to go change," Luke said.

Sam carried Charley out of the pool and set her down on the patio. Maddie told her to go inside the house, change into dry clothes, and then go watch TV while the grown-ups talked. She whined a bit, but I could see how tired she was.

27

Luke

I changed out of my bathing suit, rushing to get back to Lily and the others to announce that I'd be buying Bernie's Bar. I couldn't believe that I was actually going to do it, and I knew it was going to be a lot of hard work, but with Lily by my side, it would be worth it. As I walked down the stairs, I saw Charley curled up on the couch, watching cartoons. I walked over to her, kissed her on the head, and as she looked up and smiled, her eyes were ready to close. As I grabbed a beer from the kitchen, I sat down next to Lily, taking her hand in mine.

"I have an announcement that I'd like to make"—looking around the room—"I've decided to buy Bernie's Bar."

"Dude! That's awesome!" Sam exclaimed.

Lily looked over at me, smiled, and put her hand on my cheek. I knew she was happy.

"Luke, my boy, that's wonderful news. If you need any help, let me know," my dad said proudly.

My mom got up from her chair and hugged me. "I'm so proud of you, son. You're finally going to put that settlement money to good use."

Maddie stood up and high-fived me because she'd be managing the bar once I took over, which meant better hours for her. I leaned over and kissed Lily on the lips.

"It makes me happy that you decided to follow your dreams," she said.

"It's because of you, babe." I smiled.

My good news didn't last long as my father decided to say something to Maddie about Charley's dad.

"Charley tells us that her dead beat dad is coming to visit in a couple of days."

Maddie looked at him and said she didn't want to talk about it right now. Maddie was good at avoiding things, believing that if she didn't think about it, then the issue didn't exist. But Charley's dad did exist, and she needed to learn to deal with it.

"He said he's changed, that he's off the alcohol and the drugs, he wants to form a relationship with his daughter, and he wants a better relationship with me," Maddie said.

I didn't believe it for a second because I knew Adam too well. We used to be friends in high school, until he started hanging with the wrong crowd. Maddie was infatuated with him because he was the *bad boy* with the tattoos and piercings all over his body. I warned her to stay away from him and told her he was trouble, but she didn't listen. They went on a few dates, and she ended up pregnant. He was her first, and I'd never forget the night she told our mom she was pregnant. Of course being the dead beat that he was, he denied the baby was his, and my mom cried all night while I went out and beat the shit out of him. Lily sat there and didn't say a word while we went back and forth about what a loser he was. As I got up from my seat,

I asked Lily if she was ready to leave. It was getting late, and I just wanted to spend time with her alone.

***

The next morning I found Lily arranging bagels and muffins on the kitchen table.

"Good morning, babe," I said, kissing her.

"Good morning." She smiled.

"What's all this?"

"I went out and grabbed us some breakfast," she said as she held up the plate to me. "We have blueberry, banana, and chocolate chip muffins on this side. Now, on this side"— turning the plate—"We have plain, salt, and cheese bagels, with your choice of regular, honey-walnut, strawberry, or non-fat cream cheese."

"Who's going to eat the non-fat cream cheese?" I asked.

"Gretchen will because her and Sam are coming over. They should be here in a few minutes."

"Do I have time to jump in the shower?"

"Yes, just make it quick," she said as she kissed me.

"I really wish you would have woke me up earlier and told me."

"Sorry, baby, it was sort of last minute!" she yelled as I already made my way down the hallway.

After I finished my shower and getting dressed, the voices I heard grew quiet as I entered the kitchen. Looking around, Sam and Gretchen were sitting at the table, and Lily was staring at me with tears in her eyes.

"Babe, what's wrong?" I asked her as I walked over to where she was sitting.

"I'm sorry, Luke. I had to tell her about Giselle seeing her mom in Seattle. I got a phone call from her mom saying that she's on her way here and she wants to talk to Lily," Gretchen confessed.

Lily looked at me with sad and disappointed eyes as she got up from the table and walked into the kitchen area. "I can't believe you knew and didn't tell me."

"I'm sorry. I wanted to tell you, but I didn't want to upset you," I said as I went to hold her.

She moved away from me and looked down. "There's one thing I will *not* tolerate in a relationship and that's keeping secrets. I *hate* secrets. They do nothing but ruin your life."

I moved closer, but she still continued to back away. "Lily, please. I think you're overreacting," I said.

Gretchen and Sam got up from their seats. "Hey, bro, I think we should leave. Call me later," Sam said.

Gretchen walked over to Lily and put her hand on her arm. "Don't stress, we're all here for you."

When they left, my attention had immediately gone back to Lily. I wanted to wrap my arms around her and take away her pain, but she wouldn't let me.

"Lily, tell me what you're feeling," I pleaded with her.

She walked over to the table and started cleaning up the plates.

"I feel betrayed that you didn't tell me about this. I feel sad because I trusted you to tell me everything, and I feel angry because you knew something about my family that I didn't."

"Babe, seriously, don't you think you're overreacting just a little bit? Come on, so what if Lucky told her where you are. So what if she comes here and finds you. She's your mom, and you should talk to her. You were with my family last night. That's how a family should be, not full of anger and resentment. I understand what she did was wrong, but you have to find it in your heart to forgive her at some point."

She turned around and looked at me with rage in her eyes. "Don't you dare tell me that I need to forgive her! I told you about my family and what kind of childhood I had. She was going to ruin my life by letting me marry that cheating bastard!" she yelled.

"You need to calm down, Lily," I said as I cautiously approached her.

"Don't you tell me what I need to do! You have no idea what path of destruction my family has left inside me, so you don't get to tell me to calm down."

I was getting angry by her unreasoning, and I raised my voice to her. "Don't yell at me. I'm not Hunter, your mom, or Brynn!"

"Since you're so big on forgiveness, why don't you take your own advice and forgive Charley's dad?"

"That's different, Lily, and you know it," I said as I shook my head.

"No it isn't. What you feel for him is what I feel for my mom and sister. Why is it so easy for you to tell me to forgive and forget when you can't do it yourself?!" she spat.

"It's a totally different situation, babe."

"No, it isn't, Luke."

As I walked closer to her to tell her that everything was going to be all right, she folded her arms and turned away.

"Lily, I'm sorry, but you're being really childish right now."

"Then leave this child alone," she replied.

"Do you really want me to leave you alone?" I asked.

She spun around and looked at me. "Yes, I do!"

"Fine, then consider me leaving you alone. You won't hear from me until you decide you want to talk, but I don't know if I'll be around when that happens!" I yelled as I opened the door.

"You're an asshole!" she spat.

"Watch your mouth!" I yelled as I walked out and slammed the door.

I stood there for a second with my hand on the knob, listening to her yell, "Fuck you—fuck you—and a triple *fuck you*!"

28

Lily

Taking in a deep breath, I stood in the middle of my living room and pondered over our first fight. Hunter and I fought all the time, and it wasn't healthy. I should've known then the relationship was toxic. Our fights always consisted of him having to work late and canceling plans at the last minute because of some business deal that came up. The more I thought about it, the more I knew those were just lies to see my sister or some other woman who may have been in his sights. As I sat down on the couch and brought my knees to my chest, I realized that I didn't even know why I got so mad at Luke. I knew he was only trying to help, and yelling at him wasn't right. It was hard for him to understand the dysfunction of a family when his was so perfect. I jumped up off the couch and ran to the door. I needed to apologize. As I pulled open the door, I saw Luke leaned up against the wall, staring at me.

I threw my arms around him as fast as I could.

"I'm so sorry. I didn't mean anything I said. Please forgive me," I begged, tears forming quickly in my eyes.

"Shh, babe, it's alright," he said as he held me tight. "I'm sorry. I didn't mean to push you."

I looked at him as he brushed my hair out of my face and gently kissed my lips.

"Does this mean that we get to have make-up sex?" he asked.

I lightly laughed as I pulled him into my apartment, and he kicked the door shut with his foot. He broke our kiss long enough to lift my shirt over my head. A low growl came from the back of his throat when he saw I wasn't wearing a bra. As he unbuttoned my shorts and slid them off my hips, he pushed me up against the wall.

"I don't think we're making it to the bedroom," he said breathlessly.

"I don't think we are either." I smiled.

As Luke wrapped his mouth around my breast, I unbuttoned his jeans and slid them off his hips, wrapping my hand around his cock and feeling the extreme hardness against my palm. My body shuddered as he dipped one finger into me and then another. I tilted my head back as his lips traveled up to my collarbone, licking and light sucking my skin, sending intense vibrations throughout my body. As he lifted me up, I wrapped my legs around his waist, and he entered me with a long, hard thrust. My body tightened when his thrusts became accelerated, and I found myself moving my body with his as his tongue traveled from my neck, down my jawline, to my chin, and finally, to my lips. Our breathing became shallow, and our hearts were racing as we moved in-sync and our taut bodies gave way to the inevitable pleasure of release we both desperately wanted. Luke buried his face into my neck as he tried to catch his breath.

"I love you, Lily," he whispered.

"I love you too, Luke," I replied as tears filled my eyes.

He looked at me and softly kissed each eye. "No tears."

I smiled as I unwrapped my legs from his waist, and he gently lowered me down and pulled up his boxers and jeans. As he handed me my clothes, I heard my phone chiming. I quickly got dressed and walked over to where my phone sat, noticing there was text message from Sam:

"Is everything good between the two of you? Because the wall was vibrating, and if it wasn't from the two of you, then it had to be a minor earthquake!"

I couldn't help but laugh out loud as Luke walked over, and I handed him my phone. He shook his head and responded back:

"Dude, don't you have anything better to do than listen to us have sex?"

Luke grinned when he read Sam's reply:

"Bro, when a fucking picture falls off the wall, what the hell do you want me to think?"

"I'm going to go change," I said as I walked towards the bedroom.

"And I'm coming to watch." Luke smirked as he followed behind.

Suddenly, there was a knock on the door, and he quickly turned around to answer it.

"I'll get it, babe. It's probably Sam."

Just as I pulled my white sundress from my closet, my body started to tremble at the familiar voice I heard in the next room, my heart beat out of control, and my hands began to shake. I took in a deep breath before walking into the living room and facing my mother for the first time in over a year. I stopped dead in my tracks as I saw her standing there, staring at me.

"Hello, Lily," she said in a mild-mannered tone.

"What the fuck are you doing here?" I asked. Turning to Luke, I put my hand up and spoke, "If you tell me to watch my mouth, you're out of here."

"I wasn't going to say anything," Luke said as he stood by my side.

She stood there in her beige pant suit, looking at me. Her long, brown-dyed hair still looked the same, but her face had aged quite a bit.

"I've missed you so much, baby girl."

"Don't you ever call me that!" I said sternly as I put up my finger in disgust.

"Please, Lily, let's talk. It's been far too long, and I want to talk to my daughter."

"Maybe you should have thought about that before you let me spend a year planning a wedding with a lying, cheating bastard!"

Suddenly, out of nowhere, Luke spoke up. "I think that both of you need to get everything out in the open, but here's not the place because it's too easy to start screaming and yelling. I'm taking the both of you out to lunch to a restaurant, where you will do nothing but embarrass yourselves if you raise your voice. That way you can talk calmly."

"Thank you, Luke," my mother said.

"If you think for one second I'm going anywhere with that woman, than you're delusional!" I yelled.

"Come on, babe. We need to talk," he said as he lightly took hold of my arm and led me to the bedroom. "We'll be right back, Mary," he said.

As we walked into the bedroom, Luke pulled me into an embrace.

"Listen to me, if you ever want her to leave you alone, then you need to talk things out with her. Just listen to her, ask her questions, get your answers, and then be done with it. If you still want nothing to do with her after you talk, then you can walk away with no regrets."

"I can't, Luke. You don't understand," I said as I began to tremble.

Instantly, he broke our embrace and placed his hands on each side of my face. "Close your eyes, and take in a deep breath, babe."

I did what he said, then I slowly opened my eyes. "Feeling better?" he asked.

I nodded my head, and he kissed me on the lips. "I'll be there with you. I'll be there for you, and I'll be there to catch you if you fall. You've suffered enough and you need to do this. Okay?"

"Fine, I'll go. Just let me get myself together," I said.

"That's my girl." He smiled, kissed me on the head, and walked out of the room.

Luke pulled into the parking lot of a restaurant called The Garden Bistro. I was still unsure about this, but I had Luke there to help through it if things got rough. We walked into the restaurant and were promptly seated at a table. I stopped to see which seat my mother was taking because I didn't want to sit next to her, then I took the seat across. As the waitress greeted us and handed us our menus, she asked us for our drink orders.

"I'll have a melon ball, please." I smiled.

Luke looked at me with knitted eyebrows and then looked at the waitress. "Doesn't that have vodka in it?" he asked her.

"Yes, it does," the waitress replied.

"No melon ball for her. She'll have a glass of red wine."

I looked at him, cocked my head, and then looked up at the waitress. "Just bring the bottle, please." I sighed.

I looked across the table at my mother as our eyes met and she took that opportunity to begin her sad attempts at changing my mind about her.

"I miss you, Lily. You have no idea how hard this has been for me since you left."

I felt the fire starting to rev up in my body. "This has been hard on *you*?" I asked as I raised my voice, and Luke grabbed my hand. I took in a deep breath because I wasn't going to embarrass myself or him. I made a promise to him, and I was going to keep that promise. Just as I was getting ready to speak, the waitress set the glass and bottle of wine down on the table. Luke grabbed the bottle, pouring some into my glass. I took a sip and asked my mother the question that I've wanted the answer to.

"Okay, mother. *Why*? Why didn't you tell me about Brynn and Hunter?"

She looked down at her glass that held her gin and tonic. "They both promised me they'd end it, and I thought that they had. You already had trust issues with men, and I didn't want to hurt you."

"Once a cheater, always a cheater. You of all people should know that!" I spat.

I could see the tears beginning to form in her eyes. Luke looked over at me. "Lily," he said.

"What? It's the truth. Dad promised you that he wouldn't see other women, but he did anyway, and he did it until the day he died. I remember walking past your bedroom almost every night and hearing you cry yourself to sleep. How could you live like that? How could you want that life for me, your own daughter?"

Mary took in a sharp breath. "You put up with certain things when someone is your life and consumes you. I know Hunter loved you, and that's why I didn't tell you. You deserved to have a good man love you after what your father put you through."

As I couldn't comprehend where she was coming from, I blankly stared at her. "I have a question for you mother, and I want you to be honest with me… Are you on drugs?"

"Lillian Grace Gilmore! How *dare* you speak to me like that!" she spat in a loud enough voice that managed to turn a couple of heads.

"Lillian?" Luke smiled as he asked.

"I was named after my grandmother. Be warned that you are *never* to call me that!" I said sternly as I held up a finger to him.

The waitress walked over with our food and sat our plates down in front of us as I got ready to spit fire back at my mother.

"Brynn misses you. She's torn up over everything that has happened," she said calmly.

I finished the last of my wine, grabbed the bottle, and poured more into my glass. "*She's* broken up? What about *me*? Don't you even care how this has affected me? Why is everything about you and Brynn? What about *my feelings* and what happened to *me*? Jesus Christ, Mother, sometimes I think we aren't even cut from the same cloth."

She looked at me, and a single tear fell from her eye as she quietly spoke, "We aren't."

In that instant, every part of me froze. My pulse starting racing, and I felt my throat constricting.

"What the hell, Mary!" Luke said as he looked at her.

As I glanced at Luke, I got up from my seat. "I need to get out of here," I said as I grabbed my purse and ran out of the restaurant.

I had only made it to the parking lot when I needed to stop to try and catch my breath. My legs felt like lead, and they didn't want to move anymore. My stomach was tied in knots, and I wanted to vomit. Luke came up behind me, placing his arms around me, but I broke away from him.

"Don't, because if you do, I'll lose it, Luke, and I can't lose it!" I started raising my voice.

Suddenly, I heard my mother's voice in the distance. "She was only seventeen years old and a baby herself."

As I started to take a few steps forward, I stopped and turned around. With sarcasm I responded, "Let me guess…you swooped in and saved the day!"—raising my voice—"Or better yet, her life!

"The two of you aren't going to do this in the middle of the parking lot," Luke snapped. "Get in the Jeep, and we'll go back to the apartment where you two can talk about this."

As much as I hated her at this moment, I needed to hear everything she had to say. I couldn't spend the rest of my life wondering about the truth Mary had kept hidden all these years. As hard and painful as it was going to be, I needed some answers.

"Luke's right. Let's go back to my apartment. I want to hear about what a lie my life has been."

The three of us climbed into the Jeep, and Luke drove us back to my apartment.

29

We walked into my apartment, and I immediately took out a bottle of wine. As I was taking a glass from the cupboard, my mother looked at me and said, "You seem to drink a lot. Do you have a drinking problem?"

I gasped as I set the glass on the counter. "Considering everything I've been through in my life, I should have one."

She shook her head and sat down at the table. Luke sat down across from her, and I stayed at the kitchen counter.

"So, go ahead and tell me how my whole life's been a lie," I said.

She cleared her throat as she began to speak. "I had some problems, and the doctors told me that I would never be able to conceive a child. You have no idea how much that devastated me, because the only thing I wanted was a child with Johnny. I started drinking a lot, I stayed in bed all day, and I isolated myself from the world. One night, Johnny came home with this seventeen- year-old girl, Allison. He told me she was pregnant with his child, and that she'd agreed to give us the baby. Her mother was a prostitute and a drug addict, and her father had run off after she was born. She could barely take care of herself, let alone a child. So, Johnny paid for her medical care and after you were born, he gave her money to start a new life."

Her eyes filled with tears as she continued. "I know you're probably to going ask me why I stayed after that. It was because of you, Lily. I may not have given birth to you, but you were *my* baby, *my* daughter, and you were a part of Johnny, which made you even more special."

I gulped before throwing back my glass of wine. I closed my eyes and Luke got up from the table and walked over to me.

"Lily, are you all right?" he asked as he put his hand on top of mine.

"I raised you, Lily. You're *my* daughter, and you cannot say otherwise! *I* loved you and nurtured you. *I* took care of you when you were sick, and *I* was there for you when you cried, while your father was out playing his shows and having sex with any woman that looked his way."

Luke tightened the grip on my hand.

"Mary, I think Lily's heard enough."

As I removed my hand from his, I looked at him. "It's okay, Luke. Let's go sit down."

I walked over to the table and sat across from my mother as I actually had a moment where I felt incredibly sorry for her.

"Mom, please just tell me why you were going to let me marry Hunter if you knew about him and Brynn. All I want is an honest answer."

Mary looked at me with pursed lips as she tilted her head. I could see the pain in her eyes as she spoke to me.

"You seemed happy with Hunter, and I couldn't ruin that for you. All I wanted was for you to be happy. I know I was wrong, and I should have told you when I first found out," she said as she shook her head.

"When *did* you find out?" I asked.

"Does it really matter at this point, Lily?"

"Yes, Mother, it does. It matters to me."

She took in a deep breath before spilling the words I didn't want to hear. "I found out the day we went shopping for your wedding dress."

My stomach instantly felt sick as I put my shaking hand over my mouth and my eyes swelled with tears.

"But, Brynn was with us that day and she was trying on maid of honor dresses. How did you find out?"

"I received a text message from Mrs. Kendall with a picture of Hunter and Brynn going into a hotel room together. She said she saw them, and she thought I should know. Why do you think I broke down and cried when you came out in your dress? Part of it was because you were so beautiful, and I couldn't believe you were getting married, and the other part was because I knew it would destroy you, and I couldn't let that happen. So, one day, not too long after that, I confronted the two of them and warned them that they were to end it immediately."

Luke leaned over and clasped my shoulders with his hands, rubbing them gently. I took in a deep breath, and I buried my face in my hands. As I thought of something, I lifted my head and looked at my mother.

"If you couldn't get pregnant, then how did you with Brynn?"

She looked at me and smiled lightly. "Brynn was a complete surprise. The doctors couldn't explain it either. They just said she was a gift from God."

"Yeah, a real gift," I mumbled as Luke kissed me on the head.

Mary reached over, put her hand on mine, and I instantly froze. "Lily, what your sister did was wrong, and please don't think that I'm defending her, but you also need to remember that you're supposed to love your children unconditionally."

As I slid my hand out from under hers, I got up from the chair and walked over to the window. There was a part of me that understood where she was coming from and why she didn't tell me. As I turned around and looked at my mother, I saw a weak woman who was scared and alone. I saw a forgiving woman who took in someone else's child, as her own, because she so desperately wanted a baby with the man she loved. I walked over, sat down in the chair, and grabbed her hand.

"Our relationship is going to need a lot of work. It's going to take time to get back to where we were before all of this happened. I just can't instantly forgive you and pretend it never happened. I need time to process everything you've told me."

She tilted her head and gave me a small smile. "At least it's a start. I want our relationship back, Lily."

"We'll get there eventually, but you're going to have to give me space, and as for Brynn, don't expect miracles, because I don't think I'll ever be able to forgive her."

As Mary and I got up from our chairs, she hugged me.

"I'm going to go now and give you the space you want, but please keep in touch. You're a very lucky woman to have such a wonderful man in your life. Even though I don't know him very well, I can tell he's a great man, and he's very sexy too." She winked.

Smiling at her, I walked her to the door. She turned to Luke.

"I'm counting on you to take care of my daughter."

"Don't worry, Mary, I'll take excellent care of your daughter." Luke grinned as he winked at me.

Shutting the door behind her, Luke walked over and pulled me to him.

"I'm so proud of you. It took a lot of strength to try and mend things with her." He kissed the top of my head. "That's one of the qualities I love about you, Lily."

"Oh yeah?" I smiled as I looked up at him. "Tell me what other qualities you love about me."

His hands began to travel up and down my sides as he softly kissed my lips.

"I love how soft your skin is," he whispered as his lips traveled to my neck. "I love how perfect your ass is," he said as he squeezed it with both hands. "I love how beautiful and firm your tits are." He smiled as he pulled the strap to my sundress down and exposed one breast, taking it in his mouth and lightly sucking my nipple. "But most of all, I love how wet you get when I touch you," he whispered as his finger dipped into me.

I moaned as I ran my fingers through his hair, threw my head back, and brought one leg up to his waist so his finger would deepen inside me. My body instantly knew pleasure when he touched me. Hell, it knew pleasure just by the way he looked at me. As he removed his finger, he looked at me and smiled.

"Come on, babe, let's take it to the bedroom this time." He picked me up, carried me, and gently laid me down on the bed.

30

Luke

As Lily and I were snuggled against each other in bed, I heard my phone beep. I reached over, grabbed it, and read a text message from Maddie.

"Adam just called and talked to Charley. He said that he's sorry and something came up, so he won't be able to come visit her. She's devastated and won't stop crying."

I sighed and Lily asked what was wrong. I showed her the message from Maddie. I was relieved because I didn't want him anywhere near her, but I felt sorry for Charley. I kissed Lily on the forehead and sent a message back to Maddie.

"Typical douchebag, Adam. I'll be up there in a second."

As we climbed out of bed, Lily and I got dressed and headed upstairs to Maddie's apartment. Opening the door, Maddie walked over and told us Charley was in her room. I could hear Charley crying down the hallway. As Lily and I stepped into her room, we saw Charley lying face down and crying into her pillow.

"Hey, peanut," I softly spoke as I rubbed her back.

"Go away, Uncle Luke. I don't want to talk to anyone," she sobbed.

"Your mom told me about your dad, and I think it's pretty crappy what he did, but he'll come see you soon."

"You don't know anything!" Charley snapped at me.

Lily walked over to the bed and motioned for me to move down. "Let me try," she whispered.

Sitting next to Charley, she began to tell Charley about her father.

"I know what it's like to be disappointed by your dad, Charley. My dad disappointed me almost my whole life."

Charley turned her head, looked at her, and sniffled. "Really?"

"Yeah, really," Lily answered her in a soft, sweet voice.

"But he promised, Lily. He promised me that he would come see me."

Lily took her hand and started stroking Charley's hair. "I know he did, sweetie, but sometimes when you're grown up, things come up, and it can hurt the ones you love. My dad made me a lot of promises that he didn't keep. Sometimes, he wouldn't be home for my birthday, even though he said he'd be."

"What did you do?" Charley asked as she sat up and Lily handed her a tissue.

"I cried, just like you are right now, and then I got over it, because I had plenty of people at home who loved me, just like you do."

"But I wanted to see him," she whined.

Lily pulled Charley into an embrace and kissed her on the top of her head.

"I know you do, sweetie, but sometimes certain things can't be helped. You have to be a big girl and try to understand."

As Lily looked at me, I smiled. Seeing her with Charley was incredible, and all I saw when I watched her was the mother of my children.

"Thank you, Lily." Charley spoke as she hugged her.

"You're welcome, baby."

"Hey, what about me?" I asked as I leaned over and began tickling her.

Charley giggled and tried to push my hands away. "Thank you, Uncle Luke."

"How would you like to spend the night over at my apartment tonight? We can dance, eat a bunch of junk food, sleep on the floor and, best of all, we can watch scary movies!" Lily said with excitement.

"Really?!" That would be so fun! Can Uncle Luke spend the night with us?" Charley asked.

Lily looked at me and then she twisted her face as she looked at Charley. "Are you sure you want *boys* at our sleepover?"

"Only Uncle Luke." Charley giggled.

Lily leaned over and kissed me. "I guess he can come, but he has to behave himself."

"Is that so?" I growled at her.

As Lily and I got up and walked out of the room, I told Charley to pack her bag. We walked into the living room, where Maddie was sitting on the couch.

"Charley is going to have a sleepover at Lily's tonight. If that's ok," I said.

She looked up at me and smiled. "That's great, Luke. Thank you, Lily. I'm sure that made Charley very happy."

Charley came running down the hall with her bag. "I'm ready!" she squealed as she kissed Maddie goodbye.

* * *

The next morning, I rolled over and looked at Lily as she slept next to Charley on the floor. We had a great night and Charley was happy. Before getting up, I softly kissed Lily on the head and walked back to my apartment to take a shower. While standing under the warm water, I kept thinking about Callie and how she'd be happy that I'd moved on. I grinned as I thought about Lily and how all I saw was my future with her. As I was turning off the water and wrapping a towel around my waist, there was a knock on the bathroom door.

"Bro, I have to take a piss! Can you hurry it up?"

"I'm done, man, relax," I said as I opened the door and walked to my bedroom. After getting dressed, I saw Sam sitting on the couch, alone.

"Where's Gretchen?"

"She had a photo shoot."

I walked into the kitchen and grabbed what I needed to make pancakes because I wasn't sure if Lily had everything.

"Dude, come over to Lily's for pancakes; Charley's there."

Sam turned his head. "Why is Charley there?"

"Adam called her yesterday, said something came up, and that he wouldn't be able to come visit her. She was upset and crying about it, so Lily asked her if she wanted to sleep over at her place."

"I bet she loved that." He smiled.

"We had a lot of fun."

"Hold on a second and let me throw on some clothes." He got up from the couch and headed to his room.

We walked back to Lily's place and I set the stuff on the counter. Lily wasn't on the floor anymore, and Charley was up watching cartoons.

"Hi, Uncle Sammy." She smiled.

"Good morning, darling."

"Charley, where's Lily?" I asked as I plugged in the griddle.

"She's in the shower. Are you making pancakes?"

"I sure am." I smiled.

As I measured out the pancake mix, Sam cracked the eggs and put them into the bowl. Lily emerged from the bedroom with a smile on her face.

"If I didn't know any better, I'd think you two were gay."

Love in Between

I looked up and smiled at her as she walked over and kissed me on the lips.

"Maybe I am, and you just don't know it yet."

She hit me on the arm with the back of her hand as she walked over and kissed Sam on the cheek. "Where's Gretchen?"

"She's at a photo shoot. We're leaving tomorrow afternoon for San Francisco. I'm taking her home to meet my parents."

"That's great, Sam." I smiled.

As Lily reached up in the cabinet, Sam grabbed her and hugged her.

"Dude, what the hell are you doing?" I said as I looked over at them.

"I'm just thanking her for moving in next door, because if she didn't, I never would have met the love of my life."

"Uncle Sammy! Lily is Uncle Luke's girlfriend. You shouldn't be hugging her like that."

"Yeah, Sammy, hands off." I chuckled.

"It's okay, Charley. It's just a friendly hug," Lily said as she set the plates on the counter.

I made the pancakes exactly the way Charley loved them, and the four of us had a nice breakfast. As we were cleaning up, and Charley was gathering her things, my phone rang and my mom appeared on the screen.

"Hey, Mom," I answered.

"Good morning, Luke. Your father and I were wondering if you and Lily would like to go to Bernie's bar tonight for a couple of drinks."

I told her to hold on as I looked at Lily and asked her if she wanted to go. She smiled and nodded her head as she took a sip of her coffee.

"Sounds good, Mom. How about we meet around seven?"

"Excellent! We'll see the two of you tonight. I love you, Luke."

"I love you too, Mom."

31

Lily

After spending the day with Charley, Luke took her back to her apartment as I got ready to meet his parents at the bar. I couldn't stop thinking about how devastated Charley was when her father told her that he couldn't visit. It was a feeling that I knew too well, and how I wish I didn't. As I stood in front of my full-length mirror and stared at the girl looking back at me, I thought that she looked happy and fulfilled. *Had fate finally led me to where I was supposed to be?* I'd never been this happy, and now that I'd settled things with my mother, an overwhelming sense of peace had landed in my life; it was a feeling I never wanted to lose.

"What are you thinking about?" Luke asked as he came up from behind me and wrapped his arm around me, burying his nose into my neck.

"I was just thinking about how my life has worked out and how happy I am because of you." I smiled.

A low growl came from the back of his throat as he took in my scent. "Do you have any idea how good you smell?"

"Judging that you have one hand squeezing my boob and the other up my dress, I think I have a pretty good idea." I laughed.

"Can you feel that?" Luke whispered as he pushed his body against me, looking at me through the mirror.

"Yes, I can feel how hard you are, baby, but we don't have time." I smiled as I turned around and kissed him on the cheek. "Look at the clock. It's six forty-five and we have to meet your parents in fifteen minutes." I walked over to my closet and grabbed my shoes.

"Damn, Lily, you sure know how to give a guy blue-balls!" he exclaimed as he adjusted himself.

"Sorry, baby. I don't want to be late for your parents. I promise I'll make it up to you when we get home." I winked.

"I just want you to know that you're mean, babe!" he yelled as he stood in the bedroom.

"Yep, and I'm going to show you how mean I am later!" I yelled back, walking towards the living room.

Suddenly, Luke came up from behind me, grabbed me, and spun me around.

"You better keep that promise, because that's all I'll be thinking about all night," he said as he kissed my neck.

"Do you ever think about anything else besides sex?" I laughed.

"Not when I'm around you. You're all I want 24/7, babe." He put me down and kissed me.

As Luke grabbed his keys off the counter, I grabbed my purse, and we headed out the door.

***

Walking hand in hand and Luke carrying his guitar, we strolled into the bar and over to the table where his parents were sitting. Before sitting down, I gave them each a hug while Luke went to the bar and grabbed us a couple of beers.

"It's so good to see you again." I smiled at Annie.

We sat at the table and talked as Luke showed his father around the bar. I could tell how excited Annie was that Luke was finally going to buy it. She reached over and placed her hand on top of mine.

"You have no idea how happy I am that you're in Luke's life. The past year has been so difficult for him; for all of us, really."

As I tilted my head, I smiled at her. "I'm sure it's been very difficult. It seems the past year wasn't good for any one of us."

"No, it wasn't, but the only thing that matters is that you and my son found each other, and you're both happy. I'm thrilled he's decided to buy this bar. It's all he ever talked about for years. Now, he'll finally put that settlement money to good use."

"He never mentioned the settlement money to me."

"He doesn't like to talk about it. I think it's a reminder of the accident. The man who ran the red light was drunk and driving on a suspended license. He was a partner at a prestigious law firm in Los Angeles. Needless to say, he'll never be practicing law again. Luke settled for five hundred thousand dollars. His attorney said he could probably get more, but Luke just wanted to be done with it. It was settled out of court to avoid publicity."

As I sat there, pondering the fact that my boyfriend had five hundred thousand dollars that he didn't tell me about, Luke and his dad sat down at the table.

"What have the two of you been talking about?" Luke asked.

"Just girl talk." I smiled. "You haven't told Bernie yet that you're buying the bar, have you?"

"No, I just sent him a text message, telling him that I need to meet with him tomorrow and that I've made my decision."

I reached over and kissed him on the cheek, leaving a lipstick mark on his face. I laughed as I grabbed a napkin and wiped it off. We ordered some chicken wings, had a couple of beers, and enjoyed the company of his parents. Luke leaned over and told me he'd be right back as he got up from his seat. As I continued to have a conversation with Tom and Annie, the lights on the stage caught my eye. I looked up, and Luke was sitting on the bar-stool in front of the microphone.

"Good evening, everyone." He smiled and waved to the patrons in the bar.

Everyone cheered and said hello as Luke strummed his guitar. "This song I'm going to sing for you tonight is a song I wrote for a very special woman in my life."

Annie looked over at me and smiled as she placed her hand on mine and gently squeezed it. My eyes started to swell with tears before he even started singing. He strummed the chords as our eyes met, and he began to sing the words he wrote.

Even the Clouds will say

There's nowhere we can get away from everything

Love in Between

There's nowhere we can practice positivity

When all I see is me

So let's drop let's stop this teenage rivalry

And every heart will break

There's just no way to keep it safe from anything

If the only thing that makes it break is somebody

Please don't give it to me

'Cause seeing you cry makes me want to leave

But losing you scares the shit out of me.

Or maybe, I'll sail the ocean blue

Or I'd fly a rocket to the moon

But I'm good for nothing without you

It doesn't matter what you say

I think about you every day, girl, I

Am good for nothing without you

Even the clouds will say

That Saturdays and rainy days were meant to be

If you're indoors and in the arms of somebody

Under the blankets and sheets

Sandi Lynn

Well the sky is clear; it's the middle of the week

So come my dear, let's make believe.

Or maybe, I'll sail the ocean blue

Or I'd fly a rocket to the moon

But I'm good for nothing without you

It doesn't matter what you say

I think about you every day, girl, I

Am good for nothing without you

Cause I want you

I want you

I want you

To want me to

I want you

I want you

I want you

I do

But I won't fool this heart anymore

Or maybe, I'll sail the ocean blue

Or I'd fly a rocket to the moon

Love in Between

But I'm good for nothing without you

It doesn't matter what you say

I think about you every day, girl, I

Am good for nothing without you

Even the clouds will say

There's nowhere we can get away from everything

And if the only thing that breaks your heart is somebody

Please don't give it to me

'Cause seeing you cry makes me want to leave

But losing you scares the shit out of me.

Annie and Tom both looked over at me as the tears that swelled in my eyes slowly fell down my face. The crowd cheered as Luke strummed the last chord and exited the stage. I stood up from my chair and wrapped my arms around him when he approached me.

"I love you," I whispered in his ear as I tightened my grip around him.

"I love you too, babe. I'm glad you liked it."

"I loved it, Luke. It was perfect. You're perfect."

As he sat down, he brought me onto his lap and kissed me.

"That was a beautiful song, honey," Annie said.

"Great tune, son." Tom smiled as he held up his glass.

We talked for a while longer and then called it a night. I had work in the morning and Luke had a meeting with his lawyer to talk about the purchase of the bar. As we hugged Annie and Tom goodbye, we climbed into the Jeep, went back to my apartment, and I made sure Luke received his punishment for calling me mean.

32

One Month Later

Lily

My life was perfect. Luke and I were perfect. I'd never been more in love with anyone like I was with him. He consumed me and he owned me. He owned my heart and my soul, and I thanked God for him every day. He had completely changed my life. When I didn't think it was possible ever to trust someone again, he walked into my life and showed me that it was.

As Luke was still sleeping, I slipped out of bed and headed to the kitchen to make a pot of coffee. When the coffee began to brew, I walked over and opened the blinds. It was cloudy outside, and I could already smell a hint of rain as I opened the window. It was the perfect day to stay in bed and watch movies. Walking back into the bedroom, I took off my nightshirt and climbed into bed, wrapping my arms around Luke and softly kissing his back. He rolled over and smiled.

"Good morning, beautiful."

"Good morning," I whispered as my lips traveled across his chest.

Reaching down, I stroked his erection through the soft fabric of the sheet.

"Someone's horny." He smiled as he ran his fingers through my hair.

"I'm always horny when you're around."

"I know you are and I love it." He flipped me on my back and climbed on top of me.

As Luke ran his tongue behind my ear and softly nipped my neck, I could feel the warmth deep in my belly. His hard cock pushed against my thighs as his lips made their way down to my breasts. His hand cupped me down below, before his fingers found their way inside of me.

"Someone is more than ready." He smiled as he looked at me.

My hips moved in sync as his fingers moved in and out of me slowly. He was teasing me; I could tell by the smirk on his face.

"How bad do you want me inside you?"

"Very bad. Can't you tell by how wet I am?" I said breathlessly.

"Yes, but I want you to tell me how bad you want me inside of you."

"If you don't put that hard cock inside me now, you're not going to have one anymore."

The look on his face was priceless. "Well, that wasn't the answer I wanted to hear, but it'll do."

He asked me to put my arms above my head, then he locked my wrists tight with his hand as he pushed himself into me. I threw my head back as he did it with such force that it made me gasp. His eyes gazed into mine while he pounded into me and gave me exactly what I wanted. I needed to run my hands through his hair, but his grip was too tight, and I couldn't free my hands.

"You want to touch me, don't you?" He smiled.

"You know I do."

"Should I let your hands go?"

"Yes. Please," I spoke breathlessly as my heart raced at full speed.

The grin on his face grew wide. "I'll let go if you come first."

I wrapped my legs around his waist as he took in a sharp breath. He took his free hand and placed it flat on my breast, with his palm face down and pressed hard against my nipple. He began rubbing it in slow circles as he moved fluently in and out of me. My body was ready to release and he knew it.

"That's right, baby, let go, and come all over me."

His words were all I needed to hear as a moan escaped my lips, and my body shook, releasing my pleasure all over him.

"That's it, Lily. I can't hold back anymore, baby," he grunted as his grip tightened around my wrists, and I felt the warmth of him spill into me as he pushed himself one last time deep inside me.

Letting go of my wrists, he brought each one to his lips and softly kissed them.

"I hope I didn't hurt you."

I gently rubbed the side of his face with the back of my hand. "You could never hurt me."

As he leaned down and kissed me, I heard my phone chime. He broke our kiss and looked at me.

"Why are we always getting interrupted by someone?"

"It's probably Sam telling us to shut the hell up." I laughed.

Luke climbed off of me and we both got out of bed and headed to the kitchen for some coffee. As he poured some in our cups, I checked my phone and saw a text message from Giselle.

"Lunch, 1:00 p.m. at The Southside Grill. You have no choice, and don't be late. It's important."

I read her text with a twisted a face, wondering what the hell was going on, and what could be so important.

"I'll be there at 1:00 p.m. sharp!" I replied back.

"What's wrong?"

"I just got this weird text from Giselle," I said as I handed him my phone.

"Hmm, I'm sure it's nothing serious. She's probably having a bad hair day."

I rolled my eyes as Luke looked over at his beeping phone.

"It looks like I'll be upstairs, fixing Mrs. Blake's Toilet again while you're at lunch with the girls."

"That's the third time this month. I swear she does it on purpose just to get you up to her apartment."

Luke held up his coffee cup and smiled. "Maybe she does. The women in this building can't seem to resist me."

"Very funny." I shot him a dirty look and got up from my chair.

He extended his arm, grabbed my waist, and pulled me onto his lap. He made me straddle him on the chair so we were face to face. Pushing the strands of my hair behind my ears, he kissed my lips.

"You know how much I love you, babe. It's only you. It will always be you, and you better never forget that," he spoke as his deep brown eyes stared into mine.

"I know, and I love you too. I love you so much that sometimes it hurts, and I get scared."

"There's nothing to be scared of, Lily. You know my feelings for you and I know your feelings for me." He lifted my nightshirt over my head.

I bit my bottom lip and smiled as I felt his erection underneath me. He leaned his head slightly forward and took my nipple between his teeth while he looked up at me. He wrapped his lips around my breast, tenderly sucking and circling his tongue around my nipple, making it harder than it already was.

"I only want these beautiful breasts in my face." He smiled as he reached down and dipped one finger inside of me, lifting me up. "And I only want my fingers inside you."

I let out a hiss and tilted my head back as he found my G-spot and started moving his finger back and forth. I moaned with desire as a warm flushing sensation resonated throughout my body, and I released myself on him.

As Luke looked at me and smiled, he whispered, "And I only want your come all over me."

He had me so hot that I could barely stand it. After removing his finger, he scooted me back a bit and pulled his hard cock from his boxers. Grabbing my hips, he pulled me forward and gently set me on him. I slowly pushed myself down as I cupped his face in my hands and we stared into each other's eyes.

"And last, I only want to be inside of you."

Once he was fully inside me, he lifted my hips slightly as I moved back and forth. He made sure to keep a tight grip on my hips as he started to swell inside me. As I felt the warmth of him shoot through me, he wrapped his arms around me and held me tightly on him as he finished himself off, pouring every last drop of pleasure inside of me.

Gazing into my eyes, he placed his hands on my face. "Do you understand?

I nodded my head and spoke softly. "Yes."

Luke pulled me into an embrace as he whispered in my ear, "You better."

***

Walking into the restaurant, I saw Gretchen and Giselle sitting over at a table in the corner. I made my way through the restaurant and joined them.

"You're exactly five minutes late," Giselle said as she looked at her watch.

"Sorry, but I couldn't find a place to park. This joint is busy."

A waitress with long black hair walked over to the table and set a glass of red wine down in front of me.

"I took the liberty of ordering your drink," Gretchen said.

"Thank you. Do you want to tell me what's going on? You sort of have me freaked out."

"I'm pregnant," Giselle blurted out as I was in the middle of taking a sip of wine.

I spit out my wine all over the table and started choking. "What?! Did you just say you were pregnant?"

I must have said it too loudly because a few heads turned and looked in our direction. Gretchen took her napkin and started wiping the spilled wine from the table.

"Yes, Lily. You heard right. She's pregnant."

"Who's the baby's daddy?" I asked.

Giselle looked at me. "You don't have to say it like that, and the father is Lucky."

"WHAT?!" I exclaimed as a few heads turned once more.

"Will you please keep it down," Giselle whispered.

"How far along are you?" I asked quietly.

"About six weeks."

"How do you feel about this?"

"I'm not sure."

I looked at Gretchen who was sitting there in silence.

"Have you told, Lucky, yet?"

"No, not yet, and I don't know how to."

"How did this happen? I thought you were on birth control?"

"I am, but sometimes I forget to take it. You know I have a hectic schedule."

"Yeah, and it's about to get busier," I said.

Giselle reached across the table and took my hand. "Listen, Lily, I'm thinking about getting an abortion and I need your support."

"You know how I feel about that, Giselle."

"I know and that's why I'm begging you."

"There's always adoption. Do you know how many couples can't have children?"

Suddenly, this conversation hit home as tears started to form in my eyes.

"Listen, I'm not getting into this discussion with the two of you right now. I'm about to say something and I don't want you to ask any questions. We'll discuss it further at my apartment, over dinner, one night. Mary isn't my biological mother."

Giselle and Gretchen looked at me as shock took over their faces. I held up my finger.

"If my biological mother decided to have an abortion, I wouldn't be sitting here with the both of you."

Gretchen picked up her phone off the table. "Everyone look at their schedules right now because we're setting up a dinner night over at Lily's."

I let out a light laugh while Giselle took a sip of her water and looked at me. "Lily, I promise I'm going to tell Lucky tonight, and the two of us will make our decision together."

"I'm here for you, Giselle. Don't get me wrong, I will always be here for you, no matter what you decide."

"We're here for you, Lily, and you can't keep something like that from us," Gretchen said.

"I know, and I'll tell you everything. Let's have dinner at my place next Tuesday, and we'll do Chinese take-out. No guys. Just us girls."

***

As I opened the door to Luke's apartment, I saw him lying on the couch watching TV. I threw my purse on the table, walked over to where he was and lay down next to him, snuggling into his chest.

"How was lunch, babe?"

"A clusterfuck," I mumbled.

"Watch your mouth," he said as he kissed me on the top of my head.

"Sorry, but wait until I tell you something."

"Did something happen?"

I propped myself up and kissed him. He smiled as he nipped at my bottom lip.

"Giselle is pregnant, and Lucky's the baby's daddy."

Luke's eyes widened and his mouth dropped open. "Are you serious?"

"Yes. I wouldn't make something like that up."

Luke pushed himself up into a sitting position as I laid my head across his lap.

"Does Lucky know?"

"She's telling him tonight, and she wants to have an abortion. I told both of them about Mary not being my biological mother, and we're having dinner at my place Tuesday night so I can tell them the whole story. I couldn't stop thinking about it, because what if my birth mother had an abortion?"

Luke ran his fingers through my hair. "I don't want to think about that. I'm sorry lunch was such—"

"A clusterfuck?" I said, knowing he'd tell me to watch my mouth.

As he looked down at me, he tapped me on the mouth with his fingers. "Watch your mouth, babe."

Just as I grabbed Luke's fingers and stuck them in my mouth, Sam and Gretchen walked through the door. I sat up and looked over at her.

"Long time no see, Gretch."

"Ugh, what a clusterfuck of a day!" she exclaimed as she fell into the recliner.

I stared at Luke. "Aren't you going to tell her to watch her mouth?"

"No. Why would I tell her that?"

"You tell me that all the time!"

"That's because you're my girl, and I don't want you talking like that." He smiled as he kissed me on the nose.

"Wait a minute!" I exclaimed. "I wasn't your girl when you were telling me that in my bathroom while you were fixing my shower."

"Well, I sort of liked you."

"Sort of?" I asked.

"Babe, drop it."

I rolled my eyes and sighed as I got up and Luke slapped me on the ass. Sam laughed, and Gretchen followed me to the kitchen to grab a beer.

"What do you think Giselle's going to do?" I asked her.

"I honestly don't know. You know Lucky is totally not her type, and our parents will die when they find out."

"Well, let's hope they make the right decision." I walked over to Luke and handed him a beer.

33

Luke

"Congratulations, Luke. You are now the owner of this bar!" Bernie smiled as he handed me the keys.

"Thanks, Bernie," I said as I shook his hand.

"This was my legacy, and my passion for many years, son, and now it's your turn. Do whatever you need to and make this bar *your* legacy."

"I will, Bernie. Enjoy the retired life," I spoke as I hugged him.

"I will, Luke. You two take care." Bernie smiled as he tipped his hat and walked out the door.

As I picked up Lily and swung her around, I kissed her. "I can't believe it, babe. I can't believe this is all mine!"

"I'm so happy for you."

The door to the bar opened and my mom, dad, Maddie, and Charley walked in.

"Uncle Luke!" Charley exclaimed as she ran over to me.

I picked her up and kissed her on the cheek. "Welcome to Luke's Bar and Grille, peanut."

"Yay!" she exclaimed.

I put her down as my mom and dad walked over and hugged me.

"We're so proud of you, Luke."

"Damn proud, son," my dad said.

"Congratulations, manager." I smiled as I threw the extra set of keys at Maddie.

I stood there and looked around the bar. My life was exactly where I always wanted it to be. I was the owner of a bar, and I had a woman that I was madly in love with standing by my side. As I was in deep thought, Lily looped her arm around my neck.

"What are you thinking about?" she asked.

"Just how lucky I am to be able to share my dream and this moment with you."

She leaned into me and softly kissed my lips. "I'm the lucky one." She smiled.

As we were having our little moment, Candi burst through the doors of the bar.

"Hey, boss." She smiled as she hugged me. "You have no idea how happy I am that you bought this joint."

Candi was one of the best bartenders I knew. She was forty-two years old, and she had never been married. Maddie had always been jealous of her long, curly black hair, and the two of them worked together for years. Both being single, they were constantly getting hit on by the customers. Candi used to be a prostitute. She stumbled into the bar one night after being beat up by her pimp. She was only twenty-two years old at the time. When Bernie saw her, he took her to the hospital. After she was released, they had a long talk, and Bernie brought her back to the bar, taught her how to make drinks, and gave her a job. That was twenty years ago, and she told us every day how Bernie saved her life and gave her a second chance.

I decided to have a celebration party with family and friends tonight. I put up a sign on the door, saying that the bar was closed for tonight only and would re-open tomorrow. Lily walked over to me and gave me a kiss goodbye. Chris, the principal of the school, had called her in for a meeting. As I looked over at the stage, I chuckled when I saw Charley up there, pretending she was holding a microphone, and singing her little heart out. My mom and dad left just as Sam came walking in.

"Dude, congratulations!" he said as we fist-bumped. "I never thought I'd see this day."

"Me either, Sam. You and Gretchen are coming tonight, right?"

"Of course we are, and depending on how Giselle is feeling, her and Lucky will be here."

"Oh yeah, that's right. Today's the day of her appointment at the clinic. Lily wanted to be there with her, but Giselle told her that Lucky was taking her."

"It sucks that they got themselves into this situation in the first place," Sam said as I handed him a beer.

"Uncle Sammy!" Charley shrieked. "Did you hear me singing?"

"I sure did, and I think you're going to be the next Taylor Swift."

Charley's eyes widened as she smiled. "Do you really think so?"

"Yes, I do. In fact, I'm going to call up *American Idol* and tell them I have a nine-year-old celebrity sitting next to me."

I chuckled as I poured Charley a coke. "Here, peanut. Take this and go sit over at the table."

"Thanks for the beer, man. I'm going to head home, get changed, and then wait for Gretchen to finish her photo shoot. I'll see you later," Sam said as we did our handshake.

***

As I was sitting in my office, going over some paperwork, Lily walked in, and I immediately knew something was wrong.

"Hey, babe. What's wrong?" I got up from my chair and wrapped my arms around her.

"The teacher that I'm subbing for is coming back to work on Monday. Her husband passed away sooner than they thought and she said she needs to come back to teaching to take her mind off of it."

"Aw, babe, I'm sorry," I said as I held her tight.

"I mean, I can understand her needing to come back, and I'm sorry her husband passed away, but I'm going to miss my students." She started to cry.

"I know you will. I know how much they mean to you." I kissed her head.

My heart broke for her. She loved her job and her students. I wanted to take away her sadness, but I didn't know what to do for her.

"You can work here at the bar."

She broke our embrace and looked at me.

"Thank you, but no. As much as I love you, I don't want to work for you. Anyway, Chris said that one of the teachers will be retiring at the end of the year, and when they move some other teachers around, there will be a position available, and she said it's mine. I'll just focus on photography for a while."

"That's my girl." I smiled.

I tilted my head as I looked at her and gently wiped away her tears. I brought her face closer to mine and softly kissed her lips.

"You know, in order to make this place perfect, we have to have sex here."

"Is that so?" She smiled as she bit her bottom lip.

"I think my office is the perfect place to start, Miss Gilmore." I grinned as I slowly undid the buttons on her shirt, then pushed it off her shoulders.

"I agree, Mr. Matthews." Her smile grew wide as her fingers grabbed the bottom of my t-shirt and she lifted it up over my head.

34

Lily

Luke and I left the bar and headed back to my apartment to change, and get ready for the party. The whole staff was going to be there along with all of Luke's family and friends. It was going to be a great night, and I wasn't going to ruin it for me or Luke. As much as I loved my students, maybe it was best that I focused on what I'd always wanted to do—photography. Walking into my apartment, and Luke following behind, I set my purse on the counter and grabbed a bottle of water from the refrigerator. Turning around, Luke put his hands on my hips and looked at me.

"Are you all right?"

"I'm fine, Luke." I smiled.

"I'm going to run next door and grab some fresh clothes. I'll be right back," he said as he kissed me on the forehead and walked out the door.

I couldn't stop thinking about Giselle and what she must be going through right now. She told me and Gretchen that she didn't want us to go with her to the clinic because it was something her and Lucky needed to do alone. She told me that she'd call me when she had the chance. As I was heading to my bedroom to change my clothes, Luke opened the door and walked in.

"That was quick," I said as he followed me into the bedroom.

"I'm a guy. Give me a pair of jeans and a t-shirt and I'm happy. We're not like you women who spend hours deciding what you're going to wear, how you're going to do your makeup, and how you're going to style your hair."

"I don't do that!" I exclaimed as I took a dress from my closet, looked at it, and then put it back. "Okay, guilty as charged." I smiled.

Walking over to my dresser, I looked at Luke as he was getting dressed.

"I'm worried about Giselle. Have you heard from Lucky?"

"No, not yet," he replied, slipping his dark gray t-shirt over his head.

"What are your feelings about all this?"

Luke sat on the edge of the bed and watched me as I ran a brush through my hair. "I don't know what to think. I'm not happy about the decision they made, but it's their life, and they have to live with it. Who knows? Maybe fatherhood would have changed Lucky."

"Their relationship is weird. They're more friends with benefits than anything else," I said as I twisted my hair up in a clip.

"Some people prefer their relationships that way. It's way less complicated."

"Are you saying our relationship is complicated?"

"Yes, our relationship is very complicated because I can't just have sex with you and leave. You plague my thoughts and my dreams when you're not around. So, I would say that complicates things because when you're not with me, I feel like life has stopped until you're by my side again."

His words were like poetry to me, and they reached deep down to the very core of my soul. What he had just said made tears spring into my eyes. I couldn't say a word, because if I opened my mouth, I would lose it and cry like a blubbering idiot.

As Luke stood up from the edge of the bed and wrapped his arms around me, I took in a deep breath and tried not to let the tears fall.

"I'm sorry, babe. I said too much, and if you respond, you're going to cry, right?"

Once again, I nodded my head and closed my eyes.

"I love you, Lily."

"I love you, Luke."

"I hate seeing you sad. Don't worry about this teaching thing. Everything will work out, and I'll be by your side every step of the way."

The one thing I could always count on Luke for was the fact that he always made me feel better and, suddenly, losing my job as Charley's teacher didn't seem so bad anymore.

***

Luke and Maddie were behind the bar, setting up the glasses, while Candi and I were making sure the tables were set up.

"How many people are you expecting, Luke?" Candi shouted across the bar.

"About fifty or so."

"Who's watching Charley tonight?" I asked Maddie.

"She's spending the night at her girlfriend's house."

Maddie walked over to me and gave me a hug. "I'm really sorry to hear that Charley's going to have a new teacher on Monday. I haven't told her yet. She's going to be devastated."

"Thanks," I said as I looked down. "I'm really going to miss those kids, but I'll still see Charley every day, and she's more than welcome to come over whenever she wants. Just send her down."

Maddie laughed as she placed her hand on my shoulder. "That's sweet of you, Lily, but I'll give you a call first in case you and my brother are busy."

"Ah, that's a good idea." I winked.

As I looked over Maddie's shoulder, I saw Tom and Annie walk into the bar.

"Your mom and dad are here," I said to her.

"Great, keep them occupied for me." She smiled as she walked the opposite way.

Following behind them was another couple who walked over to Luke and hugged him. Luke looked over to where I was standing and he motioned for me to come over to him.

"Lily, I would like you to meet my Aunt Rose and Uncle Matt."

"My, aren't you a sight for sore eyes," Aunt Rose said as she hugged me. "We've heard so much about you from Annie and Tom that we feel like we already know you."

"It's great to meet both of you." I smiled.

Rose was Annie's younger sister, and Matt was her husband. She was a cake decorator and owned a bakery in San Francisco, and he was a retired accountant who did the books for Rose's bakery. As we were talking, Gretchen and Sam walked in.

"Hey, bro." He smiled as he and Luke shook hands.

"Hi, Sam," I said as he gave me a hug.

"Have you heard from Giselle yet?" I asked Gretchen with concern.

"I texted her and she said she's fine—she's…"

Before Gretchen could finish her sentence, Giselle and Lucky walked through the door. I put my hand on Luke's shoulder, and he turned around. The four of us stood there and stared at them.

"We're having a baby!" She smiled as she threw her hands in the air.

We stood there, unable to say anything, then Luke spoke the first words.

"Awesome." He smiled as he hugged Giselle and high-fived Lucky.

Sam followed behind Luke and did the same as I looked at her and smiled. Gretchen, Giselle, and I walked over and sat down at a table.

"I couldn't do it. I was lying down on the table with my feet in the stirrups. Lucky was holding my hand and the doctor walked in and asked me if I was ready. I told him I was and then he went to check me, and I yelled, 'stop.' I looked at Lucky, told him that I couldn't do it, and he said 'please don't.' So, I sat up, got dressed, and the two of us went out to lunch and talked about what we're going to do."

"And what are you going to do?" Gretchen asked as she grabbed Giselle's hand.

"Lucky and I are going to raise the baby together as friends, with some occasional sex thrown in." She smiled.

"Is he moving in?"

"No, we're not moving in together. We're both going to keep our separate places fully furnished with all the things the baby needs."

I leaned over and looped my arm around her neck. "If that's what the two of you want, then I'm happy for you. I can't tell you how glad I am that you didn't go through with it."

"I know you are, Lily, and I gave a lot of thought to what you said about your birth mother. By the way, nobody better cancel on Tuesday, because I want to hear all about it," she spoke as she pointed her finger at me and Gretchen.

I felt two strong hands clasp my shoulders. As I looked up, Luke bent down and kissed me. "Come on, babe. There are a few people I want you to meet."

After meeting all of Luke's family and friends, Luke walked over and got up on the stage. As he positioned himself in front of the microphone, he held up his beer and yelled, "Welcome to Luke's Bar and Grille!"

Everyone in the bar whistled and cheered as I stared at Luke's smiling face. As he looked at me and winked, I held up my beer and blew him a kiss. His happiness was the only thing that mattered to me, and I would do everything I could to make sure he stayed that way.

***

The next couple of weeks, I barely saw Luke at all. He was at the bar from morning until night. If I wanted to see him, I would have to go to the bar. When he'd come home, he would quietly slip into bed and wrap his arms around me. We'd have dinner together at the bar every night, and he still tried to convince me to work there. He even went as far as to ask me if I would play the guitar and sing a few nights a week. I didn't have to say a word, he could tell my thoughts on that just by the look on my face. I had Giselle and Gretchen over for dinner like we planned, and I told them everything about Mary. Charley cried almost every day at school because I was no longer her teacher. It had been a clusterfuck of a week, and certain emotions from my past were being stirred up. As I was sitting on the couch, feeling sorry for myself, a text message from Luke came through.

"Hey, babe. Why aren't you here yet?"

"I'm not coming to the bar tonight."

"Why not? What's wrong?"

"Nothing's wrong, Luke. I just want to stay home."

"But I miss you, Lily."

"Yeah, I miss you too, but you don't seem to care about that."

As I sat there and stared at my message to him, I couldn't believe I had just said that. I didn't know what was going on with me, and I just wanted to be left alone. When he didn't respond, I threw my phone across the table. About twenty minutes later, the door opened. I turned around as Luke walked in, threw his keys on the counter, and stood in front of me.

"What the hell was that last text supposed to mean?"

I suppose I was looking for a fight, because I jumped up without hesitation and got in his face.

"It means exactly what I said."

"What's the matter with you?" he asked as he softly grabbed my arm when I started to walk away. "Don't you dare walk away from me!"

I jerked my arm out of his grip. "Don't you dare tell me what to do!"

"Babe, please tell me what's going on with you, because right now, you're not acting like yourself."

"You want to know what's wrong. Fine. I'll tell you what's wrong. I never see much of you anymore, and when I do, it's always at the bar with everyone else. We barely eat together anymore, and we don't go out. You spend every damn, fucking minute at that bar."

"Watch your mouth, Lily."

"Oh, and that's another thing, you don't get to tell me to watch my mouth, because I can talk anyway I want. I'm an adult, and if I want to scream FUCK to the world, then I fucking will!"

"We talked about this before I bought the bar. That's why I discussed it with you first, and now you're behaving like this. Why, Lily? Are you trying to hurt me? You knew the first few months were going to be difficult."

"Yeah, but then the first few months turn into another few months, and then they turn into years. It's your passion, and that's all you'll ever do, and that's all you'll ever think about, Johnny!" I screamed.

The expression on his face nearly killed me. It was filled with pain, disgust, and anguish. As he walked to the door and put his hand on the knob, he turned around and looked at me.

"I'm not your father, Lily."

He slammed the door behind him, and I stood there with my hand over my mouth as I dropped to my knees. I couldn't believe I called him "Johnny." As I closed my eyes, the memories of my mother and father fighting became more vivid. Brynn and I would sit on the stairs and listen to them scream back and forth at each other. I remembered my mother yelling at him about never being around and how he promised things would be better. I began to sob as I buried my face in my hands. I felt two arms wrap themselves around me, and I heard Sam's voice telling me that it was going to be okay. He helped me up from the floor and led me to the couch.

"Lily, please calm down."

"Sam, I said horrible things to him. I called him 'Johnny.' I'm more fucked up than I thought I was."

35

Luke

As I hopped on my bike and sped out of the parking lot, I couldn't stop thinking about Lily's behavior and her attitude towards me. She was being irrational, and I was disturbed by the fact that she called me her father. We'd had a long discussion about how many hours I'd be working at the bar the first few months, and she told me that she understood and that she'd be with me and support me through it all. As I pulled into the parking lot at the bar, I parked my bike on the side of the building and walked through the doors. I sighed as I stepped behind the bar and poured myself a cold beer.

"Where'd you run off to?" Maddie asked as she was making drinks.

"Lily's apartment."

"You didn't bring her back with you?"

"No, we got into a fight."

Maddie stopped what she was doing and looked at me. "About what?"

"The bar and how she's sick of not seeing me and spending time with her," I said as I slammed the glass down on the counter and looked at her. "See, this is what I don't get: we spend time together, and we see each other every day. She comes here, and when I leave, I go home to her place, and I spend every night with her."

"You have to realize that things for Lily have significantly changed over the past couple of weeks. She lost her teaching job, and her boyfriend, who spent every waking minute with her, became the owner of a bar, so she barely sees him anymore. That's a lot to take in at the same time."

"She called me 'Johnny,'" I said.

"What? Why did she do that?" Maddie asked in confusion.

"I don't know. All she said was that this will consume me because it's my passion and dream."

As I looked down, Maddie placed her hand on mine.

"It sounds like she's having flashbacks of her father and how he was never around. Didn't she say that her ex-fiancé was never around either and started spending less time with her?"

I nodded my head and clenched my jaw. "You're right. Now things are starting to make sense."

"You need to talk to her, Luke. I love you both, and I don't want to see your relationship go in the toilet because of a misunderstanding. "

"I'm going to talk to her, don't worry. I'll be leaving after I finish the budget. I want to give her time to cool down."

Pulling my phone from my pocket, I swiped the screen and saw that I had a text message Sam.

"I just left Lily's and she's a mess, man. I know it's none of my business, but I'm not sure if I've ever seen a girl like that. She's pretty messed up, and if you love her, you'll get your ass back there."

"Thanks for being there for her. I'm heading over there now."

I looked at my watch and walked to my office. I shut down the computer and stacked the paperwork into a neat pile for tomorrow. I walked over to Maddie before leaving the bar.

"Starting tomorrow, I want you out of here by five p.m. You've been here late, and I appreciate it, but it's not fair to Charley. I know it's only temporary, but things are going back to normal. We need to sit down tomorrow and have a meeting, so head here right after dropping Charley off at school," I said as I kissed her on the cheek.

***

When I opened the door to Lily's apartment and stepped inside, I didn't see her. I walked down the hall, stopped in the doorway of her bedroom, and stared at her lying on the bed all curled up. My heart broke seeing her like that. She must have heard me, because she rolled over and tried to open her swollen eyes. As I walked over to her and sat on the edge of the bed, I pushed her hair behind her ear and leaned over, kissing her teary eye and moist cheek. She raised her arm up and looped it around my neck, bringing me closer as I buried my face deep into her.

"I'm so sorry for everything I said." She began to cry.

"I'm sorry for not being here for you when you needed me, Lily."

We lay there for a few moments in silence before I pulled back and looked at her. Her eyes were swollen and red. As I got up from the bed, she grabbed my hand, and I told her that I'd be right back. I walked to the bathroom and grabbed a wash-cloth from under the sink. I ran the cloth under the warm water and folded it as I walked back to the bedroom. Gently wiping her face, the corners of her mouth turned up, forming a small smile.

"That's what I like to see." I smiled back.

She sat up with her back against the headboard. I put the washcloth on the night stand, and I took both of her hands in mine, interlacing our fingers.

"We need to talk, babe. You need to tell me what you're feeling, where that last argument came from, and why you called me your father's name. Because if we don't, it's going to happen again, and that's not good for our relationship."

"I know we do," she replied.

"Are you hungry?" I asked her as I was starving.

"Yeah. I haven't eaten all day."

"How about Chinese food? I'll call and have it delivered, and we can sit on the couch, eat it, and talk."

"I love that idea." She smiled as she put her soft hand on my cheek.

I brought her hand to my mouth and kissed her palm before picking up my phone and calling in our dinner order. Lily got up from the bed and grabbed a pair of yoga pants and a tank top from her drawer. She changed her clothes and put her hair up in a ponytail.

"Ugh, look at my face!" she exclaimed as she wiped her eyes.

Wrapping my arms around her, I spoke, "You have a beautiful face, tear-stained and all."

She smiled and crinkled her nose as she turned around and kissed me on the lips. While I grabbed the bottle of wine and a couple of glasses, Lily took down two plates from the cabinet and got out the silverware. Not too long after calling in the order, there was a knock at the door. As the delivery boy handed me the brown bag, I reached into my pocket and took out some cash. Lily walked over and took the bag from my hands and sat down on the couch.

"I'm going to call a therapist tomorrow morning and schedule an appointment," Lily said as she took the cartons of Chinese food out of the bag.

"Do you really think you need to?"

"Yeah. It's something I should've done a long time ago. When I was yelling at you earlier, I felt like I was reliving my childhood and watching my mom and dad having the same argument. Mary would scream at him because he was never around, and he kept telling her that it was part of the business and that things would get better. But instead of getting better, they got worse. He would be gone for months at a time on tour, which was understandable, but then when he'd get back to Seattle, he wouldn't come home for a few days."

I set my plate down on the table, and I reached over and hugged her. "I'm sorry you had to grow up like that."

"I felt abandoned, Luke, and then I felt it again after the church incident with Brynn and Hunter. All those emotions and feelings were coming back to me these past two weeks when you were so busy at the bar and we weren't spending as much time together. That's an issue that needs to be addressed, and I think a therapist can help me."

"I love you, Lily. I don't know how to make that any clearer to you."

"I know you do, baby, and believe me, it's not you. I'm the one who has these issues, compliments of Johnny and Mary Gilmore, and I'm the one who needs to take care of them. I know you love me; I really do. It's just this change the past couple of weeks has really messed with my head."

"Then you go do what you have to do in order to free yourself of your past. I'll be here for you every step of the way." I smiled as I brushed my hand over her cheek and leaned in to kiss her.

36

Lily

After having the best sex of my life last night, I rolled over and ran my tongue along Luke's shoulder. I was extremely sore, but it was worth it.

"Good morning, babe. What time is it?"

"It's seven o'clock. Don't you have to meet Maddie at the bar?"

"Yeah, but I can be late. Just let me send her a text."

Luke did just that, set his phone on the nightstand, and then pulled me to him.

"Ouch," I said as I scooted closer.

"What's wrong?" he asked.

"I'm just a little sore down there, that's all."

"God, after what we did last night, I believe you are. I'm sorry, babe. What can I do to make it feel better?"

I smiled as I lifted my head and kissed his lips. "There's nothing you can do. It'll feel better in a few days."

"Umm, I don't think I can go a few days without having sex with you."

I rolled my eyes as I struggled to get out of bed. "You're such a guy." I smiled.

As I heard Luke chuckle, he followed me into the bathroom. I started the shower, turned around, and noticed as Luke took off his boxers.

"What are you doing?" I asked.

"Taking a shower with you like I always do," he replied with a confused look on his face.

"That could pose a problem since we can't have sex."

"Don't worry, babe. I can control myself. Let's just get in, wash up, and get out."

"All right, but you better behave yourself."

Luke smirked as we stepped into the shower. I closed my eyes and let the stream of hot water run down my hair and body. When I opened my eyes, I saw that Luke was staring at me. My eyes glanced down and noticed his hard cock. I looked at him and tilted my head.

"I can't help it, Lily. This is what you do to me. I tried to stop it, but you're standing there, naked, with the water running down that hot body of yours. What do you expect?"

I couldn't help but burst into laughter as he stood there, naked and hard, trying to defend himself. I reached my hand over and took a hold of him, stroking his entire length as his erection pressed against my palm. Taking my thumb, I skillfully circled his smooth head as I reached under and deftly stroked his balls with my other hand. A loud groan escaped the back of his throat as he threw his head back.

"Just stand there and enjoy it. This is about you, Luke."

"Babe, I need to touch you," he moaned as grabbed both of my breasts and began rubbing them.

"You can have my tits, but nothing else." I smiled as I got down on my knees and took his length in my mouth while the hot water beaded down on us.

As I sucked up and down his shaft, his moans became louder. Keeping my fingers wrapped around his base, my tongue licked its way up to his head, circling around the wet, smooth area before my lips wrapped themselves around the tip, sending him into a near convulsion.

"I'm going to come any second, babe," he moaned as he thrust his hips back and forth.

I continued to fist his base as I gave his cock one hard suck; feeling and tasting his salty liquid explode in my mouth. He pressed both hands against the shower wall as he let out one last moan and gave me every last drop he had. I looked up at him and smiled as he took my hand and helped me up. He pulled me against him as his mouth smashed with mine. His kiss was strong and forceful, letting me know that he was grateful.

"God, babe, you're amazing."

"I know." I smiled.

Luke chuckled, and we finished up our shower. He quickly got dressed, kissed me goodbye, and flew out the door. As I was in the bathroom, putting on my make-up, my phone rang. I reached over and grabbed it off the shelf, only to see that my mother was calling.

"Hi, Mom," I answered.

"Hi, Lily. I'm sure you know that tomorrow is your sister's birthday, and I was hoping that maybe you could give her a call."

I sighed, as we'd been over this a thousand times. "Mom, I don't know if I'll ever be able to forgive Brynn for what she did. Listen, I don't have time to discuss this right now. I've got a lot of things to do and I'm already running late. I'll talk to you later," I said as I ended the call.

I finally finished getting ready, so I decided to call Giselle.

"Hello," she answered sleepily.

"Hey, did I wake you?"

"No, I've just been dozing on and off. I've spent half the morning puking."

"Would you mind some company? I need to talk to you about something."

"Sure, come on over. I don't have anything going on today."

"I'm on my way," I said as I hung up.

***

"Come on in, girl." Giselle smiled as she opened the door.

I reached over and hugged her. She stood there in her white satin robe. Her long brown, normally perfect hair was pulled back into a messy ponytail.

"You look like you're not doing too well."

"I'm not. I have severe morning sickness."

"I brought some bagels. I thought the baby might like one."

"Ugh, this kid doesn't like anything," she said as she sat down on the couch and hugged the pillow.

"Have you tried crackers?"

"Yes, and they don't work either. I throw up for four hours, and then it stops."

"Your morning sickness will go away soon."

"Not soon enough." She pouted. "Anyway, what did you want to talk about?"

"Do you know the name of a good therapist around here?"

Giselle tilted her head and pushed out her bottom lip as she looked at me. "You're seeking therapy, sweetie?"

"Luke and I got into a huge fight yesterday over him not being around as much since he took ownership of the bar. It was my entire fault, and I called him 'Johnny.'"

As Giselle's mouth dropped, she reached over and grabbed my hand. "Why on earth would you call him 'Johnny'?"

"Because at that moment, I was having flashbacks of my parents, and the things my dad used to say. Music was his life and his world. It was his passion, and he put every waking moment he had into it. Suddenly, I saw that in Luke with the bar, and I freaked out, especially since Hunter never had time for me."

She sighed. "You need therapy!"

"I know I do. Now give me a name, because I know in your industry, ninety percent of the models are in therapy."

Giselle laughed as she got up from the couch and grabbed her cell phone. As she scrolled through it, she asked me if I wanted a male or female therapist. I looked at her with a twisted face because it didn't matter. I wanted the therapist who was the best.

"I would call Dr. Evelyn Blakely," she said. "Marissa sees her, and she said she's a god-send, so I'm taking that to mean she's good."

As I took my phone from my purse, I noticed a text message from Luke.

"I just wanted you to know that I can't stop thinking about your beautiful, talented mouth, and it's distracting me from my work."

I smiled as I quickly responded.

"Good, that was the plan, baby."

"Are you going to be coming to the bar?"

"Yeah, I'll be there later. I have a few things that I need to do first."

"See you later, Lily. I love you."

"I love you too."

I tapped the contact button and asked Giselle for the number for Dr. Blakely. She rattled it off as she sprang from the couch and ran to the bathroom.

I dialed the number and waited for someone to answer.

"Dr. Blakely's office, Janelle speaking. How may I assist you?"

"I would like to schedule an appointment to see Dr. Blakely, please."

"Are you a new patient?"

"Yes."

"I know this is kind of short notice, but do you think you can be here in thirty minutes? I just had someone cancel about an hour ago."

"Wow. Yeah, I can be there in thirty minutes," I said.

"Your name, please."

"Lily Gilmore," I replied.

Giselle emerged from the bathroom and sat down next to me. "I swear this kid is going to kill me."

"Aw, don't say things like that." I smiled as I put my hand on her flat stomach. "Anyway, I have to go. Dr. Blakely's office told me to be there in thirty minutes."

"Wow! Who gets into therapy that fast?"

"They just had a cancellation."

"See, it was meant to be." Giselle smiled as she got up and walked me to the door.

***

I parked the Explorer in the parking garage of the Santa Monica Sunset Medical Center. Upon entering the building, I took notice of the large salt-water fish tank that sat in the middle of the lobby. I looked over to my right at the directory and found Dr. Blakely's suite number. Upon entering the elevator and taking it up to the fourth floor, I suddenly became nervous. I hated the fact that I had to relive my past in order for Dr. Blakely to try and help me. As the elevator doors opened, I stepped out and took the long hallway down to Suite 413.

As I walked through the door, I was greeted by a small brunette who handed me a clipboard with paperwork and asked me to fill them out. Sitting down, I filled out the papers, and returned it to the desk. It was shortly after that when the small brunette called my name and walked me into Dr. Blakely's office.

Dr. Blakely emerged from behind her desk, walked over to me, and extended her hand.

"You must be Lily Gilmore. It's a pleasure to meet you." She smiled.

I politely shook her hand and told her it was nice to meet her as well. She asked me to have a seat on the beige leather couch as she offered me coffee or water. I opted for coffee as she walked over to where her coffee pot sat and poured me a cup. Looking around her meticulous office, I couldn't help but notice the burning of incense. I asked Dr. Blakely what the scent was. She told me it was sandalwood and that she burned it to help her patients relax. As she handed me my cup of coffee, she took a seat in the oversized beige chair that sat next to the couch.

"Why don't we start by you telling me why you feel like you need therapy?"

I looked down as I traced the rim of the coffee cup with my finger.

"For the first time in my life, I've met someone that I truly love, and I can't let the effects of my past ruin it. I realized that last night when we had an argument, and I called him by my father's name."

Dr. Blakeley listened intently as she nodded her head and wrote things down on her notepad. I went on to tell her about Johnny and my childhood. Before I knew it, our time was up.

"I would like to see you at least two times a week to start, if that's alright with you," she said.

"Yes, that would be fine."

"Take care, and I'll see you in a couple of days," she said as she put her hand on my shoulder.

Walking out of her office and heading towards the parking garage, I pulled out my phone and saw that I had a missed call from Luke. I quickly dialed him.

"Hey, babe."

"Sorry I missed your call. I was in an appointment with Dr. Blakely."

"Who's Dr. Blakely?"

"A therapist."

"You got in that fast?"

"Yeah, they had a cancellation. I'll tell you about it later."

"Are you coming to the bar now? There's something I want to show you."

"Yep, I'm on my way now," I said as I got into the Explorer and shut the door.

"Good. I'll be waiting, babe, and park around the back. I love you."

"I love you more." I smiled as I quickly ended the call before he had a chance to say anything.

***

I pulled into the back lot of the bar like Luke had asked, and he was standing there waiting for me. As I smiled and parked the Explorer, he walked over and opened my door. Leaning in with a smile, he brushed his lips against mine.

"I've been waiting to do that since this morning," he said.

As I got out of the truck, Luke bent down and picked me up.

"What are you doing?" I laughed.

"Close your eyes. Make sure they're closed tight because I don't want you peeking."

"Luke, what's going on?"

"I want to show you something. Just do as I say and keep your eyes closed."

He carried me through the parking lot while I kept my eyes tightly closed. He stopped, put me down, and told me to open my eyes. When I opened them, they darted to the new bar sign that read, 'Luke's Bar & Grille.' I covered my mouth with my hands in excitement as I stared at the artistry that officially made this Luke's bar.

"It's perfect, Luke!" I squealed as I threw my arms around him.

"They put it up this morning. Do you know how awesome it is to see my name up on that sign? I've dreamed of this for so long, Lily, and it finally happened."

"I know, baby, and I'm so happy for you," I said as a damn tear rolled down my cheek.

"Babe, don't." He wiped it away with his thumb.

"It's a tear of happiness. I love you so much," I whispered as I hugged him tight.

"I love you more." He smiled. "Come on, let's go have some lunch. Are you hungry?"

"I'm starving."

As Luke walked to the back, I sat down at the bar where Maddie was putting glasses away.

"Hi, Lily."

"Hi, Maddie. How are you?"

"I'm good. I'm glad to see you here today."

I gave her a strange look, and then it dawned on me that Luke must have told her about last night.

"I'm assuming Luke told you about our argument."

"Yeah. He was so upset last night when he walked in here."

"I know, and I feel awful about that, but we're good, and I'm seeking help to deal with my past."

"You have no idea how proud of you I am. You're an amazing person and Luke is deeply in love with you."

I smiled at her as Luke came up behind me. "What do you want to eat, babe?" he asked.

"I'll just have a burger. You know how I like it."

"Yes. I do," he growled as he leaned in and kissed my neck.

"Okay, that's enough!" Maddie smirked.

I got up from the bar and sat down at a table. Pulling my phone from my purse, there was a text message from Brynn. My heart started racing, and a sick feeling emerged in the pit of my stomach.

"Lily, please don't be mad. I went through Mom's phone and got your number. I really need to see you, or at the very least, talk to you."

As I threw my phone on the table and sighed, Luke came walking over with our burgers. He set the plate down in front of me and took the seat across from me.

"What's wrong, Lily? You have that look."

I picked up my phone and handed it to him. He looked at me as he set my phone down on the table.

"Don't let that upset you," he said.

"How can I not?!"

"I hate to say this, Lily, and I know your therapist is going to tell you the same thing, but you need to talk to Brynn to let go and get closure. I told you the same thing about your mom, and look how that turned out. The two of you are speaking again and trying to put the past behind you."

I took a bite of my burger. "OMG, this burger is amazing! Why is this burger so amazing?!"

Luke threw his head back and laughed. "I hired a new chef yesterday and he uses some secret ingredient. It's so secret that he won't even tell me what it is. I'll be sure to tell him that you love his burgers."

Once I got over how amazing the burger was, I went back to the subject of Brynn.

"I can't believe you would suggest I talk to her after what she did. Have you forgotten that she carried on a relationship with *my* fiancé, and then fucked him in the church on *my* wedding day?!"

"No, babe, I haven't forgotten that. But maybe you need to hear why she did it. You're carrying an awful lot of anger around with you about Brynn and Hunter, and maybe it's time you hear her out and let it all go. Besides, look at where you are right now. Just think, if you wouldn't have found them in the church, you'd be living your dream life with a big real estate agent, in a big house with a white picket fence, pretending that everything was great, and I'd be sitting in my apartment, all alone and feeling sorry for myself. It's called fate, Lily. You were meant to find out about them that day."

A part of me knew he was right. Luke was always right, and it drove me nuts. I got up from my chair and sat on his lap. He wrapped his arms around me and buried his face into my neck.

"You're right, Luke. It's time to let go," I said as I kissed him.

"Do you think that you two could either go get a room somewhere or at least go lock yourselves in the office?" Maddie said as she walked over to us.

"Go away or you're fired," Luke mumbled.

Suddenly, we heard a crash. Luke looked up as Maddie dropped a glass on the floor and stared straight ahead towards the door. I got up from Luke's lap and looked over to where she was looking at someone standing in the doorway.

"Who's that?"

"It's Adam, that motherfucker!" Luke said as he quickly got up and started walking over to him.

37

Luke

Lily grabbed my arm to prevent me from kicking Adam's ass out of my bar.

"Don't, Luke, please. Think of Charley," she said as she tried to pull me back.

As I approached Adam, he put his hands up.

"Hey, Luke, I'm not here to cause any trouble. I just want to talk to Maddie."

"Well she doesn't want to talk to you!" I spat.

"Why don't you let her decide that for herself," he said as Maddie came walking over.

"Luke, pull back," Maddie said as she looked at me.

"Maddie, you can't be serious!"

As Lily pulled me over to the side, Maddie and Adam sat down at a table.

"Luke, take your own advice!" Lily said between gritted teeth.

"What are you talking about, Lily?"

"We just had a conversation about letting things go and moving forward. You told me that I need to talk to Brynn. Well, maybe it's time you talk to Adam."

"It's different. There's a little girl involved here."

"I understand that, but he's her father, and you at least owe it to Charley to listen to what he has to say."

I rolled my eyes and turned away from her. She was throwing my own advice back in my face. Wrapping her arms around my waist, she asked me to please stay calm for her. I sighed, turned around, and kissed her forehead. I grabbed her hand, and I led her to the table where Maddie and Adam were sitting.

"Hi, Adam, I'm Lily Gilmore, Luke's girlfriend. It's nice to meet you," she said as she extended her hand to him.

"Hi, Lily. It's nice to meet you." He smiled as he took her hand and shook it.

Seeing him touch Lily made me sick, and I wanted to fucking punch him right then and there. But, I promised I would stay calm for Lily's sake.

"Would you like to explain why you just showed up here without calling?" I asked as I folded my arms and leaned back in the chair.

"Before I answer that, I just want to congratulate you on the bar. I was very surprised when I walked up and saw the sign."

I didn't say a word to him. I just sat there and stared him down as he continued to speak.

"I'm a changed man—"

"The fuck you are!" I exclaimed.

Lily looked over at me and gave me a dirty look. "Watch your mouth," she said with a serious tone.

"I'm clean, and I have been for over a year. I don't drink, I don't do drugs, and I've quit smoking cigarettes. If you don't believe me, then I can do a drug test for you."

"Why this sudden change of character?" I asked.

"Because I hit rock bottom and almost died. I guess you could say I had an epiphany, because when I woke up in that hospital bed, alone and scared, I knew I couldn't live my life like that anymore. So, I checked myself into one of the best rehab programs in the country and they helped me."

"Then why the hell didn't you come see your daughter like you promised her you would? Do you have any idea how you broke that little girl's heart?"

Adam sighed and looked at Maddie. "The reason I couldn't visit was because I'm a sponsor, and the person I'm sponsoring, who had been clean for six months, decided to shoot himself up with heroine the night before I was supposed to leave. I had an obligation to be there for him and help him."

I got out of my seat and slammed my fists on the table. "You have an obligation to your daughter!" I yelled.

Lily grabbed my arm. "Luke, that's enough!"

As I took in a deep breath, I sat down. I was angry that he would put a drug addict before his daughter, and I wanted to kill him.

"I understand you being angry, Luke; trust me, I do. After waking up in that hospital and realizing that I had almost died, the only two people I could think about were Maddie and Charley, and how I was given a second chance."

"Wow," Lily said.

I looked at her and rolled my eyes as she smacked me on the arm. "Stop it!" she spat.

"You're full of shit, Adam, and I don't believe one word of what you're saying. You've done way too much damage, and you left a trail of tears and scars with Maddie and Charley, and I will not let you walk back into their normal lives and fuck everything up!"

Suddenly, I heard a small voice from across the bar. "Daddy?" Charley said as she stood a few feet away from Adam.

"There's my baby girl." He smiled as he got out of his chair and held his arms out to her.

Charley ran to him and threw her arms around him as he picked her up and swung her around.

"Let me look at you," he said as he put her down. "You're beautiful, and you're so grown up," he said as he hugged her.

"Daddy, what are you doing here?" she asked.

"I came to see you and Mommy."

I looked over at Maddie as she took in the moment between her daughter and her daughter's father. I shook my head because I knew by the look on her face that she believed him, and she was going to let him back into their lives.

"Can I talk to you for a minute, Maddie?" I asked as I took a hold of her arm and led her to the back room.

"I know what you're going to say, Luke, but there's a part of me that believes him."

"Damn it, Maddie! I knew this was going to happen."

Maddie pointed her finger in my face. "Listen to me. I owe it to Charley to give her father a chance."

"You can't relate, Luke, because you grew up with a mother and father who loved each other and were there for you and Maddie," Lily said as she walked up behind me. "Let's go out to dinner tonight and have some general conversation; maybe you'll be able to see things differently."

"That's a great idea, Lily." Maddie smiled.

"What do you say, Luke?" Lily asked me as she wrapped her arms around my waist.

"Whatever. I have to go. I have work to do," I said as I stormed off and went to my office.

38

Lily

I could see the anger in his eyes as he stormed off into his office. Maddie looked over at me with tears in her eyes.

"He's so angry, and he has so much hatred for Adam that I don't think he'll ever accept him."

As I gave her a hug, I told her that I would talk to him. We walked back to the table where Adam was talking to Charley. Maddie excused herself as she pulled out her phone to make a phone call. When she came back to the table, she told Charley to get her things ready, because Mrs. Clements was coming to pick her up, take her to dance class, and then home with her so she could play with Allie for a while. Charley whined, and she said that she didn't want to go.

"You have to go to dance class if you're going to dance for me," Adam said to her.

"But I want to stay with you," she whined.

"I want you to stay too, but dance class is a little more important. So, I'll tell you what, you go to dance class, and tomorrow, when you get home from school, I'll take you and your mom out somewhere really fun."

Charley's eyes lit up as she looked over at Maddie. "Can we, Mom?"

Maddie smiled and patted her head. "Yeah, that sounds great," she said as she looked at Adam.

Charley gave Adam a hug and a kiss goodbye as Maddie took her outside to wait for Mrs. Clements. I looked Adam over as he watched Maddie and Charley walk out of the bar. As much as I hated to admit it, he was hot. He stood over six feet tall with a nice build, and he wore his light brown hair short. I saw a lot of him in Charley, especially in their bluish-green eyes.

Adam turned and looked at me. "Regardless of what everyone tells you, I love that little girl more than anything in this world, and I came back here to make things right with her."

"Listen, Adam, I don't know you, and I'm not judging you. But, you have a track record and a history. I came from a father that was somewhat like you, and he fucked me up, and now I'm in therapy because of him. So, I just want to let you know that I love that little girl too, and I won't stand by and let you ruin her if you decide to go back to your old life."

Luke came walking up behind me just as I finished my sentence. "Are you ready to go?" he asked me.

"Yes. Adam, we'll see you later for dinner. Maddie will fill you in on the details."

He looked down and nodded his head. "Thanks, Lily, Luke. I'll see you both later."

Luke just shot him a look and put his arm around me as we walked out of the bar. "I heard what you said to him."

"Okay. And?"

"Nothing. I just thought you were pretty bad ass." He smiled as he brushed his lips against mine.

As I climbed into the Explorer, Luke got on his bike, and we headed home.

***

"You better be nice at dinner," I said to Luke as he was in the shower, and I was touching up my makeup.

"I can't make any promises when it comes to that douchebag."

"Luke, I swear, I'll be so mad at you if you don't let him talk and explain everything."

"What's to explain, Lily? He's a drunk, a drug addict, and a thief. He'll always be those things to me."

"Wow, I never took you for the grudge type."

"Only with him, babe."

I took the towel that Luke had waiting for him off the counter, and I hid the one that was on the towel rack. As he turned off the shower, I stepped out of the bathroom. "What the hell," I heard him say as he opened the shower curtain.

"Lily, where's the towel that I had sitting on the counter?"

As Luke stood there, dripping wet, I stopped in the doorway of the bathroom and held up the towel.

"Do you mean this one?"

He tilted his head and knitted his eyebrows. "Yes, that one," he said as he held out his hand.

"Sorry, but you're not getting this towel until you promise me that you'll give Adam a chance."

"Damn it, Lily, just give me the towel," he said with irritation.

"No. Not until you promise me."

"Jesus Christ, I'm cold."

My eyes wandered down to his flaccid cock. "Yeah, I can tell." I smiled.

"That's it!" he exclaimed as he stepped out of the tub and started coming towards me.

"Oh shit!" I ran down the hall and out the apartment door, knowing he wouldn't open it.

Sam was coming out of his apartment and he looked at me. "What's going on, Lily?" he asked.

"Oh nothing. How are you?"

Sam gave me a strange look and he said he was good. Just as he was about to ask me why I was standing in the hallway with a towel in my hand, my apartment door opened, and Luke grabbed me from behind, pulling me into the apartment and shutting the door.

"Now you're in trouble, babe," he said as he took me to the bedroom and threw me on the bed.

He was in a pair of sweat shorts and no shirt. His hair was dripping wet, and he looked as sexy as hell. As he pinned me on the bed, he climbed on top and sat on my legs so I couldn't move. He took both my hands and brought them over my head as he tightly held my wrists with his hand.

"Tell me how much you love me." He smiled.

"No," I said as I tried to wiggle myself free.

"What do you mean, no?" he asked as he leaned down and smashed his lips against mine.

His kiss was rough as I parted my lips and his tongue slipped into my mouth. He stopped and looked at me.

"Tell me how much you love me."

"Let go of my wrists and I will." I smiled.

As he let go of my wrists, I brought my hand to his face, and I stared into his beautiful brown eyes. "I love more than anything and anyone in this entire world."

"I promise you, Lily, I'll be nice tonight, and I won't get out of line." He smiled.

Pulling him down to me, I wrapped my arms around him and whispered in his ear, "Thank you, baby."

***

We met Maddie and Adam at a restaurant called The Falcon's Landing. As the hostess led us to the table where Adam and Maddie were already sitting, Luke tightened the grip on my hand when he saw Maddie laughing.

"You promised," I whispered.

"I didn't do anything," he said as he looked over at me.

We arrived at the table and took our seats. I was amazed that Luke shook Adam's hand. Maddie looked over at me and smiled.

"Adam is moving to Los Angeles and he's going to attend UCLA," she announced.

I looked over at Luke as he clenched his jaw. I squeezed his thigh under the table, and he loosened it.

"That's great, Adam. What are you studying?"

"Drug abuse and alcohol counseling," he answered.

"You want to counsel drug addicts?" Luke asked.

"Yes, I do. I already have a year of classes under my belt, and they've all transferred to UCLA. I'm starting over, man. I'm walking away from my past, and I'm stepping into a brand new life; a life that includes my daughter and Maddie."

"Where are you going to be staying?" Luke asked him calmly.

"I've rented an apartment by UCLA. That way I can be close to Charley and the campus."

"I'm sorry, man, but I have to ask this: how the hell are you affording all this?"

"I've been working the past year as a computer tech, and the owner was paying me under the table. He warned me that if he caught me using drugs, he would report me to the state. He did a drug test on me once a week. I saved every dime I made so I could go to school and make something of my life."

"You always were a genius with computer." Luke laughed.

It was at that moment that Luke realized maybe Adam was telling the truth, and we had a great dinner and good conversation. As we walked out of the restaurant, Adam put his hand on Maddie's back. Luke looked at me, and I squeezed his hand. We hugged, said our goodbyes, and Luke and I climbed into his Jeep.

"They have a chance at being a real family," I said.

"I guess." Luke sighed as he pulled out of the parking lot.

As we were on our way home, my phone rang. I pulled it from my purse and saw it was Giselle calling.

"Hey, girl, what's up?" I answered and put her on speaker phone.

She was sobbing so hard, I could barely understand her. She said something about an accident. Suddenly, Lucky's voice came through the speaker.

"Hi, it's Lucky. Gretchen and Sam were in a car accident, and they've been taken to the UCLA Medical Center."

I started shaking, and instantly I felt sick.

"Lucky, how bad is it?" Luke asked as he quickly turned the Jeep around and headed toward the medical center.

"I don't know, man. The hospital called Giselle, said there had been an accident, and to get to the hospital right away. I'm freaking out, Luke. What if—"

"Stop it, Lucky, they'll be fine. We're on our way."

With shaking hands, I ended the call. Luke reached over and took my hand and brought it his lips.

"They're fine, babe. I know they're fine."

39

Luke pulled into the medical center parking garage and quickly found a place to park. As we got out of the Jeep, Luke grabbed my hand, and we ran to the entrance of the emergency room. When we approached the reception desk, Giselle came running up to me, crying.

"Lily, they won't tell me anything," she sobbed.

"Giselle, you have to calm down. Think of the baby," I said as I tried to console her.

Suddenly, Sam came walking through the automatic double doors. He had a white bandage on his forehead, cuts on his face, and his hand was wrapped.

"Sam, are you okay?" I asked.

"How's Gretchen?" Giselle cried.

"I don't know. She's still in surgery."

Luke hugged him. Giselle couldn't handle hearing that Gretchen was in surgery. Lucky grabbed a hold of her, and he made her sit down in the chair.

I looked at Sam because I needed to be strong, not only for Gretchen, but for him as well. "Sam, what happened?" I asked.

"I'll tell you as soon as we get back upstairs to the surgical waiting room."

"Did anyone call Gretchen's parents?" I asked.

"I did," Lucky said. "They're on their way down."

Lucky helped Giselle up, and we all rode the elevator to the third floor where the surgical waiting room was. It was quiet and empty, and we were the only people in there. I sat down next to Giselle and offered her some water. She wouldn't take it as she continued crying on Lucky's shoulder. I walked over to the coffee machine and put in some change. I pressed the button and nothing. The damn thing was broken. I pounded on the machine as I pressed my forehead against it and started crying. Suddenly, I felt Luke's arms from behind.

"Babe," he whispered as he laid his head on my back.

"All I wanted was a cup of coffee," I sobbed.

Luke turned me around and took my face in his hands. "I can get you a cup of coffee." He smiled as he wiped away my tears.

I was scared shitless that Gretchen wasn't going to make it, and I felt like I was on the verge of an anxiety attack. Luke went to get me a cup of coffee, and I walked over and sat next to Sam. He looked at me with tears in his eyes.

"She's going to be okay," I said, grabbing his hand.

"She *has* to be okay, Lily. If she dies, I don't know—"

"Don't talk like that. Nobody is dying here. She's a strong person, and she'll pull through."

Just as Luke walked back in and handed me a cup of coffee, a doctor in blue scrubs followed behind him.

"Are you all here for Gretchen Williams?" he asked.

Giselle jumped up from her chair. "Yes, I'm her twin sister."

We all stood up and walked closer to where the doctor was standing. "Gretchen is going to be fine."

We all let out a sigh of relief as he continued telling us about Gretchen's condition.

"She had some internal bleeding, so we had to go in and repair that, and we also had to remove her spleen. Her right leg is broken in four places, and we had to put in some pins and screws. I also believe there may be some nerve damage. She'll have to be in a cast for several weeks while the bones heal. There may be a chance she'll have to go through physical therapy to learn to use her leg again."

"When can we see her?" I asked.

"I can take you to her now, but I want you to be prepared. She's very swollen, and she's hooked up to some machines. We're keeping her comfortable on pain medication, and she hasn't woken up from the surgery yet."

As Luke put his arm around me, we all followed the doctor to the room where Gretchen was. Giselle ran to her and started sobbing. Lucky walked over to her and tried to calm her down. I instantly fell sick to my stomach when I saw her lying there. I barely recognized her since her face was so swollen.

"Are you okay, Lily?" Luke asked me.

"I'm fine. Are you?"

"Yeah, I'm just glad they're here with us."

"I know this must be bringing back a lot of memories for you," I said as I kissed his hand.

"It is, but it's cool. I'm just thankful Gretchen's going to be fine."

We walked over and stood at the end of the bed. Sam pulled up a chair, grabbed her hand, and brought it to his lips.

"Please, sweetheart. Please wake up," he pleaded.

It broke my heart seeing Sam like that. A few moments later, Gretchen squeezed Sam's hand, and she slowly opened her eyes. Lucky had to hold Giselle back from throwing herself on top of her.

"Let her wake up and focus, Giselle," he said to her.

Gretchen tried to talk, but could only mumble a few words.

"Don't try and talk, sweetheart. You're going to be fine. Just get some rest," Sam said.

She took her other hand and laid it on Giselle's arm as she mumbled, "Stop crying, I have a headache."

As we all started laughing, Sam leaned over, gently kissed her lips, and told her how much he loved her. I took a few steps back, and I looked around the room at the people I called my family. Looking at Sam, I remembered the first time I met him and how he held the door open for me as I was bringing in my boxes. Then I looked at the twins, remembering the day they moved next door, and how we instantly became best friends. As I looked at Lucky, I was remembering the night we met. I couldn't help but smile at how he tried to flirt with me, thinking he was going to get *lucky*.

"You okay, babe? You look like you're in deep thought." A small grin graced Luke's face.

As my eyes looked into his, I remembered the first time he told me to watch my mouth, and I knew at that moment, he was the one I needed to complete my life.

"I'm wonderful." I smiled as I leaned into him and softly brushed his lips with mine.

The Upside of Love

Luke Matthews and Lily Gilmore will return in the second and final book of the Love Series, *The Upside of Love*, releasing in 2014.

Please see the back of the book for the Prologue and first chapter of **Adriane Leigh's romance novel, *The Mourning After***

Acknowledgements

I would like to thank you, my readers and fans, for all your support and enthusiasm while reading my books. Without your support, I wouldn't be here giving you the story of Luke Matthews and Lily Gilmore. I cherish each message you send via Facebook and Twitter, and I look forward to connecting with you more and talking about Love In Between. I love you guys a bunch, but you already know that!

About The Author

Sandi Lynn is a New York Times, USA Today and Wall Street Journal bestselling author who spends all of her days writing. She published her first novel, Forever Black, in February 2013 and hasn't stopped writing since. Her addictions are shopping, going to the gym, romance novels, coffee, chocolate, margaritas, and giving readers an escape to another world.

Please come and connect with her at:

www.facebook.com/Sandi.Lynn.Author

www.twitter.com/SandilynnWriter

www.authorsandilynn.com

www.goodreads.com/author/show/6089757.Sandi_Lynn

www.pinterest.com/sandilynnWriter/

www.instagram.com/sandilynnauthor

The Mourning After

"ANYONE ELSE?" A deep voice echoes down the hallway.

"Please just leave her," he says groggily.

A grunt echoes up the stairs and then I shut my eyes to the world around me. I hear random screams and moans and then sometime, maybe hours later, or minutes, or days, I hear a popping noise. I don't know what it is and my brain no longer has the ability to expend the energy to figure it out. My mind has shut down and the only thing I can hear is screaming. It seems as if I scream for days. Months. I've been screaming for years.

Chapter One

"SO YOU KNOW how you said you had nothing going this summer?" I called my best friend from a coffee shop off the freeway just over the North Carolina state line.

"Yeah?" The hesitation clear in her voice.

"I've got something for you." The excitement rippled through my voice.

"Since this is the first time you've sounded excited in a while, I'm all ears."

"Great. I bought a house."

"What?" Drew's voice shrieked over the phone. I held it away from my ear with a smile on my face.

"I want you to spend the summer with me—it needs fixing up, but you can help me pick out paint colors and all that."

"Wait, you and Kyle bought a house?"

"Not really. I bought a house. Kyle didn't have much say in it."

"Georgia Hope Montgomery! Did you break up with Kyle?" Her voice rose more than a few octaves.

"No, I'm just staying at the house this summer to fix it up and then I'll rent it out next summer. You should see it Drew, it's amazing." I finished on a dreamy sigh.

"I don't know. Dad probably wouldn't be keen on me being away all summer. D.C. is far away."

Drew was the accountant for her dad's construction company. I knew she wouldn't have a problem working from the beach all summer even if she would be more than a few hours away. "Please come. You can crunch numbers from anywhere, Drew. Let's spend the summer together! We haven't spent much time together since college. Silas has already agreed; it will be a blast. And it's not in D.C."

I heard a huff from her end.

"Where is it?" She sighed.

"That's the best part, Drew—it's on the beach." My grin grew impossibly wider even though no one was there to see.

"The beach? Like, the ocean beach?" I could hear the excitement rising in her voice.

"The one and only. It's thirty minutes outside Wilmington, North Carolina. I promise there's plenty to do there, you can troll for hotties—there's plenty of clubs..." I trailed off.

"You had me at beach. Although Silas..." She groaned when she mentioned one of my other closest friends since college. Silas and I were nearly inseparable. We'd both moved to D.C. after college when Drew had moved home to Jacksonville. She'd been bummed to be moving away from us; we'd had endless amounts of fun in college, but she and Silas bickered like an old married couple most days. For whatever reason, they did not click like he and I did. Perhaps it was because she had more competition when they trolled for men at the clubs. Silas was ridiculously charming and deliciously hot and operated under the assumption that he could turn even a straight man bi for at least one night.

"I know you love him deep down." I grinned. "I'll tell him not to hit on anyone you bring home," I teased.

"Actually," I could hear the grin in Drew's voice, "I'm seeing someone."

"More than once?" I coughed on my drink.

"Yes, more than once. We're pretty serious. He's amazing in bed." She sighed wistfully.

"How long have you been sleeping with him?" I rolled my eyes. Drew was famous for her unapologetic one-night stands.

"A few weeks."

"Met him at the bar?"

"No," Drew deadpanned as if she were offended by my question. "He came into the office, he had a meeting with Dad. He's sexy, Georgia, like really sexy. Big and tall and cut, and you should see how big—"

"Great, thanks. He sounds great." I interrupted her before she could finish her sentence. "Back to the subject. Will you come? Take the summer. You, Silas, and me. We'll soak up the sun on the beach all summer." I heard an audible groan on the line.

"It won't be complete without you." I lowered my voice.

"Well, there's a bit of a minor detail I failed to mention."

"What?" I asked.

"Gavin, he's—"

"Who?" I scrunched my nose.

"The guy I'm seeing," she said.

"Oh, right. Tall, dark and handsome."

"Right. So Gavin is having a house built this summer and is a bit homeless right now until it's finished so he's been staying with me," she said the last part in a rush.

"You're living with him?" I groaned.

"I couldn't just leave him out in the cold," she said.

"Right, and I'm sure the fact that he has a big d—"

"It doesn't hurt...Unless I want it to..." She giggled and I groaned.

"How old is he, Drew?" I rolled my eyes even though she couldn't see. Drew had been known to date men far out of her age bracket and I wanted clarification before we went any further.

"Same as us—twenty-seven."

"Surprise of surprises," I mumbled.

"What?" Her irritated tone made it clear she'd heard me just fine.

"Nothing. So, you want Gavin to come too? Doesn't he work?"

"From home. He's an entrepreneur."

"Aren't they all?" I huffed.

"No, really. He does well with it if the house he's building is any indication."

"Ok, great. So Gavin can come too. I'll put you in the room farthest from mine so I don't have to hear your love romps."

"I don't know about love romps, but the man can fuck like a—"

"Great Drew, thanks. It's going to be a great summer, I can see it now."

"It will. I'll call you once I make some arrangements. When do you want me there?"

"Tomorrow…"

"Tomorrow?"

"I signed the papers today. Got the key, and I'm headed there now. I'm a few hours away. Silas is meeting me there. Just come whenever you can."

"Okay, G. I'll call you later."

"Great. I gotta go, I want to make it there before dark." I looked at the sky and noticed how late it was getting.

"Okay." Drew paused for a moment. "Are you okay, G?" A few silent beats of my heart echoed in my ears.

"Yeah." A frown crossed my face as I answered.

"Okay. Can't wait to see you." Her voice chirped in my ear.

"Me too." The frown was still whispering around my lips.

"I'll call you."

"Bye." I pushed end call on my phone and stared at it for a few moments as I stood in the coffee shop's parking lot. I knew I should call Kyle but he was not on my list of favorites right now.

He'd been more than a little angry at my spontaneous beach house purchase, especially since I hadn't consulted him on the deal. Frankly, I hadn't wanted his help. He had a tendency to bulldoze any negotiation he was part of, and he wasn't interested in heading south anyway. He worked in Washington, D.C. as an attorney seventy plus hours a week hoping to make a name for himself in the growing firm. That left me alone a lot. I managed a boutique hotel a few blocks from The Smithsonian that I loved, but evenings and weekends alone had me lonely and ready for a change.

The Carolina shore had always been my dream and suddenly I'd woken one morning and had started browsing real estate sites. I wasn't sure what I was looking for, but it didn't take long for me to land on a weathered, multistoried beach cottage outside Wilmington, North Carolina. Despite the fact that I'd gone to Duke University in Durham, I hadn't had a chance to spend much time at the shore. I was probably drawn to the beach from the Nick Sparks novels I'd devoured throughout college. Regardless, I'd called about the house that same day. The multilevel, shingled beach house with twisting staircases and whitewashed porches spoke to me.

Silas and I drove down there one Saturday while Kyle was at the office. We drove, we saw, I offered asking price, and by the time we were back in Washington it had been approved. Needless to say, Kyle was not as excited as I was. But I'd gotten a degree in hospitality and my intention had always been to own a bed and breakfast or my own boutique hotel someday. It was exactly the change of scenery I'd so desperately needed, and I reassured Kyle it would only be for this one summer. After that I would rent it out, beach rentals were big on the shore.

I was absentmindedly scrolling through my contacts list as I sipped my Frappuccino and thought about my past with Kyle.

I'd moved into the house next to Kyle's when I was twelve in a upper middle class neighborhood outside Richmond, Virginia. He had been outgoing and friendly, while I was shy and withdrawn, yet somehow we'd become fast friends, then as we'd hit puberty our hormones took over. We'd giggled and held hands and talked about getting married. He'd been my first kiss. When we were a few years older we had made out in the back seat of his car on Saturday nights and had snuck into each other's bedrooms after dark. Kyle and I had had some rough patches in high school. We'd broken up for a few months, I'd cried when he had held hands with another girl, but it wasn't long before we were back together. Kyle was my comfort, my home. The world had felt strange and awkward without him; I had felt strange and awkward without him.

Kyle had graduated a year ahead of me and had gone to Duke. He'd gotten a scholarship there and their law school was top notch in the East. The first year he'd been gone had been torture for me. Duke was nearly three hours away from our sheltered little town. He'd come home whenever he could and I had visited often, but I'd still missed him more than I had cared to remember. I'd been lost without him, so it hadn't a surprise when I had followed him the minute I'd graduated. We'd lived on campus for a few years and then had lived in a small apartment together that was tiny but clean. But the further he'd gotten into his degree, the less I'd seen of him. It had been at that point that a slow shift had begun to take place. Kyle had taken too many classes every semester, had picked up internships and had spent late hours at the library or at his advisor's office studying and setting the wheels in motion for his future. I'd known it was necessary, but that hadn't made it any less painful. I'd known a life with him would be worth it in the end and he'd promised the late nights and long hours spent away would be over soon. It had always been, "just let me get through this semester, just 'til I graduate," and then it'd become "when this internship is over, after my first promotion."

The long days and late nights still hadn't ended and things had grown strained. After more than eight years of supporting Kyle while he'd earned his law degree and then had started at a prestigious law firm in D.C., I finally broke. I saw Silas much more than I saw Kyle. I think Kyle resented coming home at midnight and finding Silas and I curled up on the couch together with ice cream watching The Notebook. Kyle would walk in and heave a sigh and then loosen his tie and head for the bedroom. Some nights I followed him in after Silas left, other nights Silas and I would stay together huddled on the couch and finish our movie before I would crawl into bed with Kyle, long after he was asleep. I knew we weren't in a good place, but he was my entire heart and I still had faith that just one more promotion, just another year at the firm, and his schedule would ease up. We could buy a house and start a family. Maybe live outside the city. I still had the dream for our future that we'd conjured together when we were fifteen and I refused to let go of it.

A part of me felt guilty for making this monumental decision in my life without Kyle, but I'd been suffocating in D.C., so I couldn't allow myself to have regrets. By the time I'd packed clothes and some essentials for the summer, Kyle was no longer mad. We were past that. It wasn't our style to shout and scream, but there had been tension. He'd kissed me and said he would visit as soon as he could. I'd nodded with a smile. I even thought these few months might be good for us. Maybe we would come back reconnected. These last few years I'd been the effect to Kyle's cause, but now I would be doing something that would be mine.

I got to his name on my contacts list and paused. The man I loved, the man who had always been there for me through thick and thin, the man I was leaving for the summer. It would be the first time we would be apart for such a long amount of time but the excitement of following my dreams eclipsed any sadness I had.

I exited my contact list and tossed my phone on the seat beside me then got back in the car and continued south.

***

"TOOK YOU LONG enough. How many potty breaks did you take?" My charming best friend leaned against his car door with a grin on his face. He looked like a natural on the beach with flip-flops, cargos, and a bright green polo shirt. His bronzed skin and perfectly styled, sandy blond hair a clear indication that he took care to look good.

I took a few steps toward him and stopped, gazing up at the sprawling beach house. My eyes locked on the white shutters, the multiple decks, the wooden staircases, and weathered shingles—it took my breath away. I closed my eyes and inhaled the salty sea breeze, caressing my face and whirling my dark hair. The call of gulls swooped overhead, a far cry from the sounds of the city that I'd just left.

"Earth to Georgia." Silas grinned, throwing an empty styrofoam coffee cup at my head.

"I stopped for coffee a while ago and called Drew."

"How's that hussy doing?" Silas mumbled as he pulled a duffel bag out of the back seat of his car.

"You can ask her tomorrow." I grinned.

"What? Fuck," Silas swore as he knocked his head on the doorframe of his car. I hadn't told him that I was going to invite Drew.

"She's bringing her new man candy."

"Of course she is." He rolled his eyes. I laughed and faked a punch on his arm before heading back to my car and getting my own duffel bag. "Ready sport?"

"Enough with the macho names," he grumbled, in a sour mood no doubt because Drew would be in his life for the rest of the summer.

"Fine, cupcake. Let's go in." I grinned and he followed me up the first set of steps to the front door.

The beach house was built on wood pilings that elevated the first floor nearly twenty feet above the sand. The ground level on the beach was semi-enclosed and served as storage space. The house was less than a hundred yards off the water and surrounded by rolling dunes and swaying grass. When the realtor walked us through the house she assured us that the water rarely made it up this far on the beach, but the house would be protected if it did. Hurricanes were another issue entirely and she'd suggested I have a hurricane safety inspection done to make sure the house could withstand hurricane-force winds. He could also instruct me on what to do in the event of an impending storm.

I unlocked the front door and we stepped into an open space that featured a spacious living room with French doors that looked out over another grand deck and the ocean. Water and waves dominated my vision. To the left was a large kitchen and to the right were the guest bath and a hallway leading to two bedrooms. Beyond the kitchen, another hallway led to three bedrooms and the stairway to the second floor. Each first-floor bedroom had an en suite bathroom, which made arrangements for this summer much more comfortable. Drew and I could log time in the bathroom, but Silas was on a whole other level—he could spend hours in front of a mirror spiking his hair with half a dozen different products.

A large island divided the kitchen and living room and the house was completely white walls and worn wood floors. The realtor had suggested I refinish the floors, but I adored their charm. Whoever had designed the house was inspired by the natural beauty of the surroundings, beautiful in its quaint simplicity. I had fallen in love at first sight.

I walked across the room and opened the French doors. I wanted these doors open the entire summer to let the ocean breeze waft in and keep the dust bunnies and stale air at bay. I wanted to wake up each and every morning to a new fresh start, and keeping these doors open would do that.

"I'm going to go throw this stuff in my room." Silas headed down a hallway.

"The corner room is mine, Silas," I called after him. He shot me a dirty look because it was the largest room on this floor with the best views. "Advantage of being the owner." I grinned. The house had two floors, but the three bedrooms on the second floor were in rough shape and I'd need to call a carpenter in to replace some of the flooring and update the plumbing. Every room in the house had access to the sprawling decks that wrapped around the first and second stories. There was also a small set of stairs off the second story deck that led to the widow's walk on the roof.

While the bedrooms on the main floor were livable, they could use a fresh coat of paint and some modern updates, just one of the summer jobs I'd roped Drew into helping me with. While Silas said he would help, I knew his version of help was more like overseeing while sipping a drink with a little umbrella in his hand. He was good for opinions though, he had plenty of those.

I continued to walk around the living room and open all the windows before lifting the sheet off the ratty, old couch. There was some wicker furniture tucked in a corner that was in need of a paint job, but I liked it and planned on leaving it.

"I'm starving. Let's order something." Silas ambled back into the kitchen. "Stop working, we just got here." He scrunched his nose.

"That's why we're here, Silas. Let's just get our stuff hauled in and then we'll talk dinner."

"Fine, Mom." Silas rolled his eyes before flashing me a playful grin. Silas always complained that I was too responsible, but on the flip side he was entirely too irresponsible, making us a perfect fit.

We both headed out the door to haul in the things we'd deemed worthy of the trip for the summer.

LATER THAT NIGHT we sat together on the couch eating pizza and drinking beer. My feet were curled up underneath me and I was angled toward him.

"I'm dying without TV, love." Silas took another slice out of the box between us. I smiled at his pet name for me. He'd begun to call me that shortly after we met our freshmen year at Duke. I'd assumed he called everyone that, but I soon found out I was the only one who'd earned that pet name. It made me feel safe and protected, loved. Silas soon became a part of me. He was there whenever the pain became too much to bear, listened with open ears, sat with me, rubbing my back without complaint when I needed silence, and started calling me love, the only thing that had helped warm my frozen heart.

"I'll work on it tomorrow, but you should know that I believe you have an entertainment addiction." I crooked a grin at him.

"I fully admit to that. If there were a twelve step program I'd be there."

"I bet." I rolled my eyes at him. "You okay with Drew being here this summer?"

"Do I have a choice?" He scowled through a bite of pizza.

"No. Maybe you could come to an understanding," I trailed off.

"Doubtful. When will she be here?" He sauntered to the kitchen and grabbed us both another beer. The boy was absolutely delectable. If he didn't like other boys I would, without a doubt, have been in trouble. I would have fallen for his mischievous grin and sexy dimples and he would have broken my naïve heart. Silas wasn't much for monogamy.

"Thanks." I took the beer. "I talked to her earlier—she and Gavin are coming tomorrow." I emphasized his name.

"Gavin, huh? Sounds like a tool."

I giggled and shook my head at Silas. "Well apparently he's a hot tool, with a big tool." Silas and I erupted into a fit of giggles.

"Can't wait." His brown eyes sparked with amusement. "Did you talk to Kyle?" Silas asked.

"Yeah." I took another sip of my beer.

"And how is he?" Silas watched me with a thoughtful expression.

"He's... okay," I mumbled.

"Still not happy about this summer's arrangements?" Silas asked.

"Not particularly." I huffed and picked the pepperoni off my pizza absentmindedly.

"Are you guys going to be okay?"

"Sure. He'll get over it."

"What if he doesn't?" Silas continued to watch me. I was fast becoming uncomfortable with this conversation.

"He will. It's just for the summer." I shrugged.

"And what about next summer?"

"I don't know, Silas. I don't want to talk about it. I'm here and he's there. That's it. That's what it is." I jumped off the couch and headed for the kitchen to dispose of my paper plate.

"I didn't mean to upset you, love." He wrapped his arms around my waist from behind and set his chin on my shoulder.

"I know. I just don't want to talk about it. We'll be fine. We've always been fine." I plastered a half-hearted grin on my face. "I'm exhausted."

"Okay." Silas regarded me with somber eyes. "If you need anything just holler. I'll come running like the valiant knight in shining armor that I am."

"Brandishing your blow dryer?" I giggled.

"Absolutely." He grinned before gathering our empty beer bottles. I slid the pizza box into the empty fridge and then flicked off the light before we headed down the hall to our respective bedrooms. Silas paused outside his door.

"Are you really going to be okay, love?"

Silas knew I always had trouble sleeping my first few nights in a new place. "Yes," I whispered. I was never good at lying.

"Come on." He wrapped his arm around mine and headed for my bedroom where we curled up together; he held me while I sobbed softly into the cool sheets.

***

"HONEY, I'M HOME!" I heard Drew's voice singing as she opened the front door the following afternoon. Earlier that morning I'd scrubbed out the fridge then had gone to the grocery store to stock up on food and drinks. I'd also bought cheap utensils and dishes and was now arranging the kitchen. Silas had just finished washing the main floor windows and was sweeping when my other best friend arrived.

I set down the glasses in my hands, skidded to the front door, and wrapped Drew in my arms. It had been months since we'd seen each other and I was beside myself with excitement, knowing we would spend the entire summer together.

"God, G, I've missed you so much." She held me tightly and we rocked back in forth. Tears sprang to my eyes as I inhaled her familiar perfume.

"Me too. I'm so glad you came. Your hair is shorter." I held her at arm's-length and took in her layered brown bob. "I love it." Drew was obstinate, opinionated, and self-centered but she, much like Silas, had the ability to set me straight. She told it like it was unapologetically. She and Silas were also the two most hilarious people I'd ever met, so unlike me I couldn't help but be drawn to them.

"Drew," Silas said behind me with a curt nod. I rolled my eyes.

"Silas." She rolled her bright blue eyes and then a small smile broke out across her face. For all their bickering I think they really enjoyed each other.

"Great house, give me a tour?" Drew looped her arm in mine and we headed down the closest hallway.

"I'll take you to your room first." She dropped a bag off in the bedroom I was giving her then we made our way through the rest of the house. At each room we talked paint colors and design schemes.

Later we made our way back to the kitchen and found Silas making margaritas.

"It's a proper girls' night already," Drew said as Silas poured the frothy drink into glasses. "Thanks for letting Gavin come, Georgia. I know it's weird since you haven't met him, but he's great. You'll love him."

"Can't wait to meet him." I sipped the cold drink.

"Tristan's great too, and off the charts hot." She rested her hip against the counter and took a drink.

"Who's Tristan?" I asked.

"Is he single? How old?" Silas asked.

"Twenty-seven, single, and straight." Drew shot Silas a warning look.

"Perfect and not a problem," Silas winked at her.

"Tristan is Gavin's best friend. They're in business together and working on a project they need to log hours on this summer. Plus he's going through this thing—so I told him that you wouldn't mind if he tagged along."

"Drew." I frowned.

"What kind of thing?" Silas cocked an eyebrow.

"Lady trouble. He just needs to get away for a while, put his past in the past kind of thing. You're not mad are you, Georgia?" Drew pouted.

"Kind of weird that I don't even know him…"

"Do you think I would invite a lunatic? Gavin's known him since they were kids."

"Technically I don't even know Gavin." I reminded her. She only rolled her eye in response.

"He's great. They both are, plus the more muscle we have here this summer the less we'll have to do." She shrugged. I heaved an exasperated sigh. That was Drew… living in the moment and getting us into situations we probably shouldn't be in. Maybe it had been a good thing she was ten hours away in Jacksonville the last few years.

"When are they coming?"

"Hopefully soon," Silas said flirtatiously. Drew shot him another dirty look.

"This weekend. Gavin's driving and Tristan's sailing up the coast." She wiggled her eyebrows at me.

"He has a boat?" I asked.

"Oh, that could make for an interesting evening," Silas said.

"Straight, Silas."

"I know, I know. Has never stopped me in the past though." He winked at her.

SOON WE FOUND ourselves seated on the porch sipping margaritas, catching up. It felt good to laugh and reminisce about old times. I'd missed having Drew in my everyday life. While we talked often on the phone, it was a poor substitute for being together in person. Silas was my best friend, and I loved him just like a brother, but it was so good to have girl time. I hadn't realized how much I'd missed that too. Apparently a lot of things had fallen out of my life over time and I hadn't realized it.

"Shopping tomorrow?" Drew asked.

"Sounds great. There are some antique stores in town I'd like to hit first." Drew and I had talked about the overall design of the house and how to maintain the cottage feel with modern updates. First we needed to start with the living room since this is where we'd be all summer. A couch was at the top of my list, as well as overstuffed chairs and end tables and an entertainment center where we could tuck a TV that would still blend with the decor. I also needed to stop at the hardware store for sandpaper and paint to refinish the beautiful wicker set that was left here.

We continued to drink while the giggling increased as the pitcher of margaritas dwindled.

"So when will be graced with the presence of Kyle?" Drew rolled her eyes.

"I know, right?" Silas huffed.

"Hey." I shot them a glare.

"Kyle's a douche, love." Silas shrugged and took another drink. I whipped my head around to him and narrowed my eyes before a giggle escaped my throat.

"Total douche." Drew laughed. "So is he coming down this summer?" She watched me intently.

"Sure, probably. Don't call my boyfriend a douche." I stumbled over the last words as a giggle erupted again.

"Is he mad that you bought this place?" Drew raised an eyebrow at me.

"Oh yeah." Silas' eyes grew wide. "He's pissed. They hardly talk."

"Silas." I whipped a throw pillow at him, causing his drink to splash in his lap.

"Is he that mad?" Drew asked softly. I chewed on my bottom lip and avoided her gaze.

"No, he's not mad, he's just not happy." I shrugged thoughtfully.

"Do you think he'll come around?" Drew asked.

"I don't know," I said softly.

"Douche," Silas mumbled under his breath. All the drinks caught up to me and my mood was suddenly crashing.

"I don't want to talk about it. I'm going to bed. Be ready bright and early sunshine." I pointed at Drew.

I BRUSHED MY teeth before stripping off my jeans and crawled into bed in my tank top and underwear. I nestled into the pillow as my thoughts drifted over the past few years of my life. A few minutes later I heard my door creak open and Drew's form was bathed in the light from the hallway. She closed the door behind her and silently curled up in the bed behind me.

"Are you okay?" Her voice was heartbreakingly sad.

"Yes," I whispered.

"Doesn't sound like it," she said.

"I am." I hugged my pillow tighter.

"Do you want to talk about it?"

"No."

"Okay." She nuzzled deeper into the pillow we were sharing.

"I'm sorry I haven't been around, Georgia."

I sucked in a sharp breath and closed my eyes as tears stung behind my eyelids. "I know." I took another deep breath and tried to swallow the painful lump in my throat.

***

THE NEXT MORNING I dragged Drew out of bed at ten and the three of us headed to town for shopping. We picked up coffee then wandered the streets, in and out of antique stores and boutiques. Our first purchase was a love-at-first-sight large cream couch. We came across some eggshell blue and cream striped chairs that complemented it. With the big items out of the way we focused on smaller decorative things. Silas spotted a weathered wrought iron and glass side table and I found a beautiful vintage mirrored lamp to place on top of it. My vision for perfect modern cottage chic was coming together.

With bright sunshine and a cool breeze, I breathed deeply and thought at this moment, I was the happiest I'd ever been; life was simple as I strolled around a small seaside town with my two best friends. Tears pricked my eyes, thankful for both of them.

After lunch we went to the hardware store to get paint samples. Silas and Drew went a little wild, bickering and stuffing dozens of colorful paint chips into my oversized purse. Kyle and I had moved into a beautiful furnished apartment in D.C. where not a single thing needed to be done, so I was embracing starting from scratch with the beach house.

We headed home mid-afternoon to meet the furniture delivery truck. They hauled the old couch away and brought the new furniture into the living room along with the oversized plasma TV Silas had insisted I get. Once the furniture was in, Silas, Drew and I spent time debating the placement of the smaller items. I cracked beers for the three of us and giggled as I watched them argue over everything. This summer would be an exercise in patience between the two of them.

The Mourning After is available now at Amazon, Barnes and Noble, and iTunes.

Manufactured by Amazon.ca
Bolton, ON

18169579R00188